C000066992

## *Copyright & Thank You*

Hope you enjoy!

Louise Murchie

## Acknowledgements:

*For my husband, kids, Tina, Nat, Bek, Aoife, Sam (my editor!) my sister, parents, in-laws and friends who I consider family, other family members who genuinely know me & have helped me write another romance; thank you!*


*Tony was inspired by an image of @hernandrago on Instagram - feel free to go & check him out!*

# *Chapters*

1 ~ Annie                                                    2

2 ~ Annie                                                    5

3 ~ Annie                                                   14

4 ~ Anthony                                                 20

5 ~ Annie                                                   27

6 ~ Anthony                                                 35

7 ~ Annie                                                   38

8 ~ Anthony                                                 55

9 ~ Annie                                                   61

10 ~ Anthony                                                68

11 ~ Annie                                                  71

12 ~ Anthony                                                82

13 ~ Annie                                                  86

14 ~ Anthony                                                94

15 ~ Annie                                                  97

16  ~ Anthony                                              106

17 ~ Annie                                                 111

18 ~ Anthony                                               115

19 ~ Annie                                                 120

20 - Anthony      133

21 ~ Annie      136

22 ~ Anthony      154

23 ~ Annie      160

24 - Anthony      168

25 ~ Annie      179

26 ~ Anthony      183

27 ~ Annie      187

28 ~ Anthony      200

29 ~ Annie      209

30 - Anthony      223

31 - Annie      229

32  - Anthony      241

34 - Annie      249

35 - Anthony      260

Epilogue      267

# 1 ~ Annie

$T$he rain falls steadily past the high-powered fluorescent street lights, soaking everything that it touches. It is the kind of rain that gets under your coat, down your neck, into your socks, and penetrates deep into your bones. If the sky is black, the street lights hide it; for nothing could be seen if one were to look up.

I pull up the collar on my tracksuit jacket to shield my neck from the cold and damp as I run to my car. Although I am going to shower when I get home, I don't want the rain to do it for free, fully clothed. Throwing my sports kit into the boot, I climb into the driver's seat as quickly as I can.

It takes a few moments for the car to start and warm up, and I rub my hands whilst I wait. The three hours I'd spent training meant the engine was as cold as ice, but I knew it wouldn't take long before I'd feel the heat. When I do, I turn on the lights and gently ease the car onto the slick roads.

The twenty-three minutes it takes for me to drive from the sports centre to home is possibly about three minutes too long. The sweat from my training session has started to dry, meaning my gi is now stuck to me like the heavy cotton suit it is. Parking the car in the drive, I air my training equipment in the usual corner of the garage and lock it, then enter my red sandstone house, dumping the soggy wet gi and other clothing at the washing machine before I head for a well-deserved, long hot shower.

At least, that was the intention. Just as I finish rinsing the conditioner from my hair, I hear my phone ring. The ring-tone tells me this is not a call to miss, at least not the second time. By the time I get to the device, it's rung out to voicemail. I wait for ten seconds, then pick it up just as it rings again.

"Julia, what can I help you with?" The women's refuge I work for only really calls on weekends when they want my help, and they pay me nicely for it. One abused woman off the streets was one they could help. I never asked who paid my fee and I doubted I'd ever be told.

I turn and sit on the bed, wrapping the huge fluffy bath sheet around me. Seeing my curtains are still open, I stand to pull them closed as Julia makes the point of her call clear. I dry myself off and start dressing as she talks on the loudspeaker.

"We've been asked to help find a runaway from the Midlands who was up here working. She left her employer in Edinburgh nearly a month ago, but she's been spotted at Buchanan Street Bus Station this evening. Her family are frantic, they want her home, especially as this pandemic is taking hold and we're about to go on National Lockdown. Can you help?"

I smiled. "Aye, ye know I can. Send me the details, and is there any chance of a sofa to crash on tonight?" I ask. I doubt I'll be in a fit state to drive back by the time I'm done and I can just hear Julia's smile, even over the phone.

"Of course, just for you. Safehouse Two has space for ye both."

I grin. "I understand. Hopefully, I'll have good news in a few hours!"

Julia chortles. "Yep, that's why I called you!"

The call ends, and I toss the phone gently onto the bed. The bed I might not see until tomorrow. I smile ruefully, not regretting that I'll not be sleeping in it for a night to save a young girl from the streets of Glasgow. The annoyance was I was going to travel from Edinburgh to do it, but it could not be helped; I'd just have to grab some food on the way, but first, there were the clothes I wanted. The rain dictated a waterproof coat, so I pull out the thick leather bomber jacket. The skin-tight black fleece-lined jeans and accompanying black vest, bra, t-shirt, and ski mask join the jacket on the bed. I grab the thigh bag from the back of the sliding wardrobe, hidden behind knee-high boots which join me on this venture. They'd keep my feet drier than the lightweight trainers I usually favoured.

I check the weather report once more, then look in the sliding door mirror. 'Lara Croft, eat your heart out!' I thought, 'You're going Highland style!'

Taking a black elastic headband and tucking my mousey brown bobbed hair back from my face, I become unrecognisable. Double-checking the technology and first aid items in my thigh bag, I quickly read the file Julia sent me on email before I lock up and drive to Glasgow, enjoying the songs from my Spotify account as the wipers swish and the motorway lights fly by overhead.

# 2 ~ Annie

It took just over an hour to drive to the edge of Glasgow, but it was nearly fifteen minutes more before I could park up in a safe place in the centre. I wouldn't contact Julia until I either gave up (it happened once or twice when the woman I'd been sent to help had managed to get on a MegaBus and head south) or the rescue was at whatever safe house Julia had directed me to get to.

The rain had followed me from Edinburgh and the same dreich drizzle coated the roads. I checked out Central Station, Buchanan Bus Station, and Glasgow Cross before turning my attention to the usual haunts the homeless and runaways occupied. I saw a few regulars I knew who would help by giving me some basic information.

"Hey, George!" I greet one homeless man and produce a cup of tea for him. I knew drinks and food made the homeless more talkative. George grumbles.

"They're putting us into a hostel!" he croaks as he takes the tea from me. I drop my five foot seven frame down to George's level.

"Are they? Which one? Why for?"

George shrugs. "Something about a damn pandemic! Not sure which one I'll be thrown into!"

I nod in reply. "Aye, I've heard about it. Have ye seen anyone new and scared about these parts, Georgie boy?"

George shakes his head. "Not tonight, naw." His accent isn't quite Glaswegian, there is a distinct Cornish lilt to it, but I never could get George to tell me what his story was.

"Keep an eye out for me, aye?"

George nods, grins at me with his missing, blackened teeth, and I rise slowly. Pulling up the ski mask from under my jacket, I roll it around my neck to try to keep the rain out. My hair is now plastered to my head and the headband is keeping it away from my face. I move on, slowly widening my circle of interest as the night wears on.

It is nearly an hour after speaking with George when I decide to grab some coffee. The late-night convenience stores haven't missed a trick with the coffee machines, and it wasn't long before I had a hot caramel latte in my hands, warming them. The fingerless gauntlets help keep my hands warm, but my fingers, not so much.

I prowl along streets and back alleys, hoping for a sign of the missing girl. It's a conversation at the back of a late-night chip shop takeaway with two homeless folks being served by the business owner which finally yields results.

"Think the police will raid the old wool mill?" asks one. He is being handed a small fried supper, which makes me remember I need food too. I ask the owner for one and produce the money, even from the backdoor. Over the fire in the burning bin, I enquire about the old wool mill.

"Naw...they'll need the meat wagons for that!" chuckles the other as his food and mine are served.

"Keep the change, and put two more on the wall?" I ask the owner. The chip shop owner nods, hands the food over, then vanishes inside.

"Nice of ye, thanks, lass!" says the first, who is maybe just able to chew his food. His mouth has a distinct lack of teeth.

"Yer welcome! Tell me, where's the auld wool mill then? I'm looking for my niece, figured she might have headed that way?"

The two homeless guys look at each other, then back at me, and I know I am onto something.

"What's she look like?" asks the second.

I smirk. "She's no dressed or equipped to be out on the streets, never mind these streets. You'll no miss her if you've seen her."

The second guy nods to the first, and I press home my advantage.

"I'll put a week's worth of suppers in here for the pair of ye if I find her alive, safe and *tonight*," I emphasise. Food is one currency the streets use. The other is alcohol and I am sure it is going to get added. I mentally count in my head and I only reach eight when the request is made.

"With McEwan's?" asks the first, tentatively. I notice his coat is tweed, rather new and very expensive. Certainly, not his normal coat, and I surmise that the mill probably isn't far away, figuring he'd have rescued it from someone there, as was often the case. I nod, quickly eating the last piece of deep-fried black pudding.

"Aye, I'll get a case so ye can share. But, only if I find her tonight."

The men nod, then tell me where to find the old wool mill and how to get entry; even though it is boarded up, they know which boards to shift to get access.

"Nice coat," I comment. The old boy shrugs in reply.

"He wanted a swap, didn't seem with it, if ye get my drift." I don't, but I nod in reply; there wasn't much I could do for a rich man walking around in a homeless guy's smelly old coat.

I hand the tray of chips to the homeless guys and reiterate my promise of food and beer, but only if I am successful.

The wool mill is only a short walk, less than ten minutes from the chip shop. As the homeless guys had instructed, the board I need can be moved neatly on a pivot and swung back silently. I take out a knife gauntlet from my thigh bag and strap it to my left hand, then test it a few times, fully aware I'd be in so much trouble if the police found me not only wearing it but intending to use it. Entering a derelict building full of known drug users, homeless people, and runaways might not be enough of an excuse, even if I could taste the weed from here.

Coming up in front of the court wasn't something I wanted, however, I needed to be alive much more. Retracting the knife, I cautiously make my way into the building.

I cross the lower floor, trying to take care to move quietly but quickly. The front part of the building is still standing, even with the broken windows. The rear of the building, however, is falling apart at the seams.

I explore and find myself in a small back room that has half a floor, a boarded window, and very little ceiling. The building is condemned for a good reason, but this section is shocking. I could hear the rain gently falling outside, though outside was relative. One wrong gust of wind and this room would be half-flooded.

On a pair of pallets is a pile of sleeping bags that stink to the high heavens of beer, body odour, and urine. The sound of footsteps nearby makes me hide in the deeper shadows where I can watch and assess.

The footsteps get louder and I realise they are coming from just above me. The voice that owns them speaks. It is a youthful voice, but not local, almost Cockney in tone but lighter somehow. "What do you mean, he's still here?!" There is more stomping. "He can't be!"

Another voice, grainier, suddenly replies. Whoever is above me has put the phone onto the speaker. "Well, he is. His phone still gives his location as right next to you," states the voice on the phone. This new voice is Scottish with an Aberdeen lilt to it, which is obvious if you know what to listen for.

The man above growls. "He's. Not. Here." Suddenly, he looks down, and I can see his shadow hit the floor before me. "Shit, he's gone through the floor and the police are arriving. I can't go looking. Let's hope I've injured him enough!"

"But..." the Aberdeen voice starts to respond, but it is either cut off or put back to the normal speaker. The man above stomps across the room, down the stairs, and comes closer towards me, and I ready my left wrist. The shouts of the police make him turn back to the stairwell, and he quickly vanishes from earshot. It takes me a few moments to breathe and then I quietly make my way across to the pallets.

Bundled deep inside the smelly pit is a man. He has dark hair which is greying around his temples, a thin face, a short beard that shows more grey than his head, and he looks to be asleep. I pull the sleeping bags off him and quickly check him out, pulling back his suit jacket. I try not to air my shock as I spot three things.

Firstly, the name of the suit manufacturer is an expensive one and they are based in Edinburgh. The second is that the coat he is wearing doesn't match his suit, though I could surmise where that smart coat now was; thirdly and more vital, he'd possibly been stabbed. I reach for my thigh bag and pull out the few bandages I carry. I realise as I check him over that he's been slashed, not stabbed, but the wounds are soaking through his shirt, his suit jacket, and the sleeping bags. "Buy a new shirt, pal," I mutter as I tear his shirt to deal with the worst wounds. Thankfully, he is easy to move and groans slightly as I turn him. It takes me a few seconds to decide I need to stitch him up, and I pull out the stitching kit I carry. Usually, I stitch myself back together, but tonight he needs it.

Taking the worst wound on his left, I thread the needle, sanitise it then stitch the wound. Something else is wrong, but I can't tell what. I am used to the pain of being stitched without any numbing agent; I'd received a few wounds so I knew. This man, whoever he was, doesn't make a sound. What the heck had happened to him to be in this state, here, tonight and not be responsive to having a needle poked into raw skin?

I put a huge sticky bandage on the wound, and I make him lie on his injured side with an old pillow on the wound to stem the flow. Then I check his other wounds. I find his phone and power it off, then I pick out a small credit card gadget from my bag and press one corner, nodding as the small indicator light flashes green. I tuck it into his waistcoat pocket, cover him back up in his damaged suit, smelly blankets, and dog-eared coat, and head off to find the girl.

"Time for me to go," I mutter, making for the stairwell to avoid the police.

Finding the girl was the easy part; she stuck out like yellow snow in a snowdrift. I watch as she tries to find a place near any of the fire pits to warm up, only to be chased off each time. As the girl makes her way to the stairs to climb up another level (where the harder drugs were used and sold) I make my move and corner her.

"It's no safe for you up there, Sarah, yer folks are worried sick. Why don't you come with me and I'll get you home?"

Sarah's eyes suddenly fill with fear, her breath hitches, and she tries to run. It takes me all of two seconds before I grab her and force her back against the wall.

"Don't try that again, please. It's been a long, cold, wet damn night looking for you as it is," I growl. Usually, I talk with them and get them to come with me on their own.

"You don't know..." Sarah begins. Suddenly, there are a lot of blue flashing lights surrounding the old mill, and I can only guess that more police have arrived.

"No, I don't. But, unless you want to be arrested and thrown in jail with this lot, please, come with me. I'm not gonna hurt ye, lass, but yer folks have reached out to me to find you. You can tell me why when I get you safe, okay?"

Sarah looks around in horror as shouts rise; cries of "Police, don't move!" and colourful expletives reach our ears. With a sharp nod, Sarah agrees and I take her hand. Three minutes later, we're heading away from the woollen mill. I remove the gauntlet and get the circulation going again. I have Sarah in one hand, my phone in the other pressed to my ear. I don't wait for pleasantries from the recipient.

"It's not me, but you need to find the signal. Code two." I hang up and don't look back.


Hours later, at Safehouse Two on the south side of Glasgow, Sarah is in a small office with a counsellor whilst I drink coffee with Julia. Sarah has been clinging to me and wouldn't leave to talk with anyone until I told her I would be here for the night. My phone rings and I sigh before I answer it, knowing who it is. I see Julia's eyes raise in concern; I hardly ever let my emotions show.

"Hey. Please tell me you got it?" I ask as I close my eyes to rest them. I have to keep my side of the conversation vague.

"Yes," says the woman in reply. "We need to talk," she states.

I sigh but smile gently, not that my verbal friend can see. "Aye, figured you'd say that. I need to sleep, so twelve hours?"

"I was hoping now," she replies in a pleading tone.

I shake my head, even if my caller can't see. "Nope, can't do it. I'm at work, o'er the other side."

The voice on the other end takes a while to come back with a reply, even though they know what I did and they know what I mean by "the other side."

"Aye, okay. In twelve hours then," she confirms before the line goes dead.

Julia looks at me strangely. I am now semi-dried but still damp.

"That was...different!" she says, almost questioningly.

I shrug. "Can't explain it to you, Jules." I pause, thinking. "I'm not sure I want to." I really don't.

Julia nods. She is aware of my military background; we'd discussed it at my interview and a few times since. "You're not in trouble for helping us, are you?" she asks me. I look at my friend, the matriarch of Safehouse Two and one of the reasons the charity exists. Equal in height, Julia was a larger than life character who ran three women's shelters across Glasgow, not counting branches in Edinburgh, Stirling, Inverness, and other cities. No one would guess that the homely looking librarian was once a corporate shark and a damn good one until a family member needed to flee and fled to a refuge, which prompted Julia to step in and run things more efficiently. Julia volunteered when they needed it and had stayed, leaving the corporate world behind her, using those skills to build another two shelters and open a charity shop in each city to support them all.

I shake my head. "No, just...other business," I casually explain. "Dinnae ask, that way I cannae lie." I sip the high-quality instant brew, trying to keep a straight face.

"Can't have that now, can we?" Julia smirks as she washes out her mug. I shrug and smile back. "Do you still need to crash here?" she asks, drying off the mug.

I nod. "Aye...I dinnae fancy tackling the M8 as I am, coffee or no. I can just about see." I know I am too tired to safely drive.

Julia nods, and I set my mug in the sink. Then she guides me to a room with two metal bunk beds in it. The words "Staff Only" on the door suggests it is for the staff on site to use as they need.

"Pick one; I'll see you in about seven hours?" she asks, and I nod, then wait until Julia has left before taking off my thigh-bag, boots, jeans, and hanging my jacket up on a hook. Tucking my things away under my bed, I crawl into the lower bunk, close my eyes, and let sleep claim me.

# 3 ~ Annie

I awoke with a start to the sounds of raised voices, mostly those of women. I don't check the time; I don't need to. I follow the sounds to find a group of women in a large room. Some are crying, others are shouting, and not all the voices are in English. I whistle sharply, making everyone go silent.

"I don't know what's going on here, but you lot could wake the dead; hell you woke me. Please, shut the fuck up!" Whether it's because I demanded, or because I'm half-dressed in black combat style t-shirt and knickers, I'm not sure, but there is the sudden sound of silence.

Julia emerges from the middle of the group, relief on her face.

"Thanks, Annie!" Julia rounds on one woman, telling her to go calm down in her room. She quietly speaks to another who skulks off to the library area, and the others, now that the drama is over with, disperse and go about their own business.

Sarah sees me and runs over to me, hugging me, thanking me over and over. I hug her back, letting her get whatever security she needs from me being here. She lets me go after ten minutes but watches my movements like a hawk.

I smile and head back to the staff sleeping area, noting I'd slept about six hours. It was better than nothing but not as good as eight, or even more. I'd have to get more once I was home. Somehow. Perhaps I'll get an early night.

Julia follows and waits by the door as I quickly dress, not saying anything. When I am ready, Julia leads the way to the kitchen and makes me sit and eat something before speaking.

"Sarah's not saying why she left her employer in Edinburgh, but we know who she worked for, so we're making an educated guess."

I simply nod. "Do I want to know?"

Julia shakes her head. "Not allowed to tell you. And if I did, I think you might do something about him."

I pause drinking my coffee, then sit back.

"You know where I am if you need me to!" I vow. My mind is working through possible scenarios as to why Sarah had run from her employer but not run home. I was sure my imagination wasn't as vivid as what she'd gone through.

Julia nods. "We have to use the proper channels, Annie."

I look at my friend and boss, knowingly. "Probably best that I go before I do or say something to embarrass us both then, aye?"

Julia nods again with a soft, knowing smile and in five minutes, she lets me out of the safehouse.


The drive back to Edinburgh is just as short as it had been the previous night. The sky still holds its rain-filled grey hue, contrasting drastically with the bright greens of the valleys below as the sun breaks through the clouds here and there. I don't push the car above the speed limit and am careful as I begin to drive familiar, albeit slick roads.

When I park on the drive, I send a text to my caller from last night, then go to make myself a coffee and change into more appropriate clothing, right after another shower. It takes a little over half an hour before the person I expect arrives at my door, on foot.

Dressed in fresh jeans, a blouse, a cardigan wrap and slippers, I now look nothing like a Lara Croft style vigilante.

We face each other as my friend closes the door behind her. We make our way silently to the kitchen where my friend places a speaker on the kitchen table. We wait until something on her phone pings, then she smiles at me.

"Annie!"

"Hiya, Blythe!"

We hug tightly and then part. Blythe hands me back the credit card transmitter, smiling.

"Do you know who you saved?" she asks, leaning back against the counter as I pocket the device.

I look at her. Her pale blue eyes shine brightly and are a contrast against her darker heritage Italian skin. Blythe looks fitter and leaner but much healthier than when we served together in the RAF.

I shake my head. "I'll be honest, Bee. I ken he was rich, his suit told me that. Beyond that, not interested. He's money; you ken how I feel about rich guys."

Blythe shrugs. "Not all rich guys are assholes, Sherlock, just because Jim is. This one has his shit together."

I grin when the use of my old force nickname comes into play. "Aye, maybe so, but once bitten, aye?" I say, smirking.

Blythe sighs at me, but I just smile. "He got separated from his shadows. Adrian wants to hear the details from ye." Her eyes are pleading. I nod, and she lifts the mobile device, flipping a switch.

"Aid, can you hear us?" she asks.

"We can." My eyes go wide.

"We?" She checks for me.

"Just Marcus and I," he states, and I relax. I know these brothers run the private security firm Blythe works for; I found her that job and I know who they are to each other.

Blythe looks at me and nods, making me aware she's asking obvious questions.

"He was slashed a good half dozen times. How did you find him?"

I go through what happened the night before, which takes a good twenty minutes and more coffee for Blythe.

"That's why it was off!" I hear Adrian rumble.

"Yeah, it was likely being used to track him," the male voice pipes up from a short distance away. Blythe mouths the name 'Marcus' and I nod, understanding.

"His attacker was speaking to someone on loudspeaker," I continue my observations, "about not being able to find him, but his signal was there." Blythe closes her eyes then opens them again. The colour in her eyes has become an even icier blue, and I know Blythe is now irritated a lot. You don't work with someone for fifteen years, be best friends for a decade longer, and not know what they're thinking or read their body language.

"I still think exactly the same as I did last night. I wish I didn't..." she states in a cold, hard tone.

"We know what you think, Bee. We don't like it, but we're coming to that conclusion ourselves," Adrian agrees.

"I have a question," I butt in, before they end the call.

"Go on, Annie," Marcus encourages. I can tell their voices apart now.

"This client of yours, I dinnae want my details being passed on. I'd appreciate being kept outta it, as best ye can?" Blythe reaches across and squeezes my hand. "Please?"

"When his head is clear, he'll pick up on it and he'll wanna know."

"Please, I've had it with folks with money telling me what I can and can't do in my life. Tell him I'm not in Edinburgh, I'm an informant or something, I don't care," I state. "But, please? Especially given what I do."

"We'll do our best on that front," Adrian promises me.

Blythe smirks. "I'll be back for my shift tonight," she confirms with them.

"We'll be close by if anything kicks off," says Adrian; his voice is closer to the speaker, to us.

"Drive back safely," they instruct in unison.

Blythe grins. "I understand," Blythe replies softly before she hangs up. I watch as the device is turned off.

"Bet they're pissed off?" I ask as we sit at the kitchen table. Blythe pulls out some shortbread from its usual high storage place as she nods in reply.

"Yep. We didn't expect the client we're contracted out to, which is who you saved, to get attacked."

I shake my head. "I didn't do any such foolish thing," I state, reaching for a shortbread finger before she scoffs the lot. "He did most of it, I just patched him up and sent you after him. I didn't know he was your client, and I had a runaway to get to safety. Why are you watching his arse anyway?"

Blythe scoffs in reply as she sips the last of the current coffee. "You really didn't know he was with us?" she asks with the shortbread halfway to her lips. I shake my head and she puts the rest of the finger into her mouth. She chews slowly, as if thinking some deep thought, but knowing her, it'll be her working out what to say.

"He received a few threats on email from someone unknown for 'causing a huge fucking problem' and saying he'd be knifed or worse, and they did it. I'm not liking how my mind is working out how they did it either." Blythe cocks her head to the side and makes a small sound of surprise, as if she's worked something out, but I don't ask for details. I'm not the one she needs to share that information with. Then she switches the subject completely.

"So, what has Jim done now?" she asks and bites the next shortbread round with determination.

"Elle mentioned I might be upgrading the car, he told me two weeks ago not to go asking him for money for it. I've got money saved for it, told him to take a fucking long walk."

Blythe shakes her head, more at his antics than at me.

"I wish," I say, whispering the biggest regret, "I'd done what you suggested and not gone to find him, or tell him I'd raise the bairn myself. Fucking hate his attitude, just because he's got money."

Blythe comes and hugs me; her silence says it all. She warned me when I was pregnant, but I wanted to give the guy a chance, give us a chance. It took me too long to see what she did. The chance was never there.

"How is my wee god-daughter?" she enquires, changing the subject onto something much better.

I smile. "Getting huge! She's eight in a few weeks. Might be the last birthday party she has for a while, given the global situation."

Blythe nods. "Aye, if the walk goes the way the talk is, we'll all be on national lockdown with a bloody curfew. Like being back on a damn base."

I shrug. "Can't stop it, from what I've heard. We're just gonna have to get on with it as best we can." I shudder, knowing how people change behaviour on a lockdown. Base life tells you that. "Might mean I'm busier than before...ye ken what I get called out to."

Blythe nods. "Aye, I know, I've seen ye when it goes south. It might also mean we celebrate our birthday before...if you're up for it? And," she pauses for a moment. "I've things to maybe share with you."

I grin. "Oh, what kind of things? It's been a while since we put on party clothes; I'm up for that! If yer shoulder is?" I ask. It's been months since it was operated on.

"It's fine, ye cannae tell they went in to fix it." Blythe grins and nods then stands to hug me. "Share with ye when I am sure," she whispers, mostly to herself. "Right, I'll see you soon, okay?" The last sentence is over-jovial, too confident.

I nod and think of asking Blythe about her client as she reaches across for her device. I stop myself from asking, but not before Blythe sees. Blythe pulls her hand back and her eyes search mine. "What is it?"

I sigh. Why do I care so much? "I ken this client is rich, but..." I hesitate; I can't have a sad ending. "He's gonna be okay?"

Blythe nods. "Yeah, he'll be fine and as Adrian said, he'll want to know about you, but we'll deflect as best we can. I think you'd like him. He's a boring git most of the time, but he's funny, and this will mean he has to keep his arse where we put it." She pauses to put on her coat. "He's being kept on morphine for today and should be off it tomorrow morning. That's gonna be a lorry full of fun!" Blythe grimaces at a memory. "Or not!" She says, grinning. "I'll catch up in a few days, okay?"

I nod as the anti-listening digital device is turned off. We hug in silence and part ways, leaving each of us to return to our routine.

# 4 ~ Anthony

My side hurts like a bitch, more so than other parts of me, and I realise other parts hurt that usually don't. The room is quiet, dark, still, and there is a horrible smell from somewhere. The main lights in the hallway aren't on, but the sidelight at the top of the landing is, which casts a soft glow through the door. I lay and listen, recognising the sights, sounds, and smells of my mansion, my bed, even my long-haired Siamese cat Hera, who is curled up on her usual cushion next to the radiator. I can hear movements downstairs, but I can't tell who is moving around. I realise I usually can, but not today. I struggle to sit up and knock something off the table next to me, causing a crash, even though whatever it was fell onto the plush bedroom carpet.

My door eases open and a face I recognise smiles at me.

"So, you're awake are you, sir? Good to see. Can you sit up a wee bit perhaps?" Morag is slightly younger, but greying around the temples even earlier than myself. She hooks an arm under one of mine and helps me sit upright, propping pillows up behind me, and turns on a table lamp not far from me but out of my reach.

"I'll be fetching you some chicken noodle soup now, sir, think you can sit there whilst it warms up? It won't take long."

I nod and lean back, resting against the pillows. My head still hurts and it takes me a moment or two to find the right word for Morag. My maid.

The sound of someone else climbing the stairs to my room makes me open my eyes. I hear low voices as both sets of footsteps pause on the staircase, then resume. A bulky figure stands in the frame of the door, partially blocking it and partially leaning against the wooden frame.

"Anthony, you look like fucking hell." He pushes through the door and comes to sit on the chair near the bed that is in the wrong place. I don't have the energy to tell him to put it back, and I have a feeling it is now the most occupied chair in my home.

"Gee, thanks! What the hell happened to me?"

He rubs a hand over his face and from the looks of him, he is not going to answer me. It seems my question has aged him five years in two seconds.

"We know some of it. And you're not going to like it." He looks me up and down. "I'll go into more detail tomorrow, now you're awake. But," he pauses, looking me over, "you were attacked. I haven't worked out how they knew where you were or who was with you, yet. You must have done something great in your previous life, because someone was looking out for you."

"Who?" I ask as my mind slowly begins to clear up. I recalled the business dinner in Glasgow, the escort to the limousine, then not a lot after.

He shakes his head then runs a hand through his light brown beard. I remember him now. He is Adrian McGowan, my head of security, one of the paid-for shadows of my life, and a business partner, along with his brother, Marcus. We grew up near each other, and I always saw potential in them.

"They don't want to be named. But thanks to them, you're alive."

I smile. "Keep working on it, would you? I want to meet them, say thank you at least."

Adrian nods. "Might not be that simple; I don't think they live in Edinburgh."

I manage a small smirk. "Does it matter?" I ask, pain running through me as I move slightly. He returns my grin.

"No, but it seems they're even more secretive and elusive than you, which says something. They've got a connection to us." I nod, understanding that it's not a connection he wants to exploit or piss off.

Morag returns at that point, carrying a tray of food. She shoos Adrian's muscular tattooed frame out of the room, closes the door then helps me visit the bathroom before helping me to eat, wash, and settle down for another bout of sleep in clean sheets, all to help me recover. But, I wonder what it is I need to recover from, and why.

Hera's yowls wake me from a restful slumber, and I recall more about the attack. I work out that I've slept nearly fifteen hours as I manage to get dressed into something that doesn't hurt any of my wounds, especially the large one on my left that hides under a large plaster bandage. After a battle with some pyjama bottoms, I stand in front of the mirror, deciding I don't look too bad. Standing at six foot three, I don't think I look too shabby since I take care of myself, and I'm only just starting to go grey. My short beard shows signs of age, but at fifty-two, I decide I still have plenty to give. Okay, so I am divorced with three grown children, a penthouse in the city, and a seven-bedroom mansion that I occupy in Edinburgh with no mortgage.

Managing myself as a philanthropist, businessman, hedge fund manager and entrepreneur requires more brains than brawn, but it would seem I'll need both if the attack the other night was any indication. I recall the knife, a fight (of sorts) and...not much else.

Gently, I slip my feet into my slippers and head towards the kitchen, allowing Hera to run on ahead. I just hope Morag is already up and busy.

Thankfully, she is and so is Adrian. I nod a good morning to them both and see Blythe patrolling outside in the garden.

"Should you be up?" asks Adrian, sounding somewhat concerned.

I shrug gently in reply. "I need to move about; I've slept enough."

Adrian sits down and starts clicking through things on his phone. "Cameras are all working. Do you want to hear more about Friday night?" he asks, glugging his coffee. Morag tsks him as she clears things away, but I am keen to hear what he thinks happened, compared to what I can now remember.

He helps himself to more coffee, and I decide we would be better discussing this situation in my office. I take my time to pad my way across the ground floor level; trying to move with healing knife wounds when you are fifty-two isn't straightforward.

By the time I make it to my office, Blythe has finished her patrol and joins us. She closes the door behind her, and Adrian once again looks like he swallowed a wasp.

"What do you recall?" he asks. I take the seat behind my desk, intending to get some trading done when they finish talking with me. Adrian is sitting in the guest chair whilst Blythe, who looks entirely dangerous and wind-swept, takes a pew on the sofa arm. I consider asking her not to do it, but she scares me. Adrian pulls out one of those anti-listening devices he is practically in love with, turning it on.

I tell them about the dinner, then getting into the limousine, vague memories that seem dreamlike of someone with a knife, then not much until I woke up being treated for wounds here at my own home.

"You don't remember getting knifed? Running into an old wool mill in Glasgow?" Blythe looks at me intently, never breaking eye contact. "Being dragged from the car? Losing your coat? The person who helped you?"

I shake my head but focus on the last part of her statement. "Someone helped me? Who?" Adrian has been carefully vague so far with any description of who it was that helped me. Blythe is being very careful as well, so this person is closer to them somehow than Adrian had suggested, I am sure.

"They don't want you to know; they don't want the attention you'll bring to them."

That statement floors me. Blythe continues. "They did hear part of a conversation of the person who attacked you. Thanks to them, we know they were using your phone to find you. However, Marcus hasn't found anything, so we're not liking where our thoughts are going as to why your attacker knew what we now know they did."

I try to recall who attacked me, but I don't recall their face.

"Do you remember anything about that night once you were in the car?" she asks, shifting herself on the arm. Her black hair is in a ponytail, her clothes fitted, allowing for ease of movement. "Any sound? Smell? Sensation?"

I try to recall the moments once I was in the car, but I only thought the car smelled super sweet, like almonds. I mention this and both glance at each other with a look of recognition.

"Go on...what's the epiphany?"

Blythe motions for Adrian to speak, but the big man baulks.

"Chloroform," he says, spitting out the word as if it were bad food. "Probably in spray form. Too much will kill you, but a quick spray of it will just knock you out. It explains why you simply don't remember. The question is, how did they get to you in the limo?"

Blithe shifts again. "The two shadows were found the following morning, not together. I think they got gassed too, but something doesn't add up. The planned route out of Glasgow was followed for a few miles. Then it was deviated from, you were doubled back. The driver was not with the other bodyguard when he checked in."

I rub my face, confused by what they're telling me. "One of them was with me, the driver was in the front with someone else," I vaguely recall seeing two heads through the driver's glass.

Adrian just nods. "Things we've discussed, I know your thoughts on that, and you know mine."

They send each other knowing looks. "Come on, I'm down but not dead, and I'm paying the bill here. I'm an adult, a big boy. I can take it."

Adrian shifts and Blythe looks at the floor. Shit, this is bad. I take a stab at the worst-case scenario. It's what I do and then I plan around or for such a situation. "It's an inside job?" I ask. The anti-listening device Adrian likes so much is sitting on my desk, blinking away as it does, calmly, unassuming, and when Adrian's eyes snap up to meet mine, I know I have assessed the situation correctly.

He simply nods. "We don't quite know who or why; so until we do, your guard will be either Blythe or myself."

I nod. It makes sense. "So you've two employees you can't always trust, or at all. What's the game plan with everything else? Meetings, travel?"

Blythe laughs. "The whole country is about to go on national lockdown, Tony. No leaving the country, not even your neighbourhood. No foreign holidays, no business meetings, and no travelling after six pm. It all kicks in from the twenty-third."

I look at them both. "You're joking?" Both of them shake their heads. "We'll let you catch up with the news," says Blythe as she deactivates the device for now.

"Will I be able to use that later?" I ask.

She simply nods and leaves it on my desk. I have a suspicion this is going to be a crazy blessing in disguise.

## 5 ~ Annie

The news pretty much said the entire country was about to head into a lockdown. Save for essential workers, we would not be allowed to leave home, unless we had to go for our hour-long daily exercise or food shopping. I got the impression the government didn't quite know its arse from its elbow, but that's nothing new. It was clear what essential services meant: the emergency lot, social workers.

Front line workers like shopkeepers, food transport people, social workers like me, will be allowed to travel out of the area to fulfil our jobs. I make a pot of tea and sit down to work out what and who can move around. Fulfilling court orders was also allowed, as was providing child care. My phone rings and my ex-husband's name appears on the screen; I sigh and answer it. Like everyone else, we have to work this stuff out quickly; might as well do it now.

"Hi, Jim," I say, trying to keep a steady upbeat tone in my head. We are divorced now, but we married quickly when I was pregnant with Elle. Then equally as quickly found out that we shouldn't have. He can be an arse and throws his weight around regarding money when I don't do as he wants. No way was I cutting our daughter off from her daddy though. Thankfully, our arrangement worked and we had it put into a court order, just to be safe; more to protect me from him than the other way around. His new wife, Fiona, is a darling and she is a second mum to Elle; she's even made Jim reasonable on a few things in my life which have made things a little easier in general. I couldn't have gotten any luckier on that front if I had tried.

"Hey, Annie! Have you heard of it?"

I scoffed. "Trying to catch up with it all now." I get comfortable and go through what I'd worked out the restrictions to be so far. He breathes a sigh of relief.

"Right, so we do as we are, but we're going to have to get creative for things to do with her. What's she into at your end?"

I laugh. "Books! She's a total worm who's migrating to a book dragon. She'll need the library from Beauty and the Beast at this rate!"

Jim laughs. "She gets that from you," he chuckles and then replies to something at his end; Fiona going by how he is talking to her. He never talked to me like he does with her, another indication we're better off as we are.

"But, she loves the movies some of the books have been turned into. *Descendents* is her current movie favourite and the many fan-based books that are out there..." I let it hang, hoping he'll get the hint.

His next statement tells me he did and I hear the key of a keyboard being pressed. "Which *Descendents*? There's a few of them. Send me a list of what she has with you? I want to order it in now, get it delivered so it's here on time."

"Sure, no problem. She'll be back tomorrow?" I ask, double-checking our agreement.

"Aye, as always, around six. We'll have fed her. Are you okay? You sound...weird."

I grin, though he can't see. "Aye, had a hard day's night, looking forward to my bed. Just hope I don't get called out again."

"Ah," was Jim's only reply. He knows what I do and that I can't always talk about it. It always bothered him that I did this, even though I got the job after our divorce, but working with domestic violence victims means I *can't* give details. When I got this job, I needed someone to talk to after a difficult shift since Blythe was away. However, Jim didn't want to know or even listen.

"I'll let you get going. Just wanted...needed to touch base with you about this lockdown. How weird is it?!" he asks. The truth was, it was weirder than finding dinosaurs walking the Earth again, and I tell him so. He laughs.

"Yer no wrong there hen! Right, I need to get going. Talk with ye tomorrow, Annie!" I am going to reply, but there is no point. He's hung up.

Between Blythe's visit, Jim's call, and work, I am on tenterhooks for the remainder of the weekend until I hand over to the weekly retrieval crew Sunday evening. Elle had returned the night before with an armload of school work, but the school wasn't closing for another week. I go through our usual morning routine. Coffee for me and a bowl of my favourite porridge, toast and jam for Elle. Then I pack her lunch, make sure she has what she needs, and take her to school before I head to the local charity offices for our usual Monday morning Zoom chat.

Julia is on the conference call as the offices connect up. It saves us all both time & fuel, though I and the other field agents for the charity go where we are needed. Thankfully, this coming weekend I know I have free time, unless this whole lockdown goes sideways, and since the instructions and decisions are coming from London, it is almost a promise waiting to happen.

We get down to business, Julia updating us on where we are at and what the lockdown might mean for us, though it is still as clear as week-old dishwater. It turns out, we might not be affected at all, as we are linked to Social Services and classed as a front line because of the domestic abuse shelters we facilitate. The question arises of how we'll reduce the time together to stay within guidelines but still get the work done. We debate for a moment, then Julia ends the meeting asking us for ideas, but calls me when everyone else has returned to their desks.

"The girl you brought in on Friday, Sarah? She's not wanting to talk to anyone, even Cat and everyone talks with Cat! Can you pop over during the week and see if you can get her to open up? You know how it goes when girls are found; they often only talk to the one that helped them."

I think for a moment, but it doesn't take me long to reply. "Yeah, I can. Has to be during school hours though. I can be there tomorrow for around ten?"

Julia's voice rises a little, relieved I think that I agreed to hang around in Glasgow for the day. I could work just as easily in Glasgow as I did at the Edinburgh facilities.

"Perfect! We'll see you then. We've moved her to number 3. Ye know where it is?" I have a vague recollection of where the newest safehouse is.

"I'll find it. I always do!" I say. Looking up the address from here on the computers and memorising the address wouldn't be an issue. I get on with the chores here in Edinburgh as the day progresses. There is food to be prepared, women to talk with, shopping to be done, toilets to be cleaned, laundry and floors to be washed. Nothing is deemed beyond our abilities or too good for us to do: If we can do it, we do. It is the same in the military, so for me, this isn't a change in mindset.

It is my turn to cook the dinner, or at least prepare it, and the request for my Spaghetti Bolognese was made last week. With four kilograms of prime Angus beef, two huge woks, half a dozen tins of tomatoes, onions, garlic, mushrooms, and spaghetti, I get to work. By one o'clock, the meat part is ready, but since it is for the evening meal, I leave it covered up on the hob. I begin thinking about what I'll be doing when this is eaten; I'll be at home with my little girl, hearing about her day, her friends, the not so nice classmates, what she liked or didn't. I am so lost in my thoughts, I jump at the sound of a text message arriving. It is from Blythe.

*B: Eastside is having a VIP only night this weekend and next before they have to close for lockdown. I have access. Wanna go for our birthday on Saturday? My treat, since we probably won't be able to spend it together this year.*

I look at the message for what feels like forever but is possibly about three seconds. Blythe and I share a birthday, though we're a year apart in age. Then my fingers reply before my brain can kick in.

*Me: Yes! Hell yes! Plain little black dress, or sparkling? Yes!*

*B: Excellent! Meet you outside there, Saturday night at eight? Sparkle, you crazy diamond :P*

*Me: Sounds ideal!*

*B: Fantastic, I'll see you then!*

With a smile on my face, I finish up and head home to pick up Elle from school.


"What did you do today, Mummy?" she asks as we meander home. I can walk to the school from home, which is why I finally picked the house I did when Jim and I divorced. The fact he was wealthy enough to pay for it outright lessened the burden on me, but as he said, I was supporting our child during the week and him at weekends; I wasn't raising a daughter of his in tenements.

"I helped out today at one of the shelters. I have to go to Glasgow tomorrow to do the same, so can I send you to the breakfast club, sweetie?"

Her eyes lit up like the sun. "Yes, please!" She starts bouncing around, and I have to remind her we're walking near the main road and she needs to be careful. She stops bouncing and walks next to me again, sensibly.

I smile at her. She's so happy, and I'm as proud as heck that she just gets on with life.

"So, what did you do today?" I listen as she rambles on about fractions in maths, the sentence constructs she's been learning in English, then she tells me a new word she's learned in Gaelic class. She was one of a few kids who wanted to learn the old language and, thankfully, one of the teachers is rather fluent in it. She devours words like a shredder eats paper: pages of it at a time.

"What word was it?" I ask. Gaelic took off when Outlander started airing and it's going through a revival. I've heard it being spoken and it's beautiful, a language I can get my head into.

"Trodaiche. It means fighter." She is rather proud of the word and she gives me a sentence or two using it. It sounds like "tro-ditch" and I like the sound of it. I love to read and I love languages just as much, a skill I discovered in the RAF.

"And why did you learn about that word?" I ask, suddenly realising her teacher never just taught them a word and how to use it.

"Oh, because Billy and Adam in year six got into a fistfight! Mr Gordain had to break it up. He *wasn't* pleased."

I smirk as she adds drama to her sentence. Mr Gordain has to be in his late fifties, nearing retirement, and how he copes with the youngsters, the pre-teens, I just do not know. It's hard enough with one nearly eight-year-old, and she's on her own!

"What did he do about it?" I question.

"He called their parents. I know because he told them he was going to, and Abbie saw Billy's folks arrive. We could hear shouting from his office, but it wasnae him shouting, or being shouted at. We didn't see Adam or Billy for the rest of the day."

I can only imagine what it was like in the office.

"You remember the skills I taught you, don't you?" I ask. We are near home now.

Elle nods at me, her wee eyes shining brightly.

"Yes, Mummy, I do. Not sure I'd ever use it, but I know them."

I smile at her. "When did we last practice them?" I'm sure it's been longer than I would care to remember.

"I..." She looks at me and her cheeks are all red. "I don't remember," she mumbles. I grin.

"It's not a telling off," I gently remind her. "I can't remember either. I want to go through the moves again before dinner, okay? But after your snack and homework, aye?"

She bobs her head, and I know full well she's trying to avoid the practice. The thing is, in my job, anything can happen and whilst Jim knows what to do if I'm hurt, neither of us wants to find out what we'll do if Elle gets hurt or involved somehow. It's part of the reason I prefer being deployed away from Edinburgh when I'm sent to domestic violence situations. Less backlash if neither spouse can find you.

We go in and decide on pasta bake for dinner, then I make her do her homework before we have a wee training session. For being extra brilliant at doing her locks, breaks, and punches, I put another garlic bread slice in for her as she showers. By eight o'clock, Elle's tucked into bed and the evening is my own. Like so many evenings before, I'm at a loss for what to do just for me which doesn't involve reading, watching the television, or being a mum. It's when I feel most alone.

# 6 ~ Anthony

Blythe stands at my office door as I continue to work into the evening. It's been just over a week since I was attacked and life has been perfectly normal. I've asked Blythe who helped me a few times and I'm now starting to insist. Although she's not called me out on asking yet, she is starting to roll her eyes when I approach her, as if she knows what I'm going to ask. The New York stock exchange is still open, so I can still trade. I stop for dinner, eating with Morag and Blythe, but I only need to look at Blythe before she rolls her eyes at me. Adrian has been checking in, but Blythe is the one assigned the personal detail whilst Adrian tries to work out which of the two shadows I had has double-crossed us. Until then, he's asked us to act and behave normally.

"Eastside have their pre-lockdown VIP Party this weekend and next. I suggest we go on Saturday evening."

I look up from the stock exchange windows on my dual-screen computer and sigh at her.

"Why would I want to do that?" I ask. I might be a shareholder in Eastside, and I certainly love the return on investment I get back from the place, but spending a night there at the weekend when it's sure to be as crazy as hell isn't my idea of a decent Saturday night.

"Because there's someone you want to meet who is also going, and you'll want to be at the Penthouse," she says, smirking at me as she pushes off the door frame, heading towards the snug. There's only one person I want to meet right now and Blythe has access to them. Access I realise she's now giving me. I finish trading the shares I want in six minutes, then I go and hunt out my bodyguard. Now I want to know why.

"How did you persuade them?" I question, finding her curled up on a chair facing the doorway with a book in her lap. She's as silent as a mouse when she reads, it's scary. She misses nothing that happens in the real world as her eyes absorb the words before her. I could open a window and she'd know, then yell at me to close the damn thing yet not lift her eyes from the book she's reading.

Blythe eyes me with a look that says, "Please, bitch!" I smirk back at her.

"It is their birthday soon, and we won't get to meet up as usual. We're about to go into a lockdown. It wasn't hard to persuade them, especially since you're providing the tickets." She grins at me again, and I haven't the will to chastise her for taking liberty at using my Eastside membership card. It's not going to break my bank if it's used.

"And I'm going to go, why?" I ask. She knows fine well I'll be going; nothing is going to stop me from being there Saturday night, not now.

"Because you've been quietly asking Adrian about the person who helped ye. Because you keep asking, and in truth, you've been a pain in the arse because of it. It's the damn elephant in the room and I'm addressing it. They don't know you're going or that you part own the place."

I smile gently. "What is your friend's name?" I ask. She's still not hinted if the friend is male or female, though I'm inclined to think they're female.

Blythe shakes her head. "Huh uh... ain't tellin' you. You get to do all the good stuff when you meet them on Saturday. Just, don't dress in *that* suit; they'll spot you a mile away."

I recall the suit she means, it's in for repair after the attack; the police found nothing on it which would identify who attacked me. I doubt I'll see it before this lockdown begins, the tailor visibly paled when he saw it.

"So how should I dress?" I ask, pouring a drink for myself. I motion to Blythe, asking if she wants one, but she shakes her head. She never does. Blythe sighs as she looks up from the tome of a book she's begun reading.

"Dress to impress, as you always do," she says, burying her face in her book again. Who the hell am I going to meet?

# 7 ~ Annie

We're up at the usual time, but Elle is bouncing because she's going to the breakfast club. She gets to eat as much food as she can at school and play on the iPads when she's done eating. I kiss her as I sign her in early and pay the fee, and I watch as she runs into the school hall.

I get back into the car, start it, select the radio station and head out towards Glasgow. The motorway is busy already, but heading into Edinburgh, not away from it. I make it to Glasgow in standard time, parking up at Safehouse 3 as if being here is normal.

I know this new unit is headed up by someone called Tina, who was told I was coming today. My access code for the bio doors works and I let myself in. The place is quiet. Two floors of old offices have been turned into private rooms, family rooms, three living rooms, there's even a library I know Elle would love.

Although I never want her to see inside a safehouse like this. I'd probably kill anyone that made her need to. That is if Jim didn't destroy them first with one of his forklifts or run them over with a lorry. I shiver and half chuckle. I shake my head to clear it and focus on what needs doing here. There are a few women residents milling about, doing their own thing.

"Has anyone seen Tina this morning please?" I ask loudly to attract their attention.

The looks I get don't shock me anymore. Women who have been abused aren't used to outsiders in their safe domain, even if I helped put them there. Most won't recognise me, which is the whole point of my dark thief set-up. However, I do see the girl I've come to talk with:

Sarah. She looks at me a moment, trying to work out where she knows me from. Then, she gasps and rushes over from the seat at the breakfast table to hug me.

"Well, hello to you!" I say. I don't use their name until they tell me I can. I hug her back and can feel her trembling in my arms, and I wonder what the hell happened to her before I found her. She's just as clingy now as she was that first morning.

"I hear you need to talk? Fancy talking with me in a wee bit?"

I put the ball, the control, in her court. I rub her back as she starts sobbing, which is how Tina finds us a few minutes later as I'm persuading Sarah to dry her eyes and clean up a bit.

"You're Annie?" she says as Sarah stands back a little, gently blowing her snotty nose.

I simply nod. I've not glanced at Tina, but I can see and sense why she's in charge. There's an energy about her that is just protective. She's not a slight lady either, but I still wouldn't want to argue white is black; I might find myself chewed up and spat out in pieces.

"Hi, Tina." I offer my hand and we shake in greeting when Sarah goes back to her breakfast. She has a firm grip, a can-do attitude just as I do. I love Glasgow for its rawness, its ability to sit on the side of the Atlantic and take a battering. However, there's something in Edinburgh that feels more like home, softer. I guess I'm a Lothian girl at heart.

"Good to meet you. Can you help with breakfast? Then you can have one of the rooms to chat."

I nod. "Who have you got on counsel for today?" I ask. I'm not qualified to chat with Sarah without a trained counsellor there, though I can listen. However, I see Sarah's reaction. Shit. This is going to be awkward, but I know it needs to be done.

"I'll check the roster when we've eaten, aye? I cannae think without food in my stomach and a coffee in my hand."

I nod and help Tina prepare breakfast for everyone at the house. I never lose sight of where Sarah is or what she's doing, even when she visits the bathroom.

Tina finds one of the counsellors and introduces us. Francis and I have a quick chat about what is needed to help Sarah, then we take drinks and snacks into a small, quiet office. The room is set back from the main hub, to avoid eavesdroppers and to ensure that once the women start talking, they're not interrupted.

Sarah curls up on a chair and the counsellor sits in another. The sofa is to the left of me and I sit down.

"Do you want a hug?" I ask her. Sarah nods and jumps over to curl up to me. I drape an arm over her and just hold her. I give her a few minutes to get comfortable. The counsellor nods at me; they're ready to just listen, though I know the questions they'll ask.

"How did you manage to get to Glasgow?" We know her employment was in Edinburgh and it took her two weeks to cross over to Glasgow. We suspect she walked, hiked and hid, probably in Stirling and the smaller towns between. Sarah sighs and then begins her story.

We sit and listen as she tells us what we suspected. She touches on why, but she won't go into the details with the counsellor. I sit and stroke her arm, providing a physical presence. She might be in her early twenties, but right now, she's just a kid, scared and full of self-blame, which is wrong, but it's going to take a little time to undo that crap.

The counsellor ends the session, saying he's here to talk whenever she is. Sarah nods and dries her eyes after being told her parents want to talk with her, to know she's safe. They organise a call to them for later that afternoon. As I'm leaving, she pipes up.

"He didn't..." She looks at her feet and my heart sinks. I don't move, I hardly breathe. I wait for her to carry on speaking, to get her thoughts sorted and onto the tip of her tongue. "He made me so scared, Annie..."

I nod. "He tried?" I ask, taking an educated guess.

She nods, still looking at her feet.

"That's why you ran?" I ask. I sit down on the chair the counsellor was occupying, wishing Francis was here. She nods again.

"Sarah, you ken it's no yer fault, aye? You're not in control of what others do. You. Did. Nothing. Wrong." I gently punctuate the last four words to try to get her to understand them. She nods, but I don't believe she understands or believes it. "Sarah, hen, will ye look at me?" I ask gently.

She lifts her head, her eyes full of tears. I slowly kneel in front of her and hold her hands which are still clasped between her clamped knees.

"You. Did. Nothing. Wrong," I repeat. The tears fall as if she understands, but I need her to repeat it, to get it into her head. I need her to start believing it.

"Say it with me, sweetie: I. Did. Nothing. Wrong."

She slowly whispers the words back to me.

I smile. "A wee bit louder. Come on, once more with feeling?" I request.

She does and smiles. "Have you ever seen Buffy?" I ask. She shakes her head. The youth today!

"Come on, let me get you that episode to watch. You can watch the whole series, we've got them here on DVD. All nine seasons! We've got Angel too, and David's not bad to look at, even if he is portraying a vampire that can barely dress. Personally, Spike's much better." She grins, laughs, and wipes away her tears.

I find the musical episode of Buffy and put it in the player for her, then show her where the entire collection is. Buffy's a great girl-power series to binge on. One of the other women complains Sarah is using the TV again, but I advise her in a harsh tone to use another TV that is not being used right now and she heads off, huffing at me in disgust.

I find Sarah's counsellor and update him on what she said after he'd left. He had left the room but stayed outside, so he'd heard everything. I sigh, thankful he did. I feel better knowing they know; they are better equipped to help her.

~

Friday night arrives and I throw myself into my mixed martial arts training session. All the frustrations, anger, angst, and every other emotion I vent out in sparring. Sometimes, I get my butt handed to me, but most of the time I forget who I am, what I do, why I felt this way, and I just live for the next move, the next lock, throw, hold, punch, whatever it is. The dojo gives me the best workout. I get to work out my body and shut my mind down. Elle's gone off to be with her dad and Fiona until Sunday, so I have time to concentrate on myself.

Nearly three hours later and the class is over. I'm hot, sweaty, tired, but most of all, I'm restored. The restless energy that's been building up within me all week is gone, reset. We bow off and I put on my tracksuit over my gi, then I head to the car, aware of my surroundings partly because of what I do, but also because I'm a woman alone. After this week and Sarah's revelations (even if she didn't name the bastard), I'm acutely aware of it. Life is messed up when one half of society has to be on alert from the other. The fact I can take care of myself is an advantage, and I am aware not everyone can.

I throw my kit bag into the boot whilst checking the back seats and get into the driver's seat, locking the door before I start the car. I head home, watching what's around me, behind me. It only takes me seventeen minutes to get home; the traffic was flowing my way tonight.

I put my kit away in the garage, pulling things out to air on the racking, then I secure the car and head inside.

It's eerie in the house; it's too quiet without the small person around causing havoc. I smile, lock the door behind me then double-check the backdoor too. Finding everything is secure, I strip off, leaving my sweaty clothes in front of the washing machine to wash when I've showered, then I head to the bathroom and take a long hot shower. Knowing I'm out with Blythe tomorrow, I preen myself. I could do with a haircut, but that's not going to happen for ages now I guess. When I'm dry, I moisturise everywhere I can, plucking my eyebrows and generally spending a little time on myself. Slipping into a kaftan and some lacy knickers, I find a bottle of wine, make myself a cheese omelette then pour myself a glass, put the laundry on, and try to find something on Netflix.

Saturday starts just like any other. I get dressed, fix myself a light breakfast, and then I contemplate leaving the house. The lockdown hasn't started, not yet. It starts at midnight on Monday; the clubs, pubs, restaurants, and anything non-essential have to be closed by 11 pm on Sunday. The two weekends Eastside thought they had to celebrate, gets turned into one. Like most venues, it had become a ticket only event. I quickly double-check things with Blythe.

A: *Tonight still on?*
B: *Yep! Just checked; it is VIP holders \*only\**
A: *Lovely! Confirm the time?*
B: *Eight. See you tonight!*

Smiling, I decide to try and get some last-minute shopping done. By the time I've found some extra toilet rolls (because everyone was buying it like there wasn't going to be a tomorrow, or a next week, but I only needed an extra four-pack), toothpaste (was my child eating it?!) and extra little bits of food and fruit, I am exhausted.

Shaking my head, I set off for home, not knowing that Saturday isn't going to end as tranquil as it had begun.

I pull onto my drive to see a long-term friend sitting there. Tears are rolling down her face and she looks like hell. I can guess what has happened, and my blood begins to boil. Only, it is more than tears. Her eye is starting to swell and there is bruising showing around her neck.

I open my arms out in a hug without saying a word. She opens her car door and runs to me, breaking down in heartbreaking sobs as I hold her.

I call the police, who are great and because I'd made the call, they send out exactly the right kind of officer to take Holly's statement and offer support. Whilst she's giving her statement, I take a moment to text Blythe.

A: *Holly's turned up at mine. Her now-ex assaulted her. Don't like to leave her on her own.*

B: *Bring her, we can look after her!*

A: *She's bruised and might not be up for it.*

B: *Don't back out. We'll find a way through. She might just want a quiet night in. I can get someone from the agency I work with to sit with her tonight? Or watch your place?*

A: *Why would you do that?*

B: *Desperate for you to come out before we're confined, purely selfish.*

A: *Shitty to leave her after she's attacked.*

B: *See what she wants to do, but I can get her in if she wants to join us, or your place watched extra. Let me know.*

I focus on Holly's words, her story. The police suggest she go to a shelter, but I can tell by the way she looks at me and the shake of her head, it's not what she wants. "I don't want to," she tells them, and I smile. We've been friends since secondary/high school and she knows her shitty ex isn't coming anywhere near her whilst she's here. He doesn't know my house, but I know already he's a coward and he's not going to be brave enough to show up.

The police sigh and give me a sympathetic nod as they leave. I smile at her. She looks like hell.

"What do you wanna do tonight? I was planning on going to Eastside with my ex-military best friend. You're welcome to come, or you can just chill out here."

Holly looks at me with wide eyes. "I didn't mean to mess up your plans, Annie!"

I smile. "You came here because it's a safe place. We'll get your car into the garage so if your ex does happen to drive by, he'll not see it. You're welcome to come either way, but this is likely to be the last night out for everyone before lockdown. It's your call."

Holly sighs. "Being honest, Annie, I think I want to stay in." She looks up at me, her eyes soft and tearful. "If that's okay?"

I nod and smile. "Sure it is. I'll get you a key, everything is going to be locked up, but the house is yours. Come on, let me show you where everything is."

She smiles and follows me as I show her the bathroom and get her to help me make up the guest bed in the spare bedroom which I use as a library. The day-bed is usually where Elle and I snuggle up on if we're reading, and it's used for guests when needed, like now.

Holly smiles at me. She looks tired with dark circles under her eyes, her usually well-kept hair looks like it's not been washed for days. She also looks a lot thinner than usual and she's curvy in general.

"When did you last eat, Holls?" I ask.

"Err...this morning...I think?" she says.

I shake my head. "I meant a meal, not stuff some food into your mouth when you can or when your stomach growls." I grin. Holly gives me a guilty look and I know it's been a while since she ate. We finish making the bed and I head to the bathroom and start running her a bath. I pour in a dollop of my French Lavender bubble bath and wink at her. As the bath runs, I head to the kitchen and warm up the oven, taking out a chicken-en-croute, some wedges and frozen vegetables for Holly, and a pasty for me. I get it all onto trays to put into the oven once I've made her have a bath.

Holly gives me this "Oh my gosh, you haven't," look as I come back up the stairs.

"Annie, you don't have to!" she protests. She knows I don't, but I do.

"That's what friends do," I say. "Elle isn't due back tonight, so I am not expecting anyone, nor have I ordered takeaway. Dinner is in the oven and the timer is set. Help yourself to whatever you want for dessert; there's some wine that I opened last night."

I smile at her. I heard what she told the police. I don't need her to tell me again unless she wants to. Like most victims, she'll want to put it behind her and just pretend it never happened, at least for now. I also know she's going to need to talk about it. Tonight though is not that night.

As Holly bathes and chills out, I begin to apply my makeup and decide on the brown smoky eye look. It's been a while since I've worn makeup this strong, but I know a night out at Eastside requires it. You don't go to a nightclub this prestigious and forget your A-game in the makeup & underwear department.

I drop Blythe a quick text to say I'm coming to Eastside as arranged, without Holly. She sends a simple thumbs-up, and I carry on getting myself ready. I'm applying the last of the smoky eye makeup to the second eye when Holly appears at my door. I smile at her. "Feel free to borrow anything that might fit you whilst yer here."

"Thanks, Annie! Here, let me help you!" She takes the makeup brush from me and continues to apply my makeup. I try not to freak out as I'm suddenly not in control, but I relax, remembering this is Holly and this is what Holly does. She's a hair and beauty technician with more vocational skills than I can ever list. After what seems like an hour, but in truth was more like five minutes, she declares I'm ready.

I open my eyes and I do not recognise the face that looks back at me. The eyes are perfect, blended better than before. My lips are lined and filled in perfectly, and being honest, I look like a model. For once, I feel like a woman!

Holly grins as I thank her, and she helps me slip on the sparkly short dress I picked out for tonight.

"Love your underwear! Are you feeling lucky or is it for someone special?" How can she comment about my sex life when her shitty ex beat her up for not wanting to sleep with his sorry ass? The lacy black bra & matching Brazilian lace knickers highlight my sporty frame, but I still blush at the compliment she gives me.

She's stronger than she realises, something I'll have to remind her of tomorrow, or another day. I feel bad for leaving her here, but this is what she chose.

It's more Christmas weather than a cold February night in Edinburgh, but the effect on me is still the same: I'm pebbling all over.

My silky hold-ups are hidden by the length of the dress, which comes to a few inches just above the knee.

"Let's get the cars sorted, then I can head off." Holly hands me her keys and I switch the cars around as the timer for our food goes off. I tell her what she needs to do next as I put on my heels and decide on a smart coat so I'll be warm. I manage to eat the pasty I warmed up for me whilst I run around, grabbing my key and remembering to give one to Holly. I check I have what I need for tonight. Cash, card, phone, key, and the best weapon of all. Me.

Eastside is in the Old Town and before you can get near the place, it's heaving. I spy Blythe who is waiting for me a few doors down, away from the line of people who are hoping to get in. I can tell by the way the bouncers are standing, they have more chances of plaiting fog than getting in there without a VIP status card tonight. Blythe hands her card over to be checked. It's swiped, then the bouncer nods. We're checked for weapons, pepper spray etc. and because we have nothing on us that's offensive, we don't have to check our bags into the cloakroom. We do check our coats in though, and Blythe leads us through to the bar. The place isn't as busy as the outside implies; it really is tickets only.

Blythe waves the card at the barman, he swipes it, and she orders drinks. A shot for each of us, with my usual rum and coke and a vodka and coke for Blythe. She got me into Vodka during our RAF days, but I'm far more of a spiced rum girl. We down the shot, letting it warm us up, then we leave the glasses on the bar. We take our regular drinks and Blythe motions upwards to the viewing area. I nod in reply; it's hard to hear anything with P!nk's dulcet tones about getting the party started blasting out at us, though the music isn't as loud as it usually is, thankfully.

Blythe is asked for the VIP card again and it's swiped, with this bouncer opening the rope barrier and letting us up. Dear God, I've never been up to the rich folks' area. I tap her on the shoulder and point to my ear. She nods whilst still climbing the stairs, and she finds us a small table in an alcove, then leans in so she can hear me.

"How the heck did we get up here? How much did that card cost you?!" Getting into Eastside is not always easy, certainly not cheap, and tonight is VIP only. This section, though, is beyond VIP only; it even has its private dance floors for crying out loud.

She leans in, her sparkly red dress refracting the lights, but she doesn't shout her reply down my ear. "It's covered with the card, don't worry about it." I give her a questioning look, but she only winks at me. She won't tell me and I don't want to spoil the night by asking her. She said this was for our birthday, so I am going to have to suck it up and do an Elsa. Christ, I've seen that movie way too many times with my little girl!

The song has changed to something else with a strong base, but it's not one I recognise. It makes me feel too old to be out clubbing, but hell, I'm a single mother, a divorcee, and a chance like this is very few and far between, given what I do for work. The song has changed again and Blythe stands up, finishing her drink, motioning to the smaller dance floor on this level. I nod, finish my drink, and go to join her.

It's been an age since I danced, and I just hope my mummy moves don't scare off the younger crowd. Then I realise, this section doesn't have the youngsters in it; this is for the folk that can afford beyond the basic entry, and there are various VIP levels so there's no one here below our age group anyway. Blythe nods towards a couple of men standing off to the side, giving us both the look that asks if we want company. I nod at them, smile, and beckon them over.

I recognise one: Adrian, Blythe's employer and one of her lovers and I nod in acknowledgment. He gives me the characteristic, short military nod in return, right before he crushes me in a hug.

His companion has caught my eye. He's just as tall with dark hair, slightly greying at the temples with some white at the chin of his short, groomed beard. His eyes are a cool blue and gorgeous. He looks collected, together, he's muscular but not overly so, and for me, hot. I carry on dancing, winking at Blythe who winks back with a sly grin on her face & a twinkle in her eye. I turn back to the guy who answered my beckoning and smile up at him. He curls a finger, beckoning to me, and I stop dancing so he can lean in.

"Let me buy you a drink," he says, his tone indicating he is not taking no for an answer. I agree and he gestures to someone off in the back I can't see. A few minutes later, some drinks are placed on the table Blythe and I had claimed earlier. Four of them. As we head over to drink them, he leans in and introduces himself.

"I'm Anthony, but my friends call me Tony." He extends his hand out in greeting and I shake it, telling him only my first name. My heart rate beats a little faster as we get closer to each other to talk. He takes my hand from the shake, turns it, and gently kisses my knuckles. There's a fire in his eyes and I know already he is wanting more than the dances and the company. The question is, do I want to sleep with him too?

The drinks are refilled when Tony calls for them, but he's only ordering as much as I say I want, which isn't many. No one goes near our drinks; at a club like this, especially tonight, there's no way drugs or anything else is getting in here easily. Even so, Tony's careful to only order when we're ready, though how he gets them to the table so fast I don't know. We're dancing to a George Ezra tune, then a Lewis Capaldi number, getting closer and closer each time. There's a point when we're that close we might as well be touching, but Tony's not laid a hand on me and I realise he's respectful, a gentleman.

A well-dressed gentleman and it makes him hotter than just his looks. I grab one of his hands and place it on my hip, nodding at him. He leans in and moves his legs between mine, Dirty Dancing style, as a rhumba style song comes on. Without me realising it, he's got me dancing to the tune and I'm looking up into his eyes, focused on his face and trusting that my treacherous body follows his lead.

The song ends and one hand comes up to caress my face, outline my jaw. I've just been gyrating on his leg for one song for crying out loud and, yes, I want him to kiss me; I'm aware I'm soaking wet, my mind is in the gutter, imagining just how good it would feel to have him above and buried in me, and I know I'm a goner, at least for tonight. I snake a hand up to run it through his hair and finally, his lips are on mine, teasing, gently opening my mouth with his tongue before his hand goes to the back of my head to angle me as his mouth masterfully assaults mine.

Good god, the man can kiss, and I'm glad he's got an arm around me. My heart is aflutter, my breaths short and fast, I'm sure I could climax on just his kiss alone: feelings and reactions I'm really not used to having. He pulls away, smiles and nods towards the booth we've claimed. I nod. Blythe is nowhere to be found, neither is Adrian. Our two drinks are left at the table, and I check my phone quickly. There's a message from Blythe:

*B: Enjoy! Giving you two space, usual protocols.*

That means she's around in a different corner or they've gone to another VIP section (I know Eastside has about three VIP areas), but she's still around if I send her the right code word. They've not changed in the twenty-five years we've known each other, but I feel no need to use them right now.

"You okay?" asks Tony, taking a sip of his drink.

I nod. "Just checking where my friend is," I say, picking up the other glass and taking a sip. The drink is temperature perfect; the spice of the rum isn't drowned out by the cola.

"I know where your friend is," he says and nods over to the far side of the level we're on. Blythe is with Adrian, as I suspected, dancing, giving us some privacy but hanging around. I smile.

"Known each other for long?" he asks.

"Aye, quite a few years," I reply, smirking, not wanting to give anything away. I've played poker with Blythe.

He still has a strong arm wrapped around my waist, holding me close to him. It's a welcome strength, but he's charming with it, not threatening. His tight dress shirt highlights his frame, and I get a slight shiver as I see his muscles pulsing beneath the fabric, which appears to be silk or very high quality. Oh heck, he's made of money! I force myself to dismiss the thought, not wanting to put a damper on the evening.

"You're very beautiful, Annie, do you know that?" he asks, leaning into my ear so I can hear him. My skin gets goose bumps of the good kind as his warm breath touches my neck and ear.

"You're quite good looking yourself, Tony," I return the compliment as I run my fingers down the shirt. He smiles at me and strokes my jawline again, then cups my face in one hand whilst the other gently massages my hips.

"I'd like to kiss you again, Annie. In fact, I'd like to do a whole lot more, but we can't here."

I smile. "A kiss, I can do," and as soon as I've given permission, his lips are on mine, firmly but not bruising. I don't know how long he has his lips exploring mine or how long we've been sat just kissing in a quiet alcove here at the club, but we break apart and I find I'm straddling him, his erection pushing again the confines of his trousers, against the thin layer of my knickers, the friction making me wet. His hands are on my thighs now, gently caressing the top of the holdups, his thumbs slowly stroking the inside of my thighs, inching higher.

"I'd say you want me too. What do you say, Annie, shall we leave?" His voice is a gentle burr of Scot and something else, his eyes are full of want and passion, and given he's made me hornier than a teenager behind the bike sheds, I nod.

I'm a grown assed woman for crying out aloud. He's not taken anything from me by force; he's asked the entire way. I nod, deciding I want to do to him what my brain has been fantasising about for the last few hours, as my body responded to his touch. I climb off him, finish my drink, and text the word to Blythe that says I'm going with this guy. She sends me back a thumbs-up and a winking emoji, then she's at the top of the stairs with Tony and me so I can go and claim my coat.

I text Holly whilst I'm waiting, letting her know I'm not going to be back tonight. She sends back an "enjoy!" message and in moments we're walking through Old Town, entwined with each other as Tony leads me to somewhere far more private.

# 8 ~ Anthony

Dancing with Annie was amazing. Seeing her when she walked into Eastside with Blythe just left me speechless.

She was stunning. Tall with shapely legs that went on forever. The dress was full-on sequin, sparkling under the lights every time she moved—and hell, could the woman move! When she beckoned me over, my heart was in my mouth and I was hard for her already. I'd never wanted to meet a woman more than I did Annie tonight. Every dance, every touch of her made me a little harder, but the first kiss sealed it for me. I had to have her, not just pay for what I thought was a much needed night out for her to thank her.

We're walking quickly through the Old Town, and I know Adrian and Blythe are behind me somewhere, ensuring we get back to my penthouse safely. Adrian texted me that they wouldn't be on guard in the penthouse tonight if Annie was with me. I assumed it was to do with giving us privacy, but there's something Blythe-like about this woman I can't quite put my finger on.

We're at the door to the penthouse building in a little over five minutes, the biometrics allowing me access without the need for a key. The elevator is at the ground level and I nod to the doorman, who simply nods back and does something on his computer. The door opens as we approach. I guide Annie in, taking out the fob that gives me access to my floor, and then the car begins to climb slowly. I turn to Annie, cup her face in my hands and kiss her deeply, crouching down a little to taste her. Her hands are on my arms, steadying her as I kiss her senseless. I've been drinking what she has, rum and cola, and whilst we've had a drink, we're not drunk. Annie only had three, which considering us Scots can usually drink, is quite lightweight.

The elevator pings as we reach the Penthouse, and I pull back, then take one of Annie's hands and guide her to my door. The biometrics let me in and as soon as we're in the hallway, I pull her to me, one hand behind her head, the other around her waist, angling her so I can kiss her as deeply as I need to. I cannot get enough of this woman and I remember, she has no idea who I am, or if she does, I'm not aware she knows.

Her hands are tugging at my coat, trying to remove it. I stop kissing her, pull back, and help her remove her coat before hanging them both up near the door.

"You can keep your shoes on," I say, eyeing up her legs. "If ye want."

She smiles and takes in the penthouse. "I think I'll take them off, so I dinnae damage yer floor." Her accent is stronger than my own; I blame my Oxford education for loosening mine. Annie's isn't quite Glaswegian, but it's more west coast. I care about taking this woman to my bed and making her come multiple times, however I can manage it.

"Another drink?" I ask, heading over to the alcohol. I notice how she takes in various areas, the split level I had built. She's muttering under her breath, and I wonder what she's saying.

"No, thanks. I've had enough for tonight." She smiles at me and looks at photos I have scattered about on a dividing bookshelf.

"Grown lads?" she asks, pointing to the photo of me and two of my kids. I nod.

"Two lads and a lassie," I say, motioning to the next frame along. She smiles again.

"My wee girl is nearly eight. They grow up so fast, don't they?"

I nod. "Aye, too fast. My eldest is just about finished University, the middle one is in his second year, and my younger son has just started. All very expensive."

She chuckles. "I never went. College was it for me, I'm not academic, far more vocational, practical."

She might not be, but I'll wager she's as bright as she is brave. I take my drink and find my favourite chair, turning the lights low with the remote. I love the technology that allows me to set the mood with the flick of a switch.

"Have you lived here long?" she asks, watching me get comfortable in my chair. I nod and indicate to the other chair, watching as she moves around my town home.

"Since I renovated the place, aye." The lights are dimmer now, but I can still see how wide-eyed she is, how she licks her lips, how she watches me. She walks over to me, then kneels before me. I open my legs and she moves so she's between my knees, then her hands are tracing the firmness of my legs from my knees up and back down, slowly. Her touch is like fire and my groin responds. She leans in and I put my glass down, lean forward and once again, cup her face. Her lipstick is gone, kissed away by me, and I feel a little primal. Her lips are swollen because of it and as our tongues dance, I run my hands slowly down her arms, reach her elbows, and I move them across so I can feel her breasts. I don't know what kind of bra she has on, but they feel full, amazingly right.

Her hands are at my shirt, slowly undoing the buttons just by touch alone. It doesn't take her long to have my shirt undone; her hands trace my pecs, and her touch sets fire to me. I groan as she walks her fingers up my abs towards my erect nipples, she pinches first one then the other; God, my dick has never reacted like this before, I can feel it pulsing in anticipation. I break the kiss and look at her as I pull her up onto my lap. I'll have her mouth around me soon enough, but I want to enjoy feeling her, touching her, setting fire to her. I have no intention of sleeping much at all tonight and I hope she doesn't either.

She reaches around to the side of the dress and lowers the zip. I'd have struggled to find it on the back and I'm as glad as heck she's done it for me. I stop her hands from removing anything else.

"Let me," I choke out, slowly dropping one of the sparky straps off her shoulder. I pull her to me and kiss the exposed skin. I kiss her collarbone as I slowly remove the strap for the other side, and the dress drops to her waist, revealing a lacey black bra.

"God, Annie, you're gorgeous lass!" I exclaim, taking a breast in my mouth whilst I pinch and fondle the other. She moans and leans back, but runs a hand through my hair, holding my head to her breast as I nip, tongue, and make her buds stand at attention. I turn my focus to the other breast and then suddenly, the bra is undone. I help her remove it and go back to my ministrations, looking up at her. Her head is tossed back; her smoky eyes are closed, though I'd love to see what her eyes look like when they are aroused, full of passion.

I take one hand and run it over the inside of her thighs, whilst wrapping the other around her waist. Her legs are just as strong here as the calves are, and I cannot wait to be between them, to have them wrapped around me, to feel her all around me. My hand teases her via her thighs, and I feel the top of the holdups. They're lacy, like her underwear, and I stroke her in circles, claiming her mouth deeply as my hand slowly reaches her sex. I run my finger over her, and she moans into my mouth. It's music to my ears, having her respond to me this way.

I push the fabric aside and slide a finger over without any barrier; the smell of her arousal reaches my nose and my cock presses painfully against the confines of my clothes. I slide a finger into her and she gasps.

"Yes..." she mews, then her hands are cupping my face, kissing me deeply. Her hands drop to my shoulders, and I slide another in to join the first, slowly making her ride my hand. "God yes!" she gasps as my hand fucks her, her fingers digging into my biceps. I pull back on the kiss and look at her. Her eyes are closed, lost in the sensations I'm giving her.

"Look at me, Annie..." She opens her eyes and they're sparkling, reflecting the soft lights around us in a million different ways. I watch her eyes change as I insert a third finger, stretching her, making her ride on my hand, and it isn't long until she is crying out her first orgasm. I feel her juices trickle over me as she calms down; I withdraw my hand, licking it clean.

She grins at me. "Certainly would have gotten us thrown out of Eastside if we'd done that there," she chuckles at me. I reach up and pull her down to me, kissing her deeply. She tries to pull away, but I hold her firmly.

"Bedroom," I say. I'm kind of asking, but more telling. She nods and climbs off me, and as I stand, she comes up close, then starts kissing my pecs, pushing my shirt off me and running her hands over my abs.

"Goodness, you're a gym bunny!" she says, smirking up at me. "I like it!"

I cup her face again and kiss her. "No, I'm not," I say. I've always been fit; I just found the need to take care of myself a long time ago, after my divorce. "This way," I say, downing my rum and coke, then taking her by the hand to my bedroom.

# 9 ~ Annie

His fingers are experienced, magical. It's been years since I've had an orgasm by someone else's hand that wasn't a machine or a vibrator, and my last lover certainly didn't make me come so hard, intensely, or expertly. He downs his drink and leads me to his bedroom. At least, it could be his bedroom. I don't know nor care. The bed, though, is huge. He pulls the top comforter quilt down, then the one beneath it to reveal the sheets, and then his lips are on mine again. His hands are making their way down to my waist, removing what is left of my clothing as he goes, and when he reaches my knickers, he slowly peels them down towards my ankles as he kisses a trail down my front from my neck to my left breast, then down to my belly-button and the top of my sex.

"Sexy as fuck!" His accent is getting stronger, a sure sign of his arousal, and I wonder what else he has in store for me.

"Lie down, lass," he says and I obey, sitting on the bed and laying back. I scoot back so my feet are on the bed, and I watch as he finally peels the shirt off his back. He's ripped, certainly, the chest hairs are slightly white or grey in places, but mostly black, like his hair. It adds to his appeal, somehow, knowing he has knowledge and experience on his side. He shakes his head, grins, and pulls me by my ankles further down the bed.

"Arse at the edge, lass," he commands.

I wiggle down so my arse is just on the bed and I'm aroused by his dominance; then he kneels, using his hands to gently spread me open; he pins my legs by my knees and exposes me to him.

"Fuck, Annie...I'm going to enjoy devouring you, lass!" His mouth is on my lower lips before I can think of a reply, and all I can do is moan as his tongue expertly laps up my juices, dives in and around me, sending sensations through me and making my body coil up for another orgasm. My hands struggle to find his head, so intense are the feelings this man is building in me. I'm about ready to explode again. My hands grab the bed sheets as I arch under his ministrations, crying out as he brings me to my second climax of the night. I hear his trouser belt being undone and I finally look at him as he drops his trousers. He's decently hung and dripping. I lick my lips. I move to try and grab him, but he firmly puts me back on the bed. "Later," he says. He goes to a bedside table and removes a condom from a box there. I come up onto my elbows as he grins at me.

"Can I?" I ask. I've always wanted to glove up a man and Tony will be my first.

He nods and I can feel my neck and cheeks go red. "You'll have to show me how," I admit, embarrassed. "I've never..." He's walked back between my legs and beckons me to sit up.

"Like this," he says, showing me how to roll it on. I hold his velvet, stiff rod and slowly guide the condom onto him, then I look up at him and smile. He cups my face and kisses me as he eases me back onto the bed. He leans over me, grabs my hips, then slowly pushes his way into me.

He fills me up, deliciously so, and he withdraws before sliding back into me again. I look at him as he slowly fucks me, watching my breasts bounce as he thrusts in. He's leaning back, making sure his pubic bone hits my clit, and the pressure within me slowly begins to build as he speeds up. His angle is perfect and it's hitting my g-spot. There's no fumbling around, trying to find where it is, this man knows how to fuck and dear God, I'm happy to let him.

His thrusts get a little more intense, a little faster, and then he's leaning over me, his face between my breasts as his pace increases. He has a breast in his mouth and a hand on the other as he speeds up. He sweeps my legs up over his shoulders and my climax builds faster as he now thrusts into me.

"Annie..." he rasps as he grabs my breasts. "Come with me!" he growls and my body obeys. I arch up, lifting myself off the bed as I scream his name and climax around him, feeling him thicken within me. The lights dancing behind my eyes are caused by him. He holds me there as he thrusts a few extra times, filling the condom. Gently he lowers my legs, my body reconnects with the bed, and with one final kiss, he withdraws, leaving me strangely empty. I open my eyes slowly to see him heading to the bathroom, removing the condom as he goes. I drape an arm over my eyes and turn to him as the bed dips.

"Come here," he says, opening his arms for me. He wants to cuddle, to hold me. Thank Christ, I hate men who can't hold a woman after he's fucked her senseless. I manage to scoot up and somehow, he's got the covers over us, trapping the warmth between us under something soft.

I can smell his scent, the earthy, fresh scent that is him. He kisses me on the head as I snuggle into a bicep. I notice he's got recent scars on his torso and a memory from a fortnight ago hits me.

I sit up and take in his profile, turn him the way the man was laying on that pallet. Then I pinch his chin and move his head to the side. I'm amazed he lets me just turn his head without a word.

No fucking way is this that rich guy who got knifed. Is it?

"Jesus Christ, it is you," I say. Then I back off a wee bit, creating some space between us as my head and body try to wrap themselves around this conundrum. This part of his bed is cold and brings me back to earth with a bump.

Tony nods, almost holding his breath. "Aye. I meant to tell you earlier, but when we kissed, my plans to do so went right out of the window. You've no idea what you do to me, Annie; I never lose focus like that. Never."

"So you knew?!" I ask, hissing the question. I'm not sure how I'm feeling right now. I look at him as he slowly nods.

"Aye, I ken who ye were when ye came in with Blythe. I gave her my spare Eastside card for tonight knowing she was bringing you. Until you walked in with her, I had no idea what you looked like. I didn't even know you were a lass until I saw ye; she's told me nothing about ye."

I swear under my breath again. I am going to kill Blythe when I see her next! Setting me up blind was a break in the sister code.

"So tonight...was a...a thank you fuck?" I ask, not quite believing what just transpired. Tonight was the best sex I've had in my life and I've been married. Hell, why did he have to be *that* rich son-of-a-bitch?

Tony shakes his head. "Hell no, lass, and please, dinnae be so crass...what we've just done, that's because I wanted you and I know you wanted me. I went hard the second I saw you, and I'm not some young hotshot who gets his head turned easily, not anymore. I've never reacted to anyone the way I've reacted to or with you tonight."

His hand is slowly caressing an arm; I hadn't noticed until I swallowed and breathed a few breaths.

"I've never had images in my head of what I'd like to do with you...still want *to* do with you, Annie. You'd be on my mind if we'd only met tonight and two weeks ago didn't happen. I'd still be finding a way to bring you back here." He pauses. "I've never brought any woman here...my ex-wife hasn't even been here."

I look across at the bedside table, the top drawer still open. He understands what I'm thinking now.

"I always like to be prepared, though it's been months since I've been with anyone. Years if you want to put it into relationship terms."

I look at him, taking him in. I was good at judging people in the RAF. I had to be, given my role. It was part of my job to believe people or prove them wrong.

I run a hand through my hair and watch him. He's still stroking my left arm, but he's not pushing himself onto me. He never forced me to kiss him, to come back with him, to straddle him in the VIP section of Eastside. I'd had lots of chances to get out of there if I had wanted to. The truth is, I hadn't wanted to go. I'd wanted to sleep with him. I'd wanted him where he was half an hour ago, above me, treating me as a woman, a Goddess, making me feel desirable, sending me over the edge.

"What are ye thinking, lass? Talk with me, tell me please."

I sigh. "Jeez...you've just dropped a bombshell and ye want me to tell you what I'm thinking?" He nods and swallows. Okay, I can take his lack of transparency, I can well believe he thought with his other head, not the handsome one with the magical mouth and the doe-like scared eyes. I trust him. I sigh and speak.

"I'm thinking I didn't want to go home. I wanted to sleep with you, it's true. I wanted to have you above me at least, maybe not just in that position. I wanted to be screaming your name, I wanted to be treated as a woman, not just... Shit, not just for what I do, though I love what I do. And I tell ye now unless I'm in the company of my daughter, I can swear like a proper scuffer."

He smiles at me, genuinely smiles. It reaches his eyes and they dance.

"You've no idea how happy I am to hear you say that, Annie. Let me hold ye, aye?" I look at him, still unsure, my head and heart in conflict. "Please?" he asks as he lays back down, opening up his arms for me to cuddle into.

I sigh and lay back down, but there's an awkwardness about the cuddles now. Before I realised who he was, I'd have gone to sleep on him, cuddled up like this, tucked in with a strong arm draped over me, let him fuck me again at least once more. Truth is, I'm a romantic. Despite all the horrors I've seen because of the women's shelters and the work I do, I still want to be romanced, dined, and danced. I still want someone to make love to me and treat me like I'm younger, wanted, not an older woman who can't possibly be fit for love. I want someone who can respect me, be there. All the things I've wanted for the last twenty years push themselves forward, making me pay attention.

"Yer still in your head," I hear Tony say.

I sigh. "Aye, you've suddenly given me a lot to think about," I reply. I'm tucking the sheets around me, trying to create a barrier so I can think, though my breasts are still sensitive and pebbled; I'm still turned on by his presence. He turns towards me and lifts my head.

"I should have said, you're right. I'm sorry." I blink. Having a man apologise without a fight is a new one for me. Usually, I have to fight like a tigress to get a man to admit he's wrong or done something to hurt me. Jim was terrible, though I think he's gotten better with Fiona. Jim is still often a swine with me and I've not worked out why. Tony leans down and chastely kisses my lips with his. No tongue, just a gentle, sensual, full on the mouth kiss.

"Let me make it up to you," he says, kissing my forehead.

"How do ye plan to do that?" I ask. I'm still not sure about this; my body and heart are dictating things here and they usually don't.

He smiles. "I'll cook for ye. Dinnae run out on me, I'm not ashamed of what we've done, or what I want to do with you in a wee bit. Let *me* take care of you, for tonight at least."

His eyes search mine, and I gently nod in acquiescence. He kisses me again and my body gives in, turning the kiss from something gentle, sensual, to something primal again. He turns us over so I'm on my back and he's above me, then he's between me, filling me, and I want it.

# 10 ~ Anthony

She kisses me after I tell her I want to look after her. I had meant it to be a slow kiss, sensual, then hold her until the small hours before I dive into her again. She has other ideas and as I turn her onto her back, I find the sweet spot to rest between her legs. She's beneath me, the quilt covering her is gone, released, and as we're kissing, I get hard again. I've never recovered this quickly from sex before and I know this time I want to make love with Annie, not just make her come.

I reach across to grab another condom, then I pull back and sit on my haunches as I roll it on, looking at her as much as I can.

"If you want me to stop," I say, but she shakes her head and beckons me down with a finger. As I lean towards her, her arms slowly wind around my neck, pulling me closer to her and making my heart race. Her hand is entwined in my hair making it impossible for me to move away. Her eyes are staring into my very soul.

The hairs on my thighs quiver as I feel her fingers' feather light strokes moving up my legs towards my groin. I'm finding it hard to think straight.

I tease her sex, moving slowly back and forth over her opening, she's warm and her wetness invites me to explore deeper; in one move I'm buried up to my balls. She wraps her legs around me, enveloping me, and if it's possible, taking me even deeper into herself, making me feel wanted, desired.

"Love me," she begs, kissing me. I kiss her deeply, keeping myself slow, enjoying the sensations of her warmth, her hands in my hair, the shivers she sends down my body. Her breathing is ragged and her kisses are deep. Then I'm building my pace, the feeling of her gorgeously fit thighs around me, holding me in place makes me feel alive. I watch her as I make love with her, glad the elephant in the room isn't there anymore. I grin as her eyes dilate, her mouth falls open, her head drops to one side, exposing her neck. I lick and bite it a little, tasting her from her hairline down across her shoulder. My dick jumps inside her as my lust begins to take over.

Her nails scratch down my back, and I lift my head to watch her as she climbs her way to another climax. I want to see her shatter around me, and I whisper her name. She opens her eyes and smiles at me, then reaches up to kiss me. I lean in, kissing her, and speed up my thrusting to match the kisses. She screams as she orgasms, and I absorb the cries in my mouth, but I don't stop. I'm not far away from my own and her nails around my arse help.

Annie arches beneath me a little, throwing her head back as another climax takes over, and I shudder deep within her. I kiss her as we calm down, tongues dancing happily, damp with sweat but happy, sated.

I leave to discard the condom, watching her from the bathroom as best I can.

As I head back to bed, I find Annie drifting off to sleep. I climb back in and snuggle up to her, and she cuddles into me again, like she did before she realised who I was. She sighs and her breathing softens, and I look down at this amazing woman, then I kiss her head and drift off to sleep.

I wake up before her, even though it's Sunday. I can't hear any of the security team downstairs, the hallway light is now off, but I can hear Hera padding around. Sliding out from Annie's arms is hard, I don't want to, but when I'm awake, I have to get up. I can't lie around and if I try, I'll just be restless and I know I'll wake her.

Annie looks so peaceful, serene and angelic lying in my ivory quilt and topper. I have to admit, I had a great night's sleep, not just because of the dancing, the drinks, and the club, but because of Annie.

There's a faint light coming from around the curtains, so it has to be near eight am. I throw on some lounge bottoms, then head out to feed Hera and see what I have in for breakfast. I gave Morag the day off with it being Sunday, and I'm glad she's not around. Annie, though, occupies my thoughts, blowing my dreams and expectations out of the water.

I take care of Hera first, partly because she'll meow the penthouse down if I don't, but she'll get under my feet until she is fed. It takes me a minute to sort her out, then I decide what I'm doing for breakfast, other than feasting on Annie again. I smile, recalling how responsive Annie was, and I loved every minute of it. I spy some English muffins, find some bacon and a jar of hollandaise sauce. The amount of eggs I have makes deciding what is for breakfast very simple. Eggs Benedict. I set the coffee machine going and I'm humming as I am about to find out how Annie likes her coffee. I bring a pan to the boil for the eggs.

It takes about five minutes to cook breakfast once the water is boiled, and I place the plates for us on a bed tray, then take it up to the bedroom. Annie's still asleep as I set the tray at the foot of the bed, then slowly I wake Annie up with many kisses.

# 11 ~ Annie

I awake to the sensation of kisses, and I turn to find Tony smiling down at me.

"Good morning, gorgeous! I brought you breakfast."

He's dressed in what seems to be dark blue silken pyjama bottoms and nothing else. I get wet again just looking at him standing there, his bare chiselled chest on full display. He bends down and picks up two mugs of something hot (which smells like coffee) and puts the mugs on the bedside tables. Then a bed tray which has two plates of food on it appears, and he nods back, telling me to sit up.

I grin. "I'm not exactly dressed for eating in bed," I say. He grins and walks over to a chair that holds the shirt to his bottoms.

"That'll cover ye, though there's just us here," he says, handing me the top half of his pyjamas.

I nod. "Aye, but I'm sitting up and I'll get cold," I say, feeling my nipples pebbling already. I lean across for the coffee. It's currently black, but there's a wee bit of cream in a milk jug and some sugar if I want it. I try it with a splash of cream and it's different but good.

"When ye said you'd cook for me, I didn't expect this," I say, looking down at the Eggs Benedict. He climbs into the bed and sits on his knees so he can use the bed tray too.

"Dig in whilst it's still hot, aye?"

I nod and do exactly as he suggests. The eggs are fluffy, perfectly runny, and the muffin is properly toasted. The bacon is crispy, which I can never manage to do, and I'm sure it took him longer to cook this than I did to eat it.

"Oh my God!" I say when I finish. "That was amazing!" I wipe my mouth on the paper napkin he's thoughtfully provided, rather than the back of my hands, suspecting he has standards I have no idea about. He smiles at me and leans across, caressing my jaw.

"I'm glad ye liked it, lass. Just going to clear these away," he says, stacking the plates then taking the tray away. I can hear him descend the stairs and talk to someone. I wonder who it is, but the question is answered when he appears a few minutes later with a gorgeous long-haired Siamese cat in tow. It jumps up on the bed and comes padding over to me, purring.

"Annie, meet Hera. Hera, be nice to Annie," he says as he fusses the cat. However, Hera doesn't care and she pads over to me, purring and head butting the hand I hold out. Cats usually love or hate me; I'm glad Hera is in the first category.

"Hallo, gorgeous kitty!" I say, rubbing her ears and letting her rub up against me. My role and my hours don't lend themselves to having a dog, but I hadn't considered getting a cat before. Hera makes herself at home on my lap, trapping me in the bed. I smirk and look at Tony. "You know, if you wanted me trapped in your bed for longer, you didn't need to pay Hera in treats to do it." He laughs at my joke and scoops Hera up, depositing her onto her bed that I now see under the window.

He turns and grins at me, then heads into the bathroom. When I don't follow, he pops his head back out and beckons to me. I hear the shower start and I sigh. My time here is coming to an end, but first thing is first: I want to make him come all over me in the shower.

His bathroom is huge; I'm sure the top floor of my house would fit in just this room. Tony's in the shower, standing tall, letting the overhead shower cascade water all over him, and I moan quietly. If there's a God, thank you! Even if this is just a one night stand, I resolve, it's been one hell of a night, a reminder that handsome, good men do exist.

I strip out of the pyjama shirt and drop it next to his bottoms, then step in to join him. He's grinning at me as I push him against the shower wall, kissing him whilst I touch his pecs, then I let my hands roam downwards, over his abs, towards his V, and I take in his moan when I grasp him. I don't have to massage him long to have him standing up to attention, and I trail kisses down his pecs to join my hand, the water now cascading over my hair, plastering it to my head. I toss my head back to remove some hair from my face, then I look up and grin.

His hands are on my shoulders as I take him into my mouth and begin swallowing him. I moan as my hand pumps him. I can see him tossing his head back as I suck and massage the length of him, rippling my tongue over the tip of his cock. It's not long before I taste some pre-cum on my tongue, and I moan at the taste of him; it's different. He is. I'm not usually one to swallow and I brace myself for him grabbing my head.

"God, Annie..." he growls as I speed up, moaning and sucking, making lots of gagging, wet noises which, judging by his reaction, he's loving. "No...wait...I..." I can tell he's close and he tries to pull away. Somehow, he manages it and covers me in sperm all over my breasts. I chuckle as it trickles down to the drain thanks to the water. "Dear God, woman, what are you like?!" he says, hauling me up to give me a smouldering kiss.

I just grin, not trusting myself with words right now.

He spins us around so my back is against the wall, his tongue and mouth assault my own like he's claiming me. He's just come so he's not going to want to again for a while. His hands are fondling my breasts, then he breaks the kiss and takes a breast into his mouth whilst he's looking at me. I moan; his tongue is amazing! There's little wonder why I always went for older men; they know what the heck they're doing!

"Ye like that, huh?" he says as his other hand finds my other lips and begin massaging me. "I'm going to taste you again, Annie," he growls into my ear. "Then I'm going to make you come on my hand like you did last night." I shiver in anticipation and it's not long until his hot mouth is exactly where he said it would be: between my legs, driving me wild! Lifting a leg, he pins me to the warm tiled wall. I can do nothing more than cry out as his tongue makes me climax and his fingers join in the encore. He's kissing me as his fingers work their magic, tearing another orgasm from me, harder than I did the previous night. His kisses are hot as he washes me down, shampoos my hair, and turns me so I'm leaning against him. Then he bends me over and I glance around.

"Condoms don't work in the shower," I say.

"I know," he says as slaps my arse. "You've a very fuckable arse, Annie." I shake my head and twist away.

"No... Just, no..." He simply nods, then leans forward and kisses my shoulder, then his lips are on mine again, turning me to him as the water shuts off. He's lifting me by my arse, his hands cupping my globes, and I wrap my legs around him. I realise he's walking us back to the bed, and he deposits me gently near the edge, just as he did last night. This has to be his favourite position. He pulls a condom out of the drawer and tells me to go onto all fours. I do and he slaps my arse again before he's filling me, his hands firmly on my hips. One hand tweaks and plays with a breast whilst the other finds my clit, and with his energetic thrusting, he's strumming me to another climax before I can think. All I can feel is him, his throbbing deep inside me. I can hear his balls slapping against me and then his other hand is on a breast, massaging it from behind as he kisses my back.

"So good...God, Annie, you feel so damn good!"

I can feel the pressure building, his breath in my ear, his head next to mine. "Come with me, lass, scream my name," he growls breathlessly and in moments, that's exactly what we're doing; crying out each other's names as we both climax, milking the other for all we're worth, then we collapse into a heap on the bed.

It's several moments before he moves off; he's pinned me down, but it's through exhaustion because he's not moved. My breathing is ragged, and I feel him stir and go limp, so he slides right out of me. Then he pushes himself off me and takes care of the third condom. I begin to wonder just how old he is. When he comes back to the bed, I've shifted but not far. I'm still face down on the mattress, unable to move. I could move before, I'm not sure I can now.

"Are you okay? I wasn't too rough?" I turn to look at him and shake my head.

"Did you take a Viagra or something last night? Where the hell did you get your stamina from?" I ask. He smirks.

"Annie, I've never been as hard as I am with you. There's something about you, lass, I'm not sure what, but I'm thinking I'm not quite done with you yet. Unless you are?"

Dear God, he's asking if I want to continue and stay with him longer. I check the time, I can stay for a few more hours. "Let me check my phone first," I say. I suddenly remember Holly and then I want a wee word with Blythe.

"Aye, I want your number, Annie," he says as I find my handbag from last night. I stop dead.

"Pardon?" I ask.

He looks at me with a straight face. "I want your number. I want to call you, date you, do all this again."

I smirk. "Do you?" I ask questioningly, sending off a text to Holly.

*A: Still at that guy's place. Are you OK?*

*H: Yes. I've done some tidying, hope you don't mind. I had the best night's sleep in forever, thank you!*

*A: No problem! I'll be back in a few more hours. Have you eaten?*

*H: Yes mum! Though, can you bring bread back? You've not much left.*

*A: Ah, right. Will do!*


Anthony shifts on the bed, sitting up against the tall leather headboard.

"God, Annie, yes. I want to know all about you."

I look at him. Whilst I forgave him last night for not telling me who the hell he was, I am not sure I want whatever nonsense he is mixed up in spilling over into my life.

"There...well..." I look at him. How the hell do I tell him what I'm thinking?

"Spit it out, lass." He leans forward, his gaze intense.

"You were knifed two weeks ago. Have ye any idea why?" I don't crawl over the bed; I keep sitting at the edge where he's just fucked me to kingdom come.

He shakes his head. "No. No, we don't."

I want to send a text to Blythe, but I decide on a phone call instead. "Let's see about that, huh? Hauld yer whisht a minute."

I dial Blythe and crawl over to Tony so he can hear.

"Annie! Did ye have a good night?" she asks. I can tell that she's on her own at her end; there's no other noise coming from the phone

"Aye...listen, tell me about two weekends ago. Any idea why he got knifed?" I ask. She doesn't know he's listening in. Let's see what they've told him.

"Ye worked it out!" she replies jubilantly. Then, her voice drops. "No, we still don't know. We think we know why his detail wasn't with him, but the money trail is coming up empty."

I sigh. "He's...asking to be more than a one-night thing. I need to know why he got hurt, Bee. I cannae be bringing trouble to my door when I dinnae ken what it is." She's my daughter's god-mum, she was at the birth and supplied one of the extra pints of blood I needed afterwards; she'll understand why I'm being guarded. I look at him as I say it. My honesty often does one of two things: Pisses people off so they push me away, or they accept it. His eyes go wide in surprise at my words, and he's not backing away or telling me to go. Is he... accepting my honesty here?

Blythe replies, cutting off my train of thought. "We don't know yet either, not exactly. There's nothing tangible showing up and to be honest, if it wasn't for what *you* heard, we'd be putting this down to a random attack and prank, malicious emails. It's only because you were there and what you heard we know it's not." I sigh at her words.

"So you didn't tell me who he was and is to you...because?" I ask.

Blythe chuckles. "He's been obsessed with you as soon as he was told he was helped. He wore me out asking about ye." I smirk at him, doubting her words.

"But you didn't tell me because..."

Blythe sighs. "Sherlock..." Tony raises his eyes and I just shake my head. I'll explain my Forces nickname later. Maybe. "You need a good man. Jim did a hell of a number on you, even though you're on semi-good terms now. Your 'dates' have all been fucking arses, proper bus drivers." I smirk at the RAF slang for bomber pilots. The constant nick-names for everything is something Blythe and I are used to. I can see Tony isn't.

"Doesn't mean you get to send me off blind into a Burton," I scold her. Tony looks very confused now. I know I am going to have to explain half these terms to him when this chat is over.

She scoffs. "He's hardly a Burton, Sherlock," I can hear her grin as she replies.

"Says you. What the hell did you expect me to do when I worked out who he was exactly?" I question her.

"Call me?" she replies. I scoff at her words and her thoughts.

"Ha! You, Grievance, bloody owe me. It was a shit thing to do. Especially to me. And given who he is."

Blythe laughs heartily. "I'll pay you back, don't you worry." Her voice drops to a low whisper. "But tell me, are ye okay? Is he good in bed?"

I laugh outright. "Aye, I'm okay and I'll be John Wayne tomorrow!" I say, which makes Tony grab a pillow and laugh into it, his eyes dancing with pride. Blythe laughs out loud too.

"See you later, Sherlock. Get a cab home, aye? I'll pay."

Tony shakes his head, touches my jaw gently, and I get his meaning. "It's covered; you better start thinking of ways to pay me back, Bee. You fucking owe me, big time. How long had ye been planning this?"

Blythe sighs. "Aye, I suppose I better think of something. And since he interviewed me," she confesses. I can hear her doing something in the background, switching ears I think.

"Laters!" I say and wait until she says the same before I hang up.

Tony throws the pillow back onto the bed as I stand up and put my phone back in my bag. Hera's still on her bed in front of the radiator, which is blasting out a serious amount of heat.

"So, let's start with Sherlock?" he says, questioningly.

I glance at him, my mind churning about the kind of danger he's in and who he is to Blythe, Adrian, and Marcus. It seems old habits die hard. I zone out for a moment as I recall Blythe's situation from months ago, but I snap back quickly enough.

"Aye, my last name is Holmes, and I was an RAF MP or a snowflake as we were often called."

He nods. "It explains why Blythe and Adrian haven't been up here this morning; I interviewed her."

I stand and pace about a bit, getting lost in my head about connections here, there, and everywhere that might connect him back to the Lloyd cousins, forgetting I'm naked until I begin to shiver slightly.

Tony lifts the bed covers and invites me to climb back in. I grab a condom out of the box at the bedside table and tuck it under a pillow as I do, allowing my hormones and libido to decide for me, at least for the moment. I have no doubt we'll be needing it in a bit. My hair is half dry and it flops over my eyes. Tony pushes it back and looks at me intently.

"Annie, I've no idea why I encountered you that night. But I do know this: I want to know you. I want you to know me. I'm smitten with you. I don't know why it's so intense. I'm fifty-two and I'm acting like I'm twenty-two. I can't seem to get enough of you." At least he's answered one question.

"I need to at least have some time to think about it. I've not..." I sigh. I have nothing to lose by telling him my lack of love life. "I've not been in a proper relationship since I divorced. Jim...my daughter's dad...we married when I found out I was pregnant. We weren't suited for anything more than a fling or a short term relationship. We tried...but it got nasty between us before it got better. It is better now and was once we decided to divorce. He's a great dad," I say, defending him. "We just weren't great together. I'm forty-two now for Christ's sake..." I let the statement hang.

Damn my emotional insecurities. Give me something I can control and I'm your gal. Give me a skip load of emotions and then leave me to work through and deal with them, I'm as good as a sunken banana boat.

Tony leans in and kisses me gently. "You're fabulous, sexy as hell, brave and..." He kisses my jaw as he carries on listing what he thinks are my qualities. "I have no doubt you're a great mother."

He pulls me on top of him, and I can feel him harden beneath me. Dear God, I am going to *be* John Wayne at this rate, never mind walking like The Duke!

His hands cup and play with my breasts which sends shivers of pleasure through me. He pulls me up a little so he can nip, bite, and lick me as his fingers have me shooting off to the moon in no time flat. I grab the condom as I become able to see and roll it onto him. Smiling, I climb up and ease my way onto him, riding him slowly, controlling how he fills me.

"Stop," he says as the pressure in me builds. He pulls my head down to his, kissing me, and then he grabs my arse with his two hands, one on either cheek, then he begins to thrust up into me from beneath. I bury my face into his neck, revealing how I feel when he has my arse in his hands like this. He bites the side of my neck and growls into my ear as I come, throbbing and clutching him within me whilst digging my fingers into his biceps.

# 12 ~ Anthony

Her walls contract, clamping around me, milking me, and that makes me come just as hard. I want to know everything about this woman. I want to know all the basic stuff, her favourite food, colour, how she takes her coffee, what movies, books...hell, the whole nine yards. And I want her screaming my name just as much.

Annie has collapsed on top of me, and I slide out from underneath her to go clean up. She moves slightly to make my exit easier, but I dare not be away from her for long. We might have the chance for another round, another quick shower before she has to go back to her normal life. I see her checking the time.

"When do you need to leave?" I ask. I don't want her to go; I want her in my bed permanently, but the time will come, somehow.

"Two, at the very latest," she says.

She watches me as I get up to go to the bathroom and clean up. Nothing escapes her attention. I wash my hands and wipe myself down after getting rid of the condom. When I get back to bed, she closes her eyes for a moment, a soft smile plays on her lips and she seems content.

"You've gotten rid of them all differently," she observes. She really doesn't miss a thing.

"Aye. It's a mixture of reasons. The influence I can provide for people is one of them."

"Oh, I see. I think," she replies sleepily. I can see her drifting off, and I check the time again.

"Alexa, set a one-hour timer," I say. Annie smiles and closes her eyes, holding my hand. When the timer goes off an hour later, Annie's gone.

# 13 ~ Annie

I awake before the timer goes off. Anthony's fast asleep, and I find his phone in his trouser pocket. I tilt the screen so I can see his unlock pattern and two attempts later, I have it unlocked. I need to mention that to Blythe. I type his number into my contacts and return it to where I found it. Then I get dressed. I need another shower, but I know what's going to happen if I try to stay. He's going to want to make me stay and goodness, his cock certainly would be persuasive!

However, I need to get back home; I have a daughter to be home for, a shower to get, and a dress to get dry-cleaned somehow in a lockdown. I know of a few businesses which might stay open for emergency service kit cleaning, and I make a note in my phone's calendar to check them out tomorrow.

Hera's meowing for food again as I try to leave and I quickly follow her to the cupboard where her food is kept. I feed her a sachet, then quickly but quietly grab my coat and shoes, then I slip out the door and make it to the elevator. By the time the thing has come up to the top floor, I've got my heels on and I've booked an Uber to take me home.

As I'm waiting for the cabbie, I fire a quick text to Tony.

*A: Great night, thank you SO much. Well, I left you my number. Give me a couple of days to decide, you know about what. Fed Hera as I left. Kinda walking funny... ;)*

I smirk at my own John Wayne joke, wondering if he'll get it. I nod to the doorman as the Uber pulls up. He just nods at me with a slight smile and carries on with his job.

I skip down to the cab and in moments, we're in a light flow of traffic. The streets are much quieter than normal. The lockdown's taking effect already.

~

I get home to find Holly's been busy.

"Honestly, Hols, you don't have to!" I admonish. She has cleaned the bathroom from the ceiling down, cleared down my kitchen, put on some laundry and got a load into the drier, hoovered, and is chilling.

"I know. But, I needed to be busy...and you're not asking me to pay anything, so..." She shrugs at me, but I know the feeling. The women who come into the shelters go one of two ways. Sit on their arses and lick their wounds (and I don't blame them, we've given them a safe place to do that!) or get stuck in with helping. Holly is clearly in the latter group.

"So, how'd it go?" she questions.

I can only grin broadly.

"Oh my God, Annie! You did it! Good for you! Was he good?" she asks.

"Fucking amazing!" is my reply. I head to the sink and run the cold tap, then I find a large glass from the cupboards and fill it. I turn the tap off and down the glass, then pour another one. I hadn't realised I was this parched. With my thirst now quenched, I realise I'm hungry. But, I'm out of bread. Damn.

"I forgot about bread," I say. "I'll get changed into something less walk-of-shame and head to the corner shop." Holly nods at me. She follows me up to my room and asks me questions about Tony. I tell her, without going into too graphic a detail, but girls always share this stuff. At least, the close friends get told.

"I lost count of the number of times he broke me. Goodness, it was amazing. I think he's ruined me for everyone else." I smirk. "If I want anyone else," I add.

"He wants to see you again?" asks Holly in a clearly excited tone.

"Oh yeah, he does." I smirk again as I pull on some nice jeans and throw on an old t-shirt. I'll get dressed properly when I'm back from fetching bread, after a shower. I can't ask Holly to go out; she's hiding from her shitty ex.

My phone pings and I grin. Is it him? Fuck, I'm acting like a teenager, but after the amount of sex we had, I'm hardly surprised. It is.

"I'll share more when I'm back, Hols. I need to go and get this bread before Elle is home and before the shops shut."

Holly hands me a scarf, and I look at her strangely.

"You need to wear a mask and since you haven't got any..." she says.

I nod. I've got a sewing machine my grandmother left me and some fabric squares. I've also got ski masks and odd bits of fabric tucked away. I might make some masks.

I slide on some socks, then my boots. "Back in ten," I tell Holly as I lock her into my house and fling my coat on. I make quick time getting to the shop, picking up what we need, then head back. In the meantime, Holly has run me a bath and I grin.

The bath is nearly the perfect temperature when I get into it. I've got an hour before Jim is due to drop Elle back, and I can finally read Tony's text.

*T: You left without saying goodbye! At least you left me your number. Why did you run off?*

*A: I woke up before the timer. And I'd be late back, I can't and won't be late for my little girl. Sorry! You looked like you needed the sleep.*

I smirk as he's not the only one that needs some sleep.

*T: So, I haven't scared you off?*

*A: Your situation is more than I'd like to deal with, but I need to decide if I want to accept whatever nonsense you're in is going to cascade into me somehow. If it hurts my little girl even remotely, we're done.*

*T: So, we're an item then? A thing? Dating? <3*

*A: One night/weekend screwing each other's brains out (sorry for being crude) does not a relationship make. Treat me as you would have done if I hadn't helped you or got Bee to you that night. We'll see and take it from there, okay?*

I sigh as my fingers and subconscious brain go into alignment and my frontal lobe catches up. I can see him responding, typing back.

*T: This lockdown is going to challenge that ability, but I'll see what I can do. When can I see you next?*

I sigh. I'm on call this coming weekend; I know I am as I was off this weekend.

*A: I'm on call next weekend, I work alternately. I have my daughter with me during the week. Schools are on lockdown so I can't during the week.*

I see the dots flash up, then stop. I put the phone on the stand next to the bath and quickly wash, my hair included. I hear Holly outside the bathroom.

"You okay, Hols?" I call out, getting a little defensive.

"Yeah...just, if you wash your hair, I'll trim the style back in for you, if you'd like?"

It takes me two seconds to think about it. "Hell yeah! I'll be out in five!" I call back.

"I'll get my scissors," she says, and I hear her head off to her room.

*T: Let me know when. Is there anything I can do for you? There are these support bubble things...*

*A: Yeah, you can be in my support bubble. Blythe would be anyway. An added benefit if you are too! :P*

I send the pokey face so he knows it's not just because of Blythe. I think I want to see him again, not just to have him screw my brains out, but I am not sure if I should. I climb out of the bath and dry off, put on a nightshirt, and wrap myself in my dressing gown. I'm sitting in a chair in the kitchen so Holly can recut my hair into the bob shape I love as Tony replies.

*T: I'd need to know where to support you, honey, not just by grabbing your fabulous arse.*

I smile at his comment for two reasons. One, he calls me honey. Two, he's talking about grabbing my arse again. Holly reads the text over my shoulder.

"Aww, Annie! That's fabulous!"

I chortle in response, feeling strangely warm to his texts.

*A: I will tell you when I decide. I need to go be a mum. Text you later.*

Holly slaps me on the shoulder. "You should carry on texting him! He sounds yummy!"

I roll my eyes at Holly as she steps before me to cut my fringe into shape, then the back of my head and sides. I lose about three inches off my length and I feel better for it.

"He is, but there's some baggage around him I haven't worked out if I want to be involved with yet."

Holly scoffs at me and gives me that friendly "Don't talk shit" look. Damn, she's good at giving that look!

"You were involved when you stayed with him once you knew who he was. You decided then. The question is, are you going to stick with your decision?"

Holly's question gives me something to think about and I'm grateful that she's a damn good friend.

Jim drops Elle off, and she has even more school books than she did last weekend. We talk for a bit and Jim notices Holly, then he notices the bruising around her neck and throat. He motions for me to step outside and I do.

"What the hell?" he asks in a low voice.

"Holly's ex attacked her. She's been here since Friday."

He looks around nervously.

"Jim, Holly's an old school friend. Her ex isn't going to be around here, he doesn't know where I live and if, by some miracle, he did, he'll have a one-way ticket to the Royal Infirmary. Hell, I can probably boot his arse to the RI from here, it's just over that-a-way!" I point in the general direction of the hospital which is just a few miles away as the crow flies.

Jim sighs and I see his jaw ticking. "Is she going to be okay?" he asks. He knows what I'm capable of doing, physically. He knows about my job but not the fights I've gotten involved with to get some women out of the situations they're put into, though most of the time it's done via negotiations; it's timing. I see the worst side of men, but still, I want to be romanced, I want my brains fucked out of me, I want what I had at the weekend with Tony. I want flowers, chocolates, breakfast in bed; I want cuddles after mind-blowing sex. But I want it regularly. I want to be treated like a queen, I want intimacy, I want someone to be there, and to be loved how I need to be. Jim and I never took the time to work that aspect out with each other. Talking with Jim makes me realise what I want, or the potential I could have with Tony. The penny drops.

I nod, getting back to the conversation I'm having, not the one yet to come. "Yeah, she'll be fine. She got out of there. I'm going to make sure she's more than fine."

Jim nods. I get his nervousness. He doesn't want anything kicking off if Elle is within range of it. Our shouting matches were enough, even though she was only a baby when we split up.

"You know who I work for. Who else is going to get her back up on her feet quickly?"

Jim smiles, his jaw relaxes and he nods. "True. I'll leave you to it," he says, heading back to his sleek Lexus. Seeing his car makes me wonder what car Tony drives, if he drives at all. They can't be living far from each other; Jim and Fiona live in Old Town, right on the edge of the New Town.

I go in and close the door; grabbing my phone, I send a text to Tony with the area I live in, just not my exact address, though I know I'm being overly cautious. I just hope I don't regret it!

## 14 ~ Anthony

My phone pings as Blythe escorts me from the penthouse to my mansion as evening draws in. It's a text from Annie. With her area and part of her postcode; not enough to pin her down exactly, but I don't push. She'll open up to me when she's ready. I let Hera out of the cat carrier, and she's off to explore the familiar territory. Her rough address puts her in Liberton, whilst I'm in Newington. It's over an hour's walk, but it's about a quick ten-minute drive from here.

I decide if I am going to be in Annie's support bubble, I am going to try and be closer. Blythe won't give me her address but said the mansion in Newington was closer, and I can work anywhere. I smile then text her.

*T: Vacated out to the Newington place. I'm only ten minutes away by car.*

*A: Really?! That's close! Half an hour on the pushbike!*

*T: You ride a pedal bike?*

*A: No! I can if I need to. You know, for extra exercise ;)*

Blythe came up to the penthouse at around three pm, after I'd changed the sheets. I told her Annie had bailed on me whilst I slept, but she did at least leave me her number. Blythe only smiled as I saved her number as Alluring Annie.

Blythe does a perimeter check as I settle in. Morag is at the penthouse, cleaning it how she likes it to be done. She'll meet us here later. There's dinner in the slow cooker, making the mansion smell mouthwateringly amazing. Morag has outdone herself again, and I decide I need to give her a raise, I have a feeling she'll be earning it fairly soon.

I wait until it's late evening before I text Annie.

*T: I want to hear your voice. Can I call?*

*A: Just heading to bed, so sure. I get to homeschool Elle tomorrow, so I figured I had better get some sleep.*

*T: I'd help!*

*A: You'd be a distraction...*

I hit the call button.

"So I'd be a distraction, would I?" I ask, grinning at the last text message.

"Hello to you too! And yes, you would." I hear her smile through her voice.

"What are you doing?" I ask. I already know she was heading to bed, and I wonder what her room looks like.

"Told you, heading to bed. I've got a nearly eight-year-old to educate tomorrow. I'm going to need some luck!" she chuckles.

"I'm sure you'll be great at it," I say. "What made you decide to text me your address?" I'm curious as to what made her come off the fence, but I can hear her let out a deep breath.

"My ex. He got funny about something which happened over the weekend and I decided I wanted to see you again. To..." she leaves the statement hanging, but I get her meaning. She wants me and a repeat of the weekend gone. I tease her a little.

"To, what, Annie?" I'm smiling, not that she can see. "Tell me, honey," I encourage in a low voice. She sighs, and I wonder why she can't tell me what she wants. She deserves anything she wants. I wait for a moment.

"You," she whispers so quietly I almost miss it. "To have you again," I hear her whisper, like I'm a forbidden secret. I smile.

"You will, you can. How are you fixed for the weekend?" I ask. We're closer to each other here but still so far away.

"I'm on call," she says, and my heart sinks as she reminds me. "So I might have to vanish to go sort things out. But, the rest of the time, I'm at home, just waiting, chilling out."

"Can you chill out with me?" I ask, hopefully. I don't know what work she does, but Blythe practically beams when she says Annie does important work.

"Aye, I can. If you don't mind me suddenly vanishing when I need to," she answers.

"I will mind, but I won't stop you from doing your job," I say, and I wonder what she does. "What is it you do, honey?" I ask.

"I'll tell you when I see you. I need to sleep. Good night, Tony."

I smile, sad the conversation is ending already. "Good night, Annie. Sleep well. Dream of me?" I ask.

She chuckles. "I'm sure I will!" she says, and the line goes dead.

# 15 ~ Annie

I hang up on Tony before I embarrass myself. I don't need him to know I feel like an insecure teenager talking to him or that I've thought about him more times this afternoon than I have thought about my daughter. I hear the light going out where Holly is sleeping, and I check the door cameras on my phone. All is quiet and my drive gate is locked shut. It won't stop anyone from stealing the car if they want it, but the extra locks I have for it should be a deterrent. Snuggling down under my quilt, I can't help but notice my bed isn't as comfortable as Tony's. Then again, I haven't a fortune to splash out on a mattress that costs me a year's council tax. It never bothered me until now, and I sigh. It's just going to have to be something else I save up for.

I hear crying and I sit bolt upright in bed, struggling to come to my senses. I listen for a moment, and I work out quickly the tears aren't coming from Elle, they're from Holly. I quickly leave my bed and walk to her room, wrapping my dressing gown around me. I open the door, expecting her to be in a nightmare and in one case, it's the truth. The horror is, she's on the phone. I can guess who has called her. Damn, I should have told her to change her mobile number yesterday. The clock says it's nearly 2 am. She doesn't hear me and she doesn't react when I take the phone from her and put it to my ear.

"You fucking bitch, who the hell are you screwing?! You won't fuck me but you will someone else!? I want to know who!" He doesn't take a damn breath. "Hey! Answer me, you fat bitch…"

"That wouldn't be your best course of action," I growl and he goes quiet. "Do not contact her again."

"I'll fucking find her," he says. I grin.

"I'm sure the police are gonna want to have a wee chat with ye if yer gonna be that stupid," I say and the static in my ear ends. He's hung up. I sit on the bed and hug Holly as she sobs into my shoulder. I rub her back and hide the phone as I hear Elle getting up. I hoped my low growls to Holly's ex wouldn't wake her. I keep Holly's phone in my hand and get up to tend to Elle, cursing her ex in my head.

"Why is Holly crying?" she asks as I take her back to bed.

"She had a bad nightmare," I say, being slightly tight with the truth, for her sake.

"Is she going to be okay?" she asks as I tuck the quilt back around her shoulders.

"Aye, she will." I grin so that she can see I'm not worried, therefore, she doesn't need to be either. "She's got yer mummy looking out for her. We're going to have a nice cup of tea whilst Holly calms down, then we're going back to bed, okay?"

Elle nods at me and lets me tuck her back in. I kiss my daughter goodnight again then I go find Holly and persuade her to come downstairs with me so I can make some tea and start sorting her life out. I check her phone settings, making sure she's not shared her location with that scumbag. She hasn't, though she has him on her contacts, and I block his number and I pay attention to her network provider. I dial their customer service number as I dig out the police reference number for Holly's case. As I wait to be connected, I half fill the kettle and put it on, then fetch Holly a blanket from the living room and wrap her up in it.

It's only a few minutes before I'm speaking with someone and Holly is verifying who she is and that I can speak for her.

"I need you to change this number in the next few hours, please. Case of domestic violence and this is the current crime number," I read the huge number out, and I hear the guy on the other end type it in.

"Certainly, Mrs Holmes, we'll have that done for her in a few hours. Has she blocked his number?"

"Oh aye, I did just afore we called you," I reply sternly. I choose not to correct him about my title.

"Good. Some folks forget to," he says.

"The shock of being contacted often makes people not think straight," I add.

"Aye, that's true. Let me just get this sorted for you," he states. A few minutes later, he breaks the silence. "That's all gone through for her," he says and he tells me about turning the phone off and restarting it in a few hours. The phone beeps in my ear, the process has already begun.

"Thank you," I say. "Have a good night."

"And you. Best of luck to your friend," he responds, and the call ends after he checks we don't need anything else from him.

I take my phone and call the non-emergency number for the police, giving them the same case number and updating them on his late-night phone call and his threat to find her. They add to the file and I'm told they'll have someone out to visit him either at work or at home, to deter him. I sigh as I hang up and Holly finishes making us both a chamomile tea.

She smiles at me weakly. "I'm sorry, Annie. I didn't mean to…" She starts to cry again.

"It. Is. Not. Your. Doing." This situation reminds me of the chat with Sarah earlier in the week. Holly looks at me and tries to smile. I go and hug my friend, and I hug her tight.

"Say it with me," I say as I hold her. "I am not responsible for his shit."

It takes her a few times to join me repeating that mantra, but she does and she breathes easier each time it's repeated. I see her visibly relax and I breathe too.

"Let's go back to bed. I'm going to keep your phone until your number has been changed, okay?" I lift her chin to make her look at me, and she nods with a weak smile and tears still threatening to escape. "I'm here for you," I say, hugging her again. "Do you want me to sleep in with you?" I ask as we head back upstairs.

"No, I'll be okay. Thanks, Annie" she whispers at her bedroom door.

I nod. "I don't mind if you want some company," I offer. It's not the first time I've laid on a bed with a victim and just held them, at least for the first night. It's often when they talk.

She shakes her head. "Nighean ghaisgeil," I mutter, and she looks at me confused. I grin. "Brave lass," I say, and she gives me another weak smile as she heads to bed. I climb into my bed too, but I'm not able to sleep for a while. That small intrusion has me very keyed up, and I'm not able to do anything physical right now to let the pressure ease off. It's gone four am when I last look at the clock, and eight am comes around all too quickly.

~

The alarm and I aren't friends today, not after Holly's verbal altercation with her ex during the night. She's likely to sleep for a while yet, given the night she had. Elle eats her breakfast then brings me all the books she's been sent home with. I inwardly swear.

"This is a lot of work, sweetie!" I say as we sit down at the kitchen table to divide it up. They'd sent home six weeks' worth of stuff and a schedule of what sheets and books were to be completed on what days, with video calls for some of the more difficult lessons like Maths and English. Not because the parents couldn't do it, but because the teaching techniques now are so different from when we were kids. Given I was last in school too many years ago, I am suddenly glad they were doing the heavy haul on those tricky subjects. I could help Elle with the homework, but trying to teach her from the ground up, with techniques she knew but I did not? It was not something I could do and I knew it, though I'd be giving her a few techniques of my own.

She ploughs through one subject worksheet with me and I check her work and make her re-write some of the answers so that she gets the spellings and letter formations correct. The first video call she has means I can fire up my laptop and see what work has to say about my employment; it is the biggest worry for me right now. Was I on this stupid furlough scheme? Or did I have to go back in and take Elle to school to be with the other small group of kids whose parents also have to work? I leave the door to the kitchen open so I can hear Elle's class, then dive into my work emails.

I lose track of time as emails fly from my outbox back to my inbox with replies. It takes me a moment to notice Elle standing by my side, and the clock says over an hour has passed since I started work. Holly still hasn't appeared, and I resolve to go check on her in a moment.

"Mummy, I'm hungry. And I've got my English lesson after lunch. Can I have a snack please?"

I sigh and kiss her on the head. "Of course you can, my darling! Let me see what we have."

I don't want to worry her that food might be scarce here at home if she is here all the time with me. The child would and could eat me out of house and home! I look down at my daughter's smooth dark brown hair. She has chosen a pink t-shirt and black jeans to wear today. I didn't see the sense in making her get dressed into uniform, but with the video calls, I told her she wasn't doing them in her pyjamas either. She didn't argue, which made me smile.

I fetch her some custard creams and a drink, which she seems happy with. She eats them on the other side of the table, away from her school work and my tablet. My heart swells with how calmly she seems to be adapting to this new requirement of life. If she can do it, damn it, so can I.

I head up and check on Holly, who is still asleep and breathing normally. I wonder when she finally dropped back off, probably not for hours. I remember her phone is still in my bedroom and go to retrieve it, turning it on as I head downstairs.

I think up a solution to the staffing question everyone has been talking about on email as I descend the stairs. I pick up my phone and call Julia.

"I've got an idea," I say as I outline my idea

"That might work," she agrees. "Two days a week in, the other two doing paperwork at home, working home cities. Are you still going to be okay doing the weekends?" she asks.

"Aye, as scheduled. I can see our services being required more; this is going to mess with people's heads as it grinds on. They're talking about this lasting more than a few months, maybe a year."

I can hear Julia sighing, though she tries to hide it.

"Yeah, I've heard the same. How are you?" she questions. I tell her about Holly and she reminds me I need to call the council to move her. She gives me a contact in Edinburgh council so I don't have to go through the call queuing system. I thank her, check Elle is still doing her school work without the Alexa device doing it for her, then call the contact Julia gave me.

It takes me all of five minutes to speak with the lady, Sharon. Then she gives me some news I am not surprised about but I know Holly won't be impressed with.

"So we've replaced the lock and secured the premises, but we're not sure what, if anything, is missing."

"Can we get the police to accompany her to check on it? I dinnae trust her to be there by herself, or we can go at the weekend when I'm able to go without hindrance." I, of course, mean Elle; there's no way I'm taking her to Holly's flat if there's any chance Holly's ex will turn up.

"If you can get them to," Sharon tells me. I smirk; I know a few officers on the force who might help.

"I'll see what I can arrange," I reply as I hear some movement upstairs. Holly's awake, at least enough to visit the bathroom. I thank Sharon and say I'll be back in touch in a wee bit, then I check on Elle, kiss her on her head, and go to see Holly. Holly's smiling as she gets dressed.

"Can I come in?" I ask as I knock gently on the door.

"Sure!" she says and opens the door for me. She's half-dressed and the bruises are starting to go yellow, meaning they're healing.

I tell her about her flat, that her ex broke in, but the locks have been replaced and the police have been updated. I'm going to enjoy the next conversation.

"Do you want the police to go with you to check it out and see what is missing? And do you want to move? The council can have you in a different area by the end of the week."

Holly's eyes are as wide as saucers. "How did you get that organised so quickly?"

I smirk. "It's down to who you know, in this case," I say. "My boss," I add, giving credit to Julia.

I see Holly thinking about things. "I think I'd like to move, but I'd like *you* there to check my flat over. And perhaps with the police too?" She nervously bites her lower lip.

I nod. "I'll see who I can organise for Friday. Elle will be at her dad's for the weekend as child-care still classes as an essential need for travel. He lives about twenty minutes from here, and I'm thinking we can check over both flats, see what's missing and what we can take with you, and see if the new place is decent."

Holly nods at me and I pull my phone out to call one of my favourite police officers.

"Sherlock!" he says as he picks up the phone.

"Wolf!" I cry back, giving Elle another kiss on her head as I check she's doing her work. She's nearly finished, and I need to make this call quick so I can make her some lunch.

"What can I do for you, Sher?" he asks.

"Need someone to go with a friend and I to a DV scene that had a break-in over the weekend. Can you help?"

"When?" he questions.

"Friday, early evening," I reply and give him the address.

"I'll find someone and call you back," he says. He's efficient; there's no good-bye.

Wolf calls me back later that afternoon after Elle's finished her classes and school work. She's curled up on the single chair with a book since we can't use the day-bed. He tells me that he and a colleague from uniform will be there on Friday. I confirm Holly's current address and arrange it for five o'clock, then I bring him up to date on her ex's threats and his call to her at stupid o'clock in the morning. Wolf literally growls.

"I'll see if we can pick him up or have a very strong chat with him. See you there on Friday," he tells me. I thank him then get on with making dinner for the three of us. It's only now I cast a thought as to what Tony's doing, how his day has gone. How the heck would he have handled me and my workload today?

## 16 ~ Anthony

I spend the day going through business proposals as I do my trade sharing. The two tie in rather well, especially if they're on the stock exchange or there are companies like them, which gives me an indication of profit sizes etc.

I'm getting close to deciding which of the last two I want to invest in. Throughout the day, I'm thinking of Annie. I wonder what she's doing and how home-schooling went. I pick up the phone and call my eldest child to see how she is. She answers me.

"Hi, Dad!" she chirps. Adaria sounds good, and we talk for a good ten minutes before she has to go to class.

"How are they doing the classes?" I ask, knowing that in-person classes are suspended.

"Live streaming. I need to get into Teams, so I've gotta go. I'll call you at the weekend! Love you!" she says. I smile as the phone goes dead. I call Carson and Evander, receiving similar responses, though they don't tell me they love me. The boys hardly seem to.

Morag comes through with tea and biscuits early in the afternoon and tells me she has no issues coming out to Newington from the City Centre. Blythe has taken one of the far bedrooms this time. I ask her why and she gives me a look, then quietly she tells me, "I don't need to hear you." I smirk and think it's fair enough. It makes me think back to the last weekend Annie and I were together, and I can feel my trousers tent up. I smile but guide my thoughts back to work.

I work until Tokyo closes and then I head to go and eat. I've not heard from Annie today, and I debate for all of ten seconds as to whether I should reach out to her or not. I do.

 *T: Hey, honey! How's your day?*

 *A: It's been...long! Not because of home-schooling though. Helping a friend get her life in order and it's been...well, it has required some resources.*

 *T: How can I help?*

I look at her text. Resources? Of what kind? I resolve to ask Adrian to check into Annie's finances, then stop. I really ought to ask her if I want to know. I can imagine Blythe kicking my arse if I don't.

 *A: Give me something good to think about, take my mind off it. Tell me something good about your day!*

 *T: I spoke with my children, it seems Universities are using video calls to do their lectures.*

 *A: I'm glad you got to speak with them.*

 *T: What about you? What's been good about your day?*

 *A: I'm not sure yet... Been a long one with police and stuff.*

 *T: And you're still standing.*

She sends me a link to Elton John's song of the same name. I smirk. We can send each other videos and I hunt out one I've been listening to. I send her a link to it, wondering why I picked George Ezra and *Paradise*. Then I listen to the lyrics.

 *A: I love that song! I'm dancing to it now! Thank you!*

I smile. She's dancing to a song I sent her. This woman... I smile and wonder who else she likes to listen to. I ask.

*A: The local station after Ken Bruce, so anything current. I have to stop for PopMaster!*

I grin. I have no idea what it is and have to Google it. Oh, it's a pop quiz show on national radio. I send her another George Ezra link, this time to *Shotgun*.

*A: I could listen to him all night! His voice... \*swoon\* Have you ever heard of Disturbed?*

*T: Yes. Loved their update to that old classic.*

*A: Both versions give me goosebumps.*

*T: What's your favourite song?*

*A: Ever ever?!*

*T: Yes.*

The dots appear and disappear, then her reply comes up on the screen.

*A: Not fair. I have two. One has my name in it, the other is Sound of Silence, by either Simon & Garfunkel or Disturbed.*

I wonder for a moment what song has her name in it and then she sends me a link to John Denver's *Annie's Song*.

*A: My dad used to play that to me when I was sad and needed cheering up as a kid.*

I smile, find the song, and save it as her ringtone. Then I sit back and listen to the lyrics... The song makes me think of all the places I'd like to take Annie, but this lockdown is going to make it impossible. Walks in the rain shouldn't be an issue; this is Scotland. I look out the window and I see the sky has darkened even more. It's a few moments before I hear the pounding of the rain onto the windows and see it turn the roads into rivers. It rains so hard it bounces a good few inches off the floor before landing again.

*T: Beautiful song. Do you know why he wrote it?*

*A: Just looked it up. He was skiing and he wrote it in 10.5 minutes after a difficult run. After an intense time, according to Wiki... How intense was their life?*

*T: I think he had cheated on her.*

*A: Oh...that's going to be intense then.*

I smile. Indeed!

*A: It came out before I was born. Not sure if that's why I'm called what I am. Must ask my folks!*

I smile and look at the clock as I reply. She'll be heading to bed soon.

*A: I need to go to sleep. See you in my dreams!*

I smile. She's killing me and she has no idea.

*T: Good night, beautiful. I'll see you there very soon.*

## 17 ~ Annie

The texting was sweet and perked me up more than I thought it would. Holly comments as we head up to bed.

"Sexting?" she asks me.

I choke on the last of my soft drink. "No!" I hand over the phone and show her the conversation.

"That's why you were dancing to George Ezra," she says.

I just nod and accept my phone back.

"It's so cute," sighs Holly as she heads for the bedroom that is currently hers.

I stop at my doorway. "Do you want to go view this flat before Friday, so we're not doing it all in one day?"

She nods. "What about Elle?" she asks.

"She can come with," I reply. I can't exactly leave her behind.

Holly nods, and we head to bed. The number change for Holly went through cleanly, and she has let only half a dozen people know her new number with strict instructions to them not to pass it to Jon, her ex. For the first time since I slept with Tony, I don't wake up until the alarm goes off the following morning.

The week settles into a routine quite quickly. I get asked if I can put some time in at one of the Edinburgh shelters for a few days, even though I'm on call this weekend, so I book Elle into school for the two days, Thursday and Friday. I send Jim a text telling him he can pick Elle up from school on Friday as I will be at work. I drive Elle and Holly to the proposed flat, and the location isn't dire, it's even slightly better than

115

where Holly is at the moment. What she can bring to this location is down to what's left at her current place. The access to the nature reserve at the bottom of her road adds to the appeal of the tenement.

Holly speaks with Sharon on Tuesday after we view the flat and tells her she'll take it. Because it's a council flat for a DV victim, they'll organise a van for Saturday to help move her stuff. We just need to ensure there's enough to move on Friday when we visit.

Elle bounds into school on Thursday as I head to one of the shelters. Holly chills out for the day at my house, and we repeat the process on Friday. Jim texts me to say he's got Elle, which leaves us free to assess Holly's old flat. As soon as I'm able, I go pick Holly up and meet Wolf.

As arranged, Wolf is there in plain clothes and so is a uniformed officer. Holly fidgets and looks around a lot, likely nervous about being back here. When she sees Wolf and the uniformed officer, I see her shoulders drop and she sighs.

"You okay?" I ask her.

She nods. "They came," she says.

"Yeah. Why are you surprised?" I ask, concerned.

"They didn't always," she tells me, and I can't think of a reply.

We check the flat over and find her ex has only taken his stuff, but he's been vile, urinating on various things, such as the bed. I throw the windows open and take in gulps of air whilst letting the smell out. I look around and wonder how many black bags we are going to need, but it's workable.

Wolf and the other officer, Adams I think he was, leave us to clear up and pack up what Holly wants to take with her. We go through the flat and work out what he's destroyed and what he hasn't, throwing away old rotten food and clearing things out. It takes us several hours and just before ten pm, we decide enough is enough. I order a large pizza to be delivered to mine and we grab some wine on the way home. We take the rubbish out and Holly grabs sheets for me to wash at mine overnight. She orders a new mattress online, and I promise to lend her an air bed to go on the base she's taking with her.

Despite the late hour when I get to bed, I text Tony.

*A: My friend is moving to her new secure flat tomorrow, I'm helping her. Won't be around too much until she's moved, I'm sorry.*

*T: I understand. I hope her move is not too stressful! Is there anything you need that I can help with?*

*A: Thank you for the offer, but we're good! What have you been doing?*

Tony walks me through his day, which is pretty much the same as it has been all week, and I wonder again why he was attacked. He hardly does anything of note. I feel for Blythe; she must be bored out of her mind.

On Saturday we spend it with the two guys from the heavy moving company the council uses. One is nearly seven-foot-tall and built like Arnie was in the seventies. The other reminds me of a slightly heavier set version of Vinny Jones. They're as sweet as anything though, and they have a dirty sense of humour, which Holly responds to.

I pay attention when the shorter of the two leaves his number for Holly, for "any emergency," and I grin at her. It takes us two-thirds of the day to move her into her new flat, and we go food shopping so Holly can buy some essentials. We take her car to the new flat, so she doesn't need me to take her anywhere. I do a quick sweep and check Holly has somewhere to sit, sleep, and food to eat. Her laundry machine was plumbed in by the guys and she's pretty much set. She insists she's okay and tells me to go visit my man, so I text Tony as she instructs.

*A: Friend wants an evening on her own in her new place. I'm still on call but I can come over once I've showered?*

*T: Shower here! Have you eaten?*

*A: Can't say I have eaten much today, no.*

*T: Come here then, let me take care of you.*

*A: It's not a problem?*

*T: If it were, I would not have told you to come here.*

I see the dots appear and disappear and he texts me his exact address. I go a little wide-eyed; I know that area and the houses there are in the several million price bracket. I pause for a few moments before replying.

*A: Okay, fair enough. Be about 12 minutes.*

# 18 ~ Anthony

I convey to Morag that Annie's coming over, and her eyes light up.

"What does your girlfriend like to eat?" she asks me as she busies herself in the kitchen.

"I'm not aware of anything she doesn't eat," I reply. The label of "girlfriend" lifts my soul and Morag nods her agreement.

"Leave it with me, I need to check with someone," she says and heads off somewhere in the house. I don't care where she's gone, but I know she'll prepare something wonderful.

Blythe appears with Morag and they head to the kitchen. I decide to leave them to it, and it's not long before the gate is buzzed. Blythe checks the cameras and lets her friend drive up. I go down to the side door to welcome Annie.

She looks tired. Suddenly, she's red in the face, embarrassed. She looks down at herself and grimaces. "I'm sorry, I really should have gone home first."

I smile. I don't care about the state she is in. Those are things we can get fixed up in a few minutes.

"Dinnae fash, yer okay," I say, holding out a hand. "Come here, lass," I command. She comes to me and I hug her, gently kissing her on the lips. I go hard as I hold her dirty, sweaty body to me.

"Morag's just started making something for you to eat. Why don't you come and get a shower?" I want Annie in my arms, but I need to behave like a gentleman, at least until Morag and her best friend have left us alone.

She nods. "If it's not going to cause issues..." she offers. I smirk.

"Tough if it does," I say. Not that Blythe or Morag will give me any stick for inviting Annie over. I lead her into the house, and the door clicks shut gently behind me.

"Don't you need to lock it?" she asks. I smile.

"It's electronically locked, but it'll be bolted before we retire." I turn to her and watch her climb the short staircase to the landing that leads into the house.

"Care for a quick tour on the way to the shower?" I offer, holding out my hand. She nods and lets me guide her to the kitchen.

"Morag, this is Annie." Already the kitchen smells wonderful. They shake hands and Annie politely says hello. Morag is easy to get along with, so it's not a surprise they're soon comparing notes about me.

"Anything I've gotta watch out for?" asks Annie, nodding towards me. Morag scoffs.

"Too much to mention for the first time meeting!" she responds, and Annie's eyes light up.

Annie chuckles. "Maybe another time then?" she asks. Morag nods and a mischievous look appears, then we head off. Blythe has left some clothes that will fit Annie on my bed, and I show her how the shower works.

"Enjoy the shower," I say, giving her a lingering kiss on her lips before I leave her in my room. I head back downstairs to the lounge and find Blythe in the library section, picking out another book.

She looks up at me and smiles. "Get Annie to leave some of her stuff here if she's going to be here every other weekend."

I smile and nod. "Good idea. If you give me her sizes..." I suggest. Blythe shakes her head.

I lean back against a bookcase and smirk. "I could just see what sizes you've given her," I suggest.

Blythe nods. "Or check out what sizes need cleaning. Good investigative work, Tony. What a good idea," Blythe sarcastically tells me as she takes a book. "I'll borrow this tonight; don't keep us all awake," she tells me as she tries not to smile as she leaves. "I'll have eyes on all the cameras but your room. I dinnae need to see what you get up to," she adds as she passes me. I sigh. I don't need an audience and I doubt Annie does too.

I hear voices from near my bedroom; I'm guessing Annie and Blythe are having a quick chat. I leave them to it and settle on the couch in the TV room. It's not long until I hear footsteps and Blythe shows Annie where I've retired to. She smiles as her friend vanishes; she looks happier.

"I really should have gone home, but your shower..." She grins. "It's amazing, thank you." Her cheeks are flushed pink, her hair is wet and I can smell something sweet and fresh.

I smile as I stand. "Let's go get you fed." I take her hand and lead her down to the kitchen table.

Annie can eat, and I'm lost just watching her enjoying Morag's cooking. It was a simple pie with steak cut chips and vegetables, but Annie polished it all off. She sits back in the dining chair with a grin on her face, a light in her eyes.

"Thank you! I hadn't realised how hungry I was!" She pours herself another glass of water. Her third.

"And thirsty?" I comment. She grins as she slowly empties the glass.

"We didn't stop today; there was a lot to move. Thank goodness the lady at the council gave us the van and the guys to move Holly. We'd still be at it if it were just her and I." She looks around, appearing to take in the room for the first time.

"I should thank Morag when I see her. The pie was fabulous!"

"Would you like dessert?" I ask. Annie's eyes dance and her eyebrows raise, only then do I understand the implication and entendre of what I've said. I chuckle and her cheeks go pink.

"Maybe later?" she replies, almost shyly.

"There's no expectations here, Annie. I'm happy like this, as we are. Enjoying each other's company." I watch her eyes and the soulful brown I see swirl as she goes wide-eyed a little more.

"Thank you," she breathes.

I smile and we stand, then she clears the dishes into the dishwasher, rinsing them as she goes. I know it's there, but I never think to clear my things away. Morag usually chases me away when we've eaten, and I am only too happy to let her. I make a mental note and begin helping, then I lead her to the TV room and we settle down to watch something. She finds her phone and checks it, keeping it close.

"Expecting a call?" I ask.

She smiles. "I'm on call, if I get a call to head somewhere, I do." I nod. Spending any time with Annie is a bonus. I spent two weeks recovering before I even learned it was this beauty who had helped me. The doctor said her stitching me up helped me.

"Do you have all you need?" I ask. Her eyebrows crinkle and she tilts her head. "I meant in terms of money or anything." It's been a while since I've wanted to really look after someone, or had someone to look after who wouldn't take advantage.

Annie smiles. "I'm comfortable in that sense, thank you."

I stroke her arm. "You'll let me know if you need anything?"

She sighs and takes me in. "I need your company and maybe, later, dessert..." She smirks and eyes up my crotch. I might be in my fifties, but her look stirs me to half-mast. She snuggles into me as she picks a movie to watch. She goes for an old classic we both probably watched at the cinema: Top Gun.

We don't quite get through the movie; her phone rings and she's fetching her boots as she talks with someone on the phone.

"Say where?" she says and heads instead to the side windows. Outside, police lights are flashing a few houses down.

"Aye. Be there in a moment or two, Wolf. I owe ye," she says, and she's got her boots on and has grabbed her jacket in seconds as she pockets her phone. The light has gone from her eyes, her lips are thin and set, her shoulders are set back. She reaches up and kisses me.

"I'll be back in a bit. Wait up for me?" she asks, stroking my crotch. I can only nod as she heads out of the door and Blythe appears at the top of the stairs.

"Who called her?" she inquiries as she strides down the stairs.

I shrug. "Someone called Wolf?" I reply. Blythe's eyes go wide and her mouth gapes before she heads to the living room to watch. I join her. What the heck is occurring on my doorstep?

# 19 ~ Annie

The phone call from Wolf is weird. Usually, the police let the shelters know they're heading to one to drop someone off. Sometimes I meet them there or meet them halfway. Tonight though, Wolf called me directly, and he sounded worried. He's never worried. I approach the police line and see the officer who helped us check out Holly's place yesterday is on duty. His eyes take in everything, his jaw square and set. What the fuck?

"What's going on? Wolf called..." He nods and motions to where Wolf is huddled over the bonnet of a police car with another officer, talking quietly. I approach but call his name out about twenty paces out; scaring Wolf is never advisable.

He's called Wolf because he's built and growls like one. He was in the Army when I was in the RAF, and we met a few times when our work paths crossed, just like now.

"Thank fuck!" he sighs. "How'd you get here so fast?"

I just smile in response.

"Never mind," he nods towards the house, "We have a situation here. The lady of the house won't let us in, but her hubby has called and says his daughter's acting weird, that she needs medical help. They called us when they couldn't get access," he nods towards a waiting paramedic unit and ambulance, "Control thinks she's been drugged somehow or taken something, judging by what the dad's told them. The mother, however, won't let us in. I need someone who can disarm her quickly and quietly, given what this might be linked to." He turns to me, his eyes wide, pleading. "I thought of you," he says. I nod, understanding he is thinking that this is a DV situation that's gone south somehow.

"Have we anything I can use to get up to the house with? Anyone got a pizza box or something?" I look around as I talk. The lights have attracted some of the locals, and they're now standing at their gates, shivering as they look on.

I see a local lady putting out a bag of takeaway boxes into the bin. I jog across to ask if I can use them. She looks at me weirdly and puts them on top of the bin, then backs away. I grab them and nod at Wolf. He calls me so he and police control can hear, then I head to the front door.

The smell of tikka-masala and Rogan Josh hits me from the bag. I knock on the door and call out, "Indian delivery!"

The woman opens the door and her eyes are all glassy, unfocused whilst she's waving about a gun. I drop the decoy bag and disarm her quickly. It's a BB replica, thank goodness!

"It's a rep. You're clear!" I speak more to Wolf, but the woman's brows furrow so I push my way in, leaving the door open and escorting her to the living room, disarming the replica as I go. On the floor, in one corner, is a man that I assume is her husband. In his lap, is a little girl, maybe about ten or so. I go to her and check her over.

"Turn her!" I say, making her lie on her left side in his lap. "Wolf, we need medics." He's not the only one who can growl. I check her airway and find her tongue has folded back. I get my little finger into her mouth and unfold her tongue, opening her airway and tilting her head back a little. Her lungs react to the sudden air and as she coughs, butterflies enter my stomach. I keep my finger in her mouth as the paramedics rush to my side. I quickly brief them and let them take over once they can keep her from swallowing her tongue. I leave them to it and focus now on the dad.

"Hey, Dad?" I say. He turns to me, but his eyes are focused on his wife. I notice he's shaking so grab a thermal blanket from one of the medic's bags, open it then wrap him up in it.

"You did good," I say. He looks at me.

"Is she going to..." He doesn't want to ask what's on his mind.

"She's in better hands now, alright? We need to let them do their job."

I can tell when Wolf walks into the room as the atmosphere changes. He deals with Mum, and another set of medics appear. I stand up and motion for Wolf to follow off to the side.

"Mum's on something. Dad's in shock, daughter..." I look around and then it hits me. How did I not see this sooner? I look at Wolf. "He's the victim here. Mum's done this." Wolf looks at me.

"How do you know?"

"It wasn't Mum holding the girl, it was Dad. He's looking at her as if she's the devil incarnate and he's mouthing the word 'why' over and over. He was cradling his daughter like she was already dead, and Mum was out of it when she opened the door to me, holding the rep." He nods and motions for another officer to join us. He quietly speaks to the uniform who nods and heads outside before radioing through what he's been asked to.

I head over to the dad. My job is to support the victims and they're usually female—tonight though, it's not.

"How long?" I ask him ever so quietly.

He looks at me, eyes wide and mouth gaping. His eyes dance as they look into mine, and I'll never forget the look in those amber green irises.

"Pardon?" he stammers.

I take a defensive position near him. "How long has she been doing this to you?" I ask. He opens his mouth to speak, then closes it.

"Three years," he whispers as he puts his head into his hands. It's heart-breaking seeing anyone fracture into a million pieces in front of you, but I know from experience, once you break down what doesn't work, you can rebuild. There's a damn difficult road ahead for this family, and it'll be as painful as all hell. He's living in a very influential part of Edinburgh; he's got money. Money he can use to help sort this problem, ease the path they need to take. He just needs to know he can and he needs to know how.

"Do you want it to end? Tonight?" Wolf hands me a box of tissues and I offer them to the dad. I don't even know his name and while I don't need to, I want to know all the people who I touch. Wolf takes a pew behind me, and I motion for him to get down. He recognises the military hand signal and drops himself quietly onto the floor behind me so he, too, is not in a threatening position.

The dad nods. "It needs to..." He looks at his little girl as she's transferred to a stretcher with bags and drip lines leading into her. I just hope whatever Mum gave her, or in the better case, whatever the girl had easy access to, doesn't cause her permanent damage.

"What's your name?" I ask. He gives it, but I intentionally don't pay attention to anything but his first name.

"Hey, Tom," he focuses on me, but also not on me, "I'm going to have someone meet you at the hospital, okay? Take their help, their guidance and support. If you do, you'll get through this much easier and maybe quicker. You *and* your wee lass, okay?"

How he gets through this depends on him, but I know he will get through it, and to do so, he's going to need help. He bows his head, and we stand.

"They'll be there for you, they'll know you," I say and quickly snap a photo of him. He doesn't notice, but Wolf does. I'll pass the photo onto the men's support refuge so they'll know who to look for. It's Saturday night and even though we're now in a lockdown, I'll wager the Emergency Room is going to be as busy as all hell. They'll need to know who to look for.

I make the call as I step outside and away from the officers, from the mess Wolf now needs to clear up. It's a quick call, but they're on route to the A&E department with the photo in hand. They've done this with me before; it's standard stuff for us. I pop back in and nod to Wolf, who acknowledges me. They've helped the dad stand and they're wheeling his daughter out with him walking with another paramedic. I head off too, behind the police cordon, and watch as they're loaded up. I slink back into the shadows then head for Tony's house as the ambulance pulls away and the numbness sets in.

There's a bench on the way up from Tony's gate to the door, and I take a seat for a few moments. I place my head in my hands, processing what I just witnessed. What I do breaks me when it's a bad one like this; though this isn't by far the worst I've ever been involved with. The sight of the little girl, drugged up and close to dying by asphyxiation would affect anyone, no matter how black their heart is. And my heart isn't black.

I don't know how long I've been sitting outside, but I start to feel the cold in my bones. I know I should head in, but I don't. I still can't face Tony like this, or even Blythe, though she's seen me after a nasty call out before, held me as I broke and rebuilt myself. I hold the tears back; I can't let them fall, not here.

Not now.

I sigh heavily and the bench sags as another weight is added. I look up. Tony's sitting next to me, wrapping his arms around me to hold me. Blythe stands before me, and she too wraps her arms around me. The pressure valve is hit, the dam breaks, and my body is wracked with sobs as my best friend and my new lover hold me on a cold, frigid Edinburgh night.

The mug of tea in my hands is scalding hot, and I can't hold it. I put it down but place my hands near it, craving the heat. We're in the house now, Blythe got me to move, and I'm grateful. I think I've cried myself out, and I ask Blythe to check my phone. I'm so cold, I can't hold the thing anymore.

"Oh, Tony's phone is easily hackable. I unlocked it in two tries," I say, recalling the previous weekend. She opens her mouth to respond, then shuts it and just nods. I stare into the mug, and Tony comes in with a woollen throw and drapes it over my shoulders. I turn and smile weakly at him; I can't share with him what happened. It's part of a police investigation now, and no doubt I'll have to give a statement tomorrow.

If he can't cope with me after a bad call like this, then I'm glad for the time I had with him. However, he sits in the chair next to me and just rubs my back.

"Bad one?" asks Blythe after what seems like hours. The tea has been drunk and I've had something to snack on, along with a glass of water. I'm grounded again and warmer.

I just nod. "Almost the worst kind. Kids..." I say. Blythe hisses, and Tony just rubs my back a little harder. I lean into him, craving his warmth. Jim offered once to listen. He lasted five minutes before he walked away, leaving me to deal with my raw emotions. I'm sure that broke me more. Blythe smiles at me gently as I lean into Tony.

"I'll leave you two to it. You know where to find me if you need me, Tony," she says, and she quietly heads off, squeezing my shoulder as she goes. I look at the clock. It's around two am and I sigh. Exhaustion is hitting me.

"Tired now?" he asks.

I nod. "Thank you," I say, though I'm not sure if he can hear me.

He kisses my head. "Come on, lass, let's sleep." I smile and wrap the blanket around me as Tony tidies up and guides me up to bed.

I check my phone, there's no text from Wolf on how the wee girl is doing. There's a message from the men's refuge. They've connected with Tom. They don't expect a response back from me. It's not customary, but I send back a thumbs up. Tonight, I'm going to respond.

I clean my teeth alongside Tony, using a spare toothbrush, and it feels strangely domesticated; somehow it's calming. He guides me to the bed and I climb in at his instruction. It's strange, having him look after me. He turns out the main lights, but the light in the hallway is left on and the door is ajar slightly.

"Why?" I ask. He looks at me weirdly. "The door?"

He smiles and comes back into the bed. "Hera," he whispers. "Come here, lass, let me hold ye." I snuggle up to him, and he wraps me in his arms, kisses me again on the head then just holds me. It doesn't take me long to get to sleep like this.

I get a text message at around five am which wakes me. It's from Wolf. The girl is going to be okay, though it's too soon to say how damaged she is, if at all. I breathe a huge sigh of relief that I didn't know I was holding onto. The noise from my phone must have woken Tony, and he speaks in whispers.

"You okay, lass?" he asks, rubbing my arms after I come back from the bathroom. I went in there to read my message and use the facilities.

"Aye. Just, good news after last night, the wee girl's made it through the night, so they're hopeful."

"That's great news!" he says happily. He kisses me gently, and I respond by turning so that he's above me. He's holding me in the crook of his arm so that he's at the side of me but above me. One hand is exploring my side, and he massages a breast. I can just see him smiling as he takes the same breast into his mouth and works his tongue over my nipple and areola, engorging them both. His hand has wandered south, but so have mine. He's as naked as I am and whilst his fingers explore my inner folds, I'm massaging the length of him.

He pulls away and opens a drawer, and I watch as he rolls on a condom. I make a mental note to check on my birth control this week. He climbs back in between my legs and kisses me deeply, firmly pushing his way into me as he does. It doesn't take much for him to slide home. He brings his head to my ear, and I can hear him rasping as he thrusts in and out of me.

He bites my earlobe and nuzzles my neck as he increases his thrusting. He hears me gasp and kisses me as the first orgasm hits. He's got some stamina as he's not quite there with me. I scratch his back and bite his earlobe as his stubble scratches my cheek. It's a few more minutes before I feel my climax building back up, and I twirl his chest hairs in my fingers as I arch against him.

His forehead is near mine, and he kisses me as I fall over the edge again, this time, taking him with me.

I awake later; my phone hasn't pinged again since Wolf's text at five am, and I notice Tony is still asleep. I smile and visit the bathroom, check my texts, then I creep back into bed and watch as he sleeps for another twenty minutes or so. I smile at him as he slowly wakes up, and I reach across to touch his face. It's Sunday and I have a few hours before I need to be home.

We kiss gently, then he just holds me, rubbing my back and stroking my hair. My stomach growls, and we chuckle.

"Let's see what Morag's made," he says and moves to get up. The smell of food reaches us, and I smile. I grab a quick shower and dress.

"I'd like it if you left some clothes here, Annie. Or, I could order you some new ones, if you'd like?" he offers.

I shake my head. "I'm happy to bring some clothes with me, but there's no need to order clothes for me. We've only just started seeing each other," I say.

He leans in and kisses me gently. "I told you I wanted to look after you," he replies. There's an intensity in his eyes when he says this. I smile gently.

"Aye, but you don't have to do it all financially. I'd prefer it if you didn't, unless it's dire straits," I respond.

He smirks. "That, I can do, though it'll be hard not to spoil you. I have a few gifts on order already," he says as he throws on a t-shirt. How can a man in his fifties look so damn good in a t-shirt and jeans?

"Oh aye?" I say. What's he ordered for me already?

He winks. "They're a surprise until you open them," he says and holds his hand out for me to take. I give him a sceptical look and sigh. Jim used to do that: throw money at me until I relented, even if it wasn't what I wanted or even needed.

"Something I said?" he asks.

I think about not telling him for a moment, then I realise holding onto it gives that situation and Jim a power it doesn't deserve.

"Jim, my ex, is quite wealthy. He has a house on the Mews with his new wife. When we were together, he'd throw money and things at me like confetti until I gave in to him. I don't want to go back to that. I want someone to be there for me, take care of my heart, of me...not stifle my soul and hold me back or down."

He nods at me as we begin to descend the stairs.

"I hear ye and I'll try to remember that. There are times though when I'm going to want to buy some things, just because I decide ye deserve them." He smiles at me.

"Then make it meaningful?" I request. We're in the kitchen now, and Morag has prepared porridge with a variety of toppings, tea, coffee, and fresh juice.

Tony kisses me in front of Morag, gently. "I'll do my best, honey," he says.

I get an hour before my phone goes off again, but it's not a call-out. It's Wolf, arranging a time for one of his officers to interview me about last night. He can't do it as he called me in. I begin to arrange for it to be done at my house before Elle comes back, but Tony says that we can do it here and use his office.

"You're sure?" I ask.

He nods and kisses the top of my head, then quietly talks with Morag about something. I can tell that they're close, but it's more like a sibling relationship. She doesn't put up with any of his nonsense and gives as good as she needs to. I like her already!

We arrange for the officer to be here in about an hour, and Wolf leaves me her number in case I need to postpone. Once Tony and I have eaten, we chill out, cuddling on the sofa, legs entwined, and wait.

The officer arrives as arranged, and she and I head into the office. Blythe lends us a digital anti-listening device, and I discreetly turn it on as I give my statement and assessment.

The officer asks me questions, and I give my observations. I don't give her my opinions; I give facts. Why Wolf called me, what I saw, how I got in, the condition of the girl, how she was nearly self-asphyxiated and how stricken her dad was, the state of Mum.

Because I've been where she is, we're done in just over half an hour, but she's made pages of notes. She massages her wrist as she tidies her notes away.

"You've some experience in giving evidence, Ms Holmes," she compliments as she packs her notes away.

I smile. "I've had some experience. I was an MP."

"Oh? For what council?" she says. I chuckle.

"Military Police. I've been where you are," I say, and she mouths an "Oh."

"I had no idea. DCI Munro didn't indicate your background."

I smile. Trust Wolf to do that. "Glad I could help," is all I can reply with.

"The mum's being detoxed, but there's a huge mess to sort out for them," she tells me. I nod.

"Aye, it's going to be a long, hard road for them to navigate. I wish them luck," I reply as we leave Tony's office. Morag shows the officer out; I turn off the listening device and look around his office. It's quite simple but tasteful, a clever mix of old and contemporary design. There's a nice high-backed leather chair sitting behind a tall modern-looking industrial-type desk. He's got two monitors linked into a computer somewhere off on the storage unit that makes the desk an L shape. There's a TV on the wall that shows current stock trades, and the leather Chesterfield the officer and I were sitting on completes the look. The walls are warm cream with detailing, and his desk faces the window which is almost floor to ceiling in height. The wooden floor looks to be solid wood, and there's a bookcase in the corner with some books and knickknacks on. It's deeply masculine.

Tony comes up behind me and pulls me to him from behind. He's just holding me, and I sink back into his embrace.

"That didn't take long," he states.

"I know how to give a statement," I say, turning my head slightly and smiling. He kisses the top of my head and then rests his head on top of mine.

"We're allowed out for an hour's exercise, according to the rules. Do you want to go for a walk or chill out here?" he asks.

I smile. "Anywhere with you," I reply. He chuckles and nuzzles into my neck, kissing me gently.

"Then let's go pick a movie, unless you want to do something else?"

I think for a moment. "Nope. Just being with you is fabulous," I say. I must've said the right thing; he's grinning like a Cheshire cat.

# 20 - Anthony

Annie and I chill out watching a movie that she picked. Thankfully, she doesn't go for a chick-flick; though for her, I'd endure such torture. I discover that she loves *The Saint*, having watched Ian Ogilvy on screen in her youth. This is a girl after my own heart!

"That's why I fell in love with the Jaguar, XJS v12, two-seater convertible in pillar-box red." Her eyes sparkle as she shares that piece of her youth with me, and I can only join in with her infectious grin. The girl is a keeper.

"No you don't!" she says, and her face drops slightly.

I give her a dumbfounded look.

"Don't you dare," she tells me again.

"What?!" I ask, holding my hands up.

"No bright ideas on the car," she says, nudging my ribs gently. Oh, I get what she thought. Though, a day driving about in one is something I'll arrange for when lockdown is over.

"No, I wasn't planning anything, but now you've given me the idea," I say, teasing her.

"Don't...please," she pleads. I kiss her gently on the head.

"I won't go buying you one," I promise. I would if she wanted it; it's pocket change for me, even the upkeep of it would not be something I'd lose sleep over.

"Okay, good," she concedes, but the idea is now there.

We snuggle up on the sofa. I put the seat into recliner mode, stretch my legs out, and she lays her head on my lap as we settle down to watch the movie. She coos over the fact that both former Saints are in the movie and seems keen to watch it. I'm not sure how far into it we get, but she's gently calling my name to wake me in what feels like moments. Lunch is ready.

Morag's made a huge Sunday roast because there are four of us here, and I realise with a start that I'm outnumbered three-to-one.

The conversation is light, and we don't talk about Annie needing time and support last night. Blythe had seen her walk up the path and sit on the bench, but she was there for nearly half an hour before we went out to her. It must've been nearly a degree or close to freezing as she was like ice when we finally got her inside.

Blythe and Annie share their work history, to some extent, and as they do, I realise why there is something Blythe-like about Annie. It's their military posture, how they handle themselves.

Annie loves her food, and I'm thrilled she does. I tell her when we've finished and we're alone again. I know she has to leave by three to be home in time for her daughter to come home.

"I do eat well," she says.

"Good," I agree. "I cannot abide women that can't eat more than a salad in company, but pig out at home in private." I recall my ex-wife being like that, though she got better as our marriage progressed. I have no idea if she still has that habit.

Annie nods. "It's often used as a control mechanism, the eating thing. Either learned young or taught by spouses. However, I have a decent metabolism, and I am used to eating large amounts, then burning the calories off. Military training does that for you," she replies as she gathers her things. "The most I'll do now is drink some tea and water for the rest of the day."

She grins at me and rises to kiss me. I hate that she has to go.

"So, next weekend, are you working again?" I ask. She shakes her head.

"No," she whispers back. "I'm all yours," she says.

"Come here again," I request. "Spend the weekend with me." I'm hoping that the secret present I have ordered for her arrives, but I'll give it to her when we're ready.

"I'd love to. And we will watch that movie, without you falling asleep. It was good," she says. Her eyes are sparkling, teasing me. She watched the whole thing and I didn't. Her head in my lap was so right, comfortable and warm, no wonder I drifted off.

"I'm a thought and a call away, Annie," I say. I kiss her gently on the mouth, holding back a little; otherwise, she'll never make it home.

"So am I, Tony," she softly replies. Then, she's driving away, and my stomach knots slowly.

# 21 ~ Annie

I drove away from Tony's with my clothes from Friday freshly laundered. I did thank Morag at dinner when she told me, and I told Blythe I'd have her clothes back. Thankfully, we're still pretty similar in size, though she's gotten leaner.

I could tell Tony didn't want me to leave, but what we have is too new. I do need to tell Elle about it though, so that's going to be fun. I wonder what she'll make of the news that Mummy has a boyfriend that's not her daddy? She took to Fiona being Mummy Fee quite well, and I hope she's just as okay with my situation as she was with Jim and Fiona.

Jim drops her off but comes inside. "I've news to share with ye," he says as he closes the door behind him. Elle starts jumping up and down so the news must be good! Jim nods to Elle and she jumps in front of me like a bouncing ball.

"Guess what, Mummy?" she asks. I get two seconds before she tells me, and I decide she's not good at this guessing game.

"I'm going to be a big sister! Mummy Fee is going to have a baby! But, Daddy says it won't be for ages yet!"

I smile and look at Jim, who nods. He seems awkward somehow.

"Congratulations, Jim! That's fabulous news!" I tell him.

"You're not mad?" he asks, following me to the kitchen and taking a seat at the dining table. I look at him confused and send Elle off to tidy her bag away.

"Why would I be mad?" I ask him. "It really is good news. I'm happy for you both. Fiona's going to be a great mum. She's proven that with Elle."

The look on his face is one of relief.

"Jim, what's been worrying you?" I question.

"I just thought..." He looks around. "Hell, I thought you'd be annoyed with me. With us."

I stare at him. "Why would I be annoyed with you becoming a dad again?"

He shrugs, but I don't want to let him off with this. Whatever his train of thought is, it's wrong and it'll eat away at him if he doesn't address it; I know him well enough.

"Nonsense," I say, forcing him to face it. "What's going through your head that you thought I'd be annoyed with you two becoming parents to your own child?"

"Just with Elle..." I sit back and let him speak out. "I thought you'd be upset with me because things will have to change for Elle, especially at the start."

I smile. "Jim, life is all about change. Elle gets to be a big sister. So there might be some changes to our arrangements regarding her for a few months when the baby first arrives, but I'm not going to be unreasonable. I have *never* kept Elle from you, and I dinnae intend to start now. You might want to not have her for the first few weeks when Fee first comes home with the little one and you settle down into a routine. That's to be expected. But, annoyed at the news or that life's going to change? No chance...life is always changing; look at this lockdown we're in." He looks at me, and I can see the tension just slip away from him.

"Jim, honestly, have I ever given you grief when things have had to change at the drop of a hat? All I ask is that you don't ignore your daughter, just include her. Though, I'm sure Fee has already thought of it since Elle is like a bouncing bean right now!"

Jim nods. "Aye, Fee and her have been planning the look of the nursery. I've got some decorating to do!"

"Jim, it's great news and I'm happy for you both, okay?" I smile at him; I'm genuinely pleased for him and Fee. I do wonder when I'll next have to walk on eggshells around him.

He nods, and Elle bounces into the room. I'm sure she's heard some of our conversation, but she doesn't indicate that she has. I'll chat with her later.

"We're due late September," he says, looking at me. I nod.

"An Autumn baby. Beautiful! Are you going to find out the gender?" I ask. We did for Elle and though this is his second, it's Fee's first.

He shrugs. "Fee's not decided on that. I'm letting her make that decision." He smiles and his eyes dance. He's clearly a happy man.

"Best idea," I reply, smirking at him.

Jim hugs Elle goodbye and sees himself out. I lock the door behind him and concentrate on Elle for a few hours. We pick a movie, I make some popcorn, and we sit and watch that damn movie. Again.

It's bedtime before Elle wants to talk about becoming a big sister. It's typical that a child wants to talk at bedtime.

"How will things change, Mum?" she asks. Ah, so she did hear, I knew she had. I sit on the edge of her bed.

"Well, when babies come home from the hospital, or when they're born, they have no idea what night and day is. They're awake every few hours to feed. They poop a lot, and it's very tiring for the parents as everyone adjusts to this new little, demanding, gorgeous person that's now in the family. It can get a wee bit stressful."

I watch her face change as she absorbs some of what I've told her.

"So what does that mean, Mummy?" she asks. I smile.

"It might mean you don't get weekend stays with Daddy and Mummy Fee for a few weeks. It will mean that you won't be able to play with the baby until they're able to move around, and they certainly won't be able to talk until they're about two! They'll follow you around when they can and you might find them annoying when they won't leave you alone!" I recall my siblings when they were born and I chuckle. I really need to call my parents.

"That sounds *so* boring, Mummy!" she groans. I chuckle.

"It's just what happens when babies are born. They can't do a thing for themselves, and they need everyone to do things for them, like dress them, change their stinky bum, wash and feed them. But, as a big sister, you can help with some of that." I smile as she turns to me and props herself up on an elbow to look at me.

"What can I help with?"

"Well, fetching things, like fresh nappies, the talc, clothes... We mums try to remember everything, but we forget a lot as we don't get a lot of sleep when babies arrive. It's hard work to bring them into the world, and our brains don't always work properly for a while. So, having someone to fetch things, help us, bring us things, pass us things, that's amazing help," I say. I also note I need to speak with Fee and tell her I've told Elle this.

Elle nods. "I can do that!" she says, cheering up.

"That's great, I know you're going to be an ace big sister! And it's your job, when they're old enough, to teach them the right way to do things. They'll copy you when they're old enough! But, you have to remember to be you too!"

Elle sighs. "That's a lot to do, Mummy! Do I get paid?" I throw my head back and laugh until tears are rolling down my face. Kids!

"No, darling, we don't!" I say, still chuckling at her indignation of not being paid.

"Then why do it?" she asks, settling back under her pink quilt.

"For love," I say.

She nods.

"Oh," I say before I get up off the side of her bed. "Mummy has some news too. I have a boyfriend. I hope that's okay?" She sits up like lightning and smiles broadly.

"You do?! So I get a second daddy?!" she squeals.

I drop an "Oh" at her, then close my mouth. I hadn't expected that reaction.

I pause before I reply. "I don't know yet. We've only started seeing each other so him becoming your extra daddy is a long way off yet, petals. But, I'll arrange a time for you to meet him soon. Is that okay?"

She nods madly at me. "Are you going to invite him over for dinner?" she asks as I make her snuggle back down again.

"That's a good idea! Dinner and a movie. But not *Frozen*! Something different?" I ask her.

She nods. "It's my birthday next weekend! I hope I get the *Descendants* DVDs," she exclaims.

"I'm sure you'll get everything on your wish list," I say, finally kissing her on her forehead and knowing that she will. I set her alarm for eight am, then close her door and let her get to sleep. I check the doors as I go downstairs, and I begin making calls.

The first is to Jim and Fee, to congratulate them both, and to tell Fee what I've told Elle.

"Oh, that's good! We'll play it by ear, aye? See how it goes?" says Fee.

"Aye, best thing. She's ever so excited. But if I need to have her for some of the weekends, I'll manage it."

"Thanks, Annie," says Fee. We talk a few minutes more about when she's due and how she's feeling. It's been a while since I was pregnant and I'm forty-two; I don't think I'll get a chance to have another. I remember about my birth control and note it down on my newly created to-do list; otherwise I am just forgetting things.

When Fee and I end the call, I call my parents and bring them up to date with my life.

"So, you've met someone?" asks my mother. She's in her mid-sixties now and she's been married to Dad for forty-five years. They married young, had the four of us.

"Aye, I have," I say, telling her about Tony. I don't mention how well off he is, just that he's comfortably well off with grown kids.

"Have you met them yet?" she asks.

"No, not yet. They're all at Uni; I've not even had a video chat with them."

"I am sure they'll like you," says Mum. I smile, though she can't see that. She's not got the hang of this video calling thing yet. I don't think many people have.

I catch up on what they've been doing down in Dumfries and what my siblings are up to. It's nearly ten pm when I finish talking with my family, and I drop Tony a text. Now, I can concentrate on talking with him until I'm ready for bed.

*A: Hey, handsome! I told my daughter that I'm seeing someone tonight. She got very excited. Asked if you were going to be her second daddy!*

My phone lights up with him calling me an instant later.

"Hey, you! How are you?" He sounds happy.

"I'm good! My daughter was super excited when I told her about you." I smile as I tell him about her reaction.

"Did she really ask that? Aww! I'd love to meet her!"

"Yeah, she'd like to meet you as well! I was going to arrange for next week? Perhaps you could come here for dinner. My house isn't anything like your mansion or penthouse," I protest. I'm not sure if I want to take Elle to his house just yet.

"I'm sure your house is just as warm, gorgeous, friendly, and inviting as you are," he whispers, and I blush, suddenly so very glad he can't see me!

"I hope you can cope with a nearly eight-year-old girl!" I chuckle at him.

"I'm sure I can, though it's been some years since my daughter was that age," he chuckles as well.

"You're not working, are you?" I ask. I know he works the stock markets, and Tokyo's just about to start trading; no doubt he'll be online trading.

"Not quite. I'm reading through the paperwork for the last two companies that have asked for investments. I can't decide between the two of them," he says.

"Ah. Do you have to decide? Can't you invest in both or are they competitors in the same field?" I question.

"They're not competitors, no. They're in two different fields, but I didn't consider investing in both. That's a good idea!"

I smile. "There you go! That was easy," I say, chuckling.

"It was. I'll do their proposals in a bit," he responds.

"Why in a bit? Was your nap that helpful?" I ask, smirking. *The Saint* was a good movie.

"I watched some of it!" he protests, understanding exactly what I am referring to.

"Huh uh! You fell asleep," I gently tease.

"Yeah, well, there was this warm, beautiful dead weight on my lap." He turns the tables back on me, and I love it. "It didn't purr, but it was so good!"

I chuckle. "A warm, deadweight that didn't purr, huh? I might give *you* Hera's food instead then!" I suggest. He laughs.

"No thanks! I would starve if I had to do that. I didn't see her much this weekend, though she was around earlier," he says.

"Has she taken to Blythe? Blythe and I always had a thing about attracting cats," I tell him.

"If Blythe's in the library, that's usually where I find Hera. Blythe won't let her into the room she's staying in," he replies.

"Yeah, we had a...small incident on base with some cats in our room once. A stray momma gave birth in one of our kit bags whilst we were out on manoeuvers. The clean-up was messy."

He laughs. "No wonder she's not keen on Hera being in her room or in her things."

I chuckle. "We lived and learned! The cats were useful on base though, has to be said."

I look at the clock and realise why my eyes are dropping. "I'm going to miss your arms around me tonight," I lament to him. I've gotten used to being held.

"Not as much as mine will miss holding you. Is Wednesday a good night for visiting you and meeting Elle? I'll bring dessert."

"It'll be a perfect night, yes. Say, about three or four in the afternoon? I did suggest dinner and a movie to her, but it doesn't have to be in that order."

"I'd love to. Goodnight, honey. See you in my dreams," he says.

"Aye," I reply, snuggling down and turning off the light. "See you there too."


Monday and Tuesday are all about school, work reports, housework, chores, tidying up. The house might not be huge, but it's mine and though it doesn't get too messy with just the two of us, I do want it to be tidy for when Tony visits. I call and speak with the doctor about birth control, and she agrees that the arm implant is probably the better option for me, given how hectic my work schedule can be. She books me in for an appointment for that Tuesday and it's done and dusted in fifteen minutes. All I have to do now is give it a month to start working.

On Wednesday as I prepare dinner for the oven, Jim drops me a text to say he's gotten Elle's present and what it is.

Elle completes her school work in super-fast time and I double-check it with her. I notice the improvement in her handwriting, and I show her my favourite pen, using it as a reward incentive, knowing she loves stationery.

So far, she's only written in pencil and she oohs over my fountain pen. I remind her why she writes in pencil and praise her for her neatness, telling her I'll buy her such a pen for using at home when her writing is good enough.

I text Tony after lunch as I square my kitchen back to tidiness again.

*A: Did I give you my full address?*
*T: No, that would be useful. Blythe is driving though.*
*A: Then she already knows where to go. See you soon?*
*T: Indeed! Can't wait to meet Elle and kiss you too.*
*A: Charmer!*

I quickly wash the few dishes I have by hand and let them dry for a wee bit, put some beers and a bottle of wine in the fridge to start chilling, then I grab a shower. At least I can be in clean clothes, smelling and looking my best when Tony turns up!

A sleek Mercedes S class pulls up into my driveway just before half-past three. It's charcoal in colour and has lines and curves that make it look like a panther on wheels. This is the kind of car the air officers would arrive on base in whilst wearing their fruit salads. Just like Tony, they'd have a chauffeur. Elle spots Blythe as soon as they're out of the car, and she's jumping around like a mad thing before they've even gotten to the front door.

I nod that she can open the door and let our guests in, and I prop myself up on the doorframe of the living room. Tony's the first to be greeted.

"You must be Elle," he says, bending down to her height so he doesn't tower over her. "I'm Tony," he says, his eyes dancing.

"Mummy's boyfriend," she retorts, pulling her shoulders back. He smiles and hands her a small bouquet.

"I am! These are for you," he says; she turns to me, her mouth wide open in awe, and she's so happy. I don't think anyone has given her flowers before.

"Let's put those in water, shall we?" asks Blythe from behind Tony. She takes Elle by the hand into the kitchen to sort out her bouquet.

Tony has stood up now, his eyes shining as he smiles at me.

"Hello, you," he says, handing me a dozen red roses from behind his back. How the hell did he get flowers like this during a lockdown? I don't care as he gently wraps a hand behind my head and angles me for a searing kiss, and I welcome his mouth onto mine, his tongue into my mouth. They dance for a moment and I'm lost.

It's Elle's "Oh boy, they're kissing!" statement that pulls us apart. I'm still holding the roses, but the smile I have is broad.

"Let's find another vase, shall we?" I say, and Elle nods. Blythe just has a huge smirk on her face, and I'm saying nothing to her as we pass in my small hallway. I turn the oven on and twist to face Tony. Blythe has been dragged off somewhere by Elle, and it leaves us alone for a moment.

"You have a very beautiful home, Annie," he says. I smile.

"It took me a while to get it how I wanted it, but with Blythe's help, I've managed it I think."

He nods. "Aye, ye have. Remind me to ask for your advice next time I need to decorate. I tend to hire people in," he says, shrugging.

I smirk. "Pinterest is good for coming up with ideas," I say. I walk him through to the living room. The silver-papered feature wall, the panelling I put in, the sofa, the light grey walls. It all looks normal to me, but suddenly, I wonder what the millionaire who stands beside me thinks and realise I *actually* care what he thinks.

The kitchen and dining area, he's seen, and I take him upstairs to the bedrooms. I show him Elle's first, and he smiles at the pinkness of it all. I show him mine, and he gets a really weird look on his face.

"What's wrong?" I ask.

"When we speak at night, is this where you are?" he asks.

I nod. "Aye, most of the time. Or, coming up to here." I take in the two-tone dove grey of the walls, the feature mirror I created from Ikea mirror panels, the colour splashes on the bed sheets and throws.

He leans in. "Now, I'll imagine you on that bed, talking with me in more detail than I did before." His eyes are dancing, and I can only imagine the thoughts going through his head.

"I'll have to get some enticing nightwear to share with you then," I say. I'm not going to tell him that all of my nightwear is only mummy-suitable. The lingerie and camisoles were gotten rid of ages ago, and I half wish I'd kept them, even if in storage. His eyes dance, and I can see his imagination has gone amok.

I guide him to the last room, the library and guest room. The white bookcases are all full of books, the bed has been remade, and the soft throws and beanbags add colour. Above each bookcase is a desk light that's bolted to the top. I switch the lights so he can see the effects, even in daylight.

"This is a lovely room," he says, smiling.

"It's a three-bed house. It's hard not to use every room we have. But, I've always wanted a library and this," I look around, smiling; "This is mine."

He nods and pulls me in close, gently kissing my mouth again, no tongues.

"You're Belle," he says, smirking.

"Yeah, just don't ask me to wear a yellow ball gown. That's so not my colour!" I giggle. I hear the popcorn machine whir, and I know that Elle and Blythe are looking to settle down for a movie.

"Movie time!" I say, smiling at him. He nods and together, we join my daughter and best friend in front of the television for a while.

Dinner is a success; we laugh and joke. Elle is a charmer and listens to stories from Tony about his three children when they were her age. I have to stop him at some points, reminding him not to go giving her ideas. He just smirks and nods.

"Mummy doesn't swear," Elle defends me as Blythe tells a simplified version of the cat story from our RAF days after Tony mentioned he has a cat called Hera. Blythe and Tony laugh, and I go red.

"Yer mummy does so! But, only when you're not around to hear her," says Blythe when she catches her breath.

Elle looks at me like I'm a naughty child. "Mummy..." she says.

I give her a look. "I do swear, yes, but Aunty Blythe has a much bigger potty mouth!" I respond, deflecting back to my best friend. Blythe gives me a look of indignation but helps me clear away the main dishes so we can get dessert.

Tony brought an apple and cherry pie with lattice topping as dessert, which was warming through in the oven whilst we ate the main course. I can only guess it was Morag who made it; I really can't see Tony making it.

We devour dessert in short order. "You are a great cook," he says as he finishes up the last of his pie. "Thank you for dinner."

Blythe chuckles. "She's always been better at this stuff. I'm terrible. Oh, Sher, do you recall that medic who burnt eggs?"

I gasp as I recall a medic burning eggs. The pot was black and the smell of burning metal and rotten egg didn't leave the mess hall for days. I nod, and she recounts the story for Tony and Elle. The medic had been out on a call on base and got the munchies. The cooks didn't mind staff using the kitchen if you cleared up and put things back. This medic, though, fell asleep whilst boiling some eggs and disaster had struck. Thankfully, there were no casualties—save the noses of everyone on base for nearly a week!

"Is that why you don't like boiled eggs?" Elle asks me, innocently.

I smirk. "It reminds me very much of that day, even though it was twenty years ago," I reply.

"Twenty years? Mummy, that was ages ago!" she exclaims, and it has the three adults around her laughing. Blythe bails me out.

"Come on, munchkin, let's go watch something and let your mum and Tony clear up, aye?" Blythe winks at me and I smile, but I don't move out of my chair.

Tony leans back, his eyes still teary from laughing at Elle's reactions and stories from Blythe and me.

"So, what do you think?" I ask.

He leans forward. "You have a wee firecracker of a lass there, ye should be proud."

I smile. "Aye, she's brilliant. And, she'll make a great big sister," I say. Tony raises an eyebrow. "My ex and his wife are expecting late September. Found out on Sunday."

He nods. "Are you okay with that?" he asks.

I nod as well. "Oh, aye. They deserve it. Elle's the only one I'm ever going to get. My pregnancy wasn't good. Neither was the birthing part; they had to go in with forceps and get her out, and I had to have a transfusion. But, she's here and that's it, I'm done. I didn't have her until my mid-thirties, which I am told is quite late," I explain.

He comes to me and hugs me. "I'm sorry that it was hard for ye," he says.

I just nod. "It was what it was. Nae regrets."

"Good for ye, lass. Let me help you clear up," he tells me. I nudge him in the ribs with my elbow.

"Morag's not here," I tease as he chuckles.

"I have to leave a mess, otherwise she complains that there's nothing to do. The truth is, I'd not eat as well or as healthy as I do if she wasn't around." He starts scooping dishes up and takes them to the sink, then he rinses them off before handing them to me to place in the dishwasher.

"What's yer favourite Scottish band?" he asks as he passes me a dish.

I grin. "Proclaimers, but it's a close call with Runrig and Texas. You?"

"Bay City Rollers," he says. I stand up straight.

"I don't think I know any of their tracks," I muse.

He takes out his phone, pulls up Spotify, and plays one of their albums from 1974. I recognise *Be My Baby* from *Dirty Dancing*, but it sounds nothing like the track from the movie! We listen as we tidy up and between the two of us, the kitchen is tidied after ten minutes, the table is cleared, the dishwasher is on, and we go to join Blythe and Elle in the living room.

Elle's picked another movie, *How to Train Your Dragon*, and snuggles up to Blythe on the single chair, as normal. I can't resist teasing her about it.

"Oh, gone to yer favourite aunty, huh?" I pout.

Elle looks at me, then back at Blythe, and nods madly. I chuckle and Tony motions for me to snuggle up to him whilst we watch the movie. I look across at Elle at the end of the movie and see she's half asleep.

"Come on, petals, time for bed," I say.

"It's not my bedtime yet, Mummy," she replies, then she lets out a huge yawn.

"Huh uh…" I give her the "don't misbehave" look and she looks at Blythe pleadingly, but I swing my legs down so I can sit up.

"I'll come and tuck ye in if you can get ready in…" Blythe checks the clock. "Five minutes! Toilet, teeth, with your pyjamas on. I'll read ye a story!" says Blythe. I can only smile; books and Elle are inseparable. Elle jumps up and hugs her, then comes to kiss me.

"Good night, Tony," she says and hugs him. He kisses her on her head.

"Good night, Elle. I hope you sleep tight and dinnae let the bed bugs bite!"

She looks at me. "Mummy, do I have bed bugs?" she asks.

I shake my head. "Not with the way I clean, petals, no." I grin.

"Oh, good. What do I do if I get them?" she asks Tony.

"You bite them back!" he says, tickling her a little before she runs off. I chuckle and follow her, but she's fast. She's half into her pyjamas as I get to her room.

"Good night, sweetie! Are you looking forward to your birthday this weekend?" I ask as I give her another kiss goodnight.

She nods. "Yes, I am! I hope my next birthday isn't in lockdown," she says.

I shrug and say, "I hope so too, petals," then I turn as I hear someone behind me. It's Blythe.

"Go on down, I've got my girl," says Blythe, touching my shoulder and smiling. I nod, then head downstairs to sit with Tony.

# 22 ~ Anthony

I hear footsteps on the stairs and turn to see Annie heading past the living room door to the kitchen. She comes into the living room a few moments later with a beer for me and something for her.

I give her a quizzical look. "Water," she says, sitting next to me. "Soft stuff already?" I ask.

"I don't drink when Elle's here, and given what I do, it's best I'm not drunk. That, and I can't abide being hungover anymore. I'm way past that stage of my life!"

I chuckle. I know Blythe is driving so I can drink this one, but if I were driving, this would put me over the low driving limit that Scotland has.

"Do you want to watch a more grown-up movie?" I ask. I'm careful about how I word that question, with Blythe and her daughter in the house; I feel it's important to keep the innuendoes to a minimum.

"What do you fancy?" she asks, pointing to the bookcase in the corner that doesn't house books, but her small movie collection.

I hadn't paid attention to the contents of that case, but I get up and browse through her extensive collection. She's got every Fast and Furious movie, off-shoot and Vin Diesel movie I have ever seen. There's a lot of Jean Claude Van Dam and Jason Statham movies to pick from. There are a few weird ones, such as *Bell, Book and Candle*. I read the back of the movie and decide against it. There are Halloween-themed ones, but I notice there are no horror movies here.

"No *Friday the 13th*?" I ask her, grinning over my shoulder.

She shakes her head. "Can't, because of Elle. Not something I like to watch on my own with a child in the house either," she answers. I nod as she makes a fair point.

Then I notice the Sci-Fi section on the lower shelves and she has three copies of *Blade Runner*: an Original, a Director's Cut, and a Blu Ray Director's Cut.

"I take it that you like this movie?" I ask. It's one of my favourites, and I stand up with the Blu-Ray Director's Cut in my hand.

"Love it. Always have," she says, extending her hand for the box. I hand it to her and make sure that our fingers touch. She smirks at me in that endearing way I've discovered she has, then pops the CD into the PlayStation that's connected up to the decent-sized television and starts playing it.

"Are we going to wait for Blythe?" I question.

Annie shakes her head. "She's seen this one as often as I have, we can pretty much recite the script by now." She smirks. I sit down and motion for her to cuddle back into me and she does.

Half an hour later, Blythe joins us and settles in to watch it from the chair, picking up exactly where we are in the movie in seconds.

"She okay?" asks Annie, and Blythe nods.

"Aye, she's better at her reading. What level is she at now?"

I grin. I'm touched by the interest Blythe has in her god-daughter.

"Dark Blue. A year or so ahead of where she ought to be," replies Annie in a low voice.

Blythe nods. "She's gonna be like you," says Blythe, and Annie grins in reply.

"Aye, a proper book dragon and word-smith!" she says, then she looks up at me and winks before turning back to the television and the movie.

It's late when the movie finishes; the Director's Cut is a good forty minutes longer. Even with both Blythe and Annie reciting the final scenes, I still enjoyed it, perhaps even more. What I don't enjoy is leaving her behind.

Blythe has gone to start the car, giving Annie and I a few precious minutes to say our farewells.

I kiss her thoroughly. "Come to mine this weekend?"

She nods. "I need to be at Jim's for Elle's virtual party for an hour or so, but that's all I need to be away from you for."

I nod. "Nae bother. I'll see ye Friday night?" I ask.

She smiles. "After training, aye, ye will!"

I kiss her again, claiming her as much as I can. "See you in my dreams," I tell her, then I pull away and head out to the car, even though I don't want to. Blythe has it on the road, engine purring, just waiting for me to climb in.

I turn at the car to see her leaning against the door, and in my head I imagine for a moment what she'd look like in a lace and silk chemise, standing as she is.

I text her the question as Blythe takes us home.

*T: Just had this image of you standing at the door with a lace and silk chemise on. Dark blue is a good colour for you.*

*A: That is a colour I like.* I'm stunned by her reply.

*T: Tell me your size again, so I get it right.*

I'm sure of her size anyway and when she replies, I smile. I remembered correctly. Then I visit the online ladies' clothing store that I have saved in my browser and order her a few things that I've seen which I think will suit her, with express delivery. A few minutes later my order was confirmed.

T: *Done! It'll be here on Friday.*

A: *Really?! Okay...*

T: *You did say to do so.*

A: *I just...didn't expect you to react that fast! ;)*

T: *Anything you want, you just need to ask.*

A: *Thank you. Remind me not to tempt or dare you.*

T: *I always see things through.*

A: *So I see. I'm just going up to bed.*

My imagination is running riot now.

A: *Good night and thank you! :x*

I smile and catch Blythe's eye in the rear-view mirror. She smirks but doesn't say anything.


I busy myself Thursday and Friday, trading stocks and preparing the two businesses I'm now mentoring. I call and speak with them both, though I get more success and time out of one than I do the other, which makes it seem like they're too important to do the background work. It happens. I trade stocks for the rest of the time on these two days, but come three o'clock on Friday, I'm itching to see Annie again.

The delivery I'm expecting is due soon too and at a quarter past three, it arrives in several large boxes. I take them to my room, helped by

Adrian. Blythe has taken the weekend off and won't be back with me until Sunday. Adrian smiles at me with a twinkle in his eye.

"What's on yer mind, man?" I ask as we move the boxes to my room. I'll open them when he's not around to see some of the contents, but hopefully, that'll be before Annie is here.

"Just wondering what it is all these are for?" He smiles. "I can tell where they're from; they're hardly discreet, Tony." He smirks.

"I'm treating Annie, that's all," I say.

He nods. "I'll stay out of your way as much as I can," he says. He's taken the bedroom furthermost from mine at the back of the house, the same room Blythe occupied when she was here on duty.

I nod. "Appreciate it," I reply, watching him as he stands at the door. "If there's anything else, I'd like to get rid of these boxes," I say. He mouths an "oh" and nods, then he leaves. I close the door over, and it opens a few moments later as Hera comes sauntering in. I empty the first box and separate the contents into their various types of clothes.

I put a box on the floor and watch as Hera jumps into it, happy with her new plaything. I chuckle as she scratches around in the box and tries to catch her tail. As she plays, I empty the other boxes, adding to the items of clothing on the bed. By the fourth box, it's clear I've maybe gone overboard on ordering Annie a few things, and I sigh.

I go to my walk-in wardrobe and decide that I can move things around, and I hang half of it in the walk-in and leave half on the bed. I'm excited and nervous about what Annie will choose to wear and what she'll think of my extravagance. Everything still has the label on it, so anything she doesn't like or doesn't suit, I can send back. I stack the boxes and take them down to the garage for such an eventuality come Monday.

I hear a car pull up to the gate and I know it's her. I walk around to the front door and smile as she comes around the top of the drive and parks behind my S class. She looks wrung out, tired, and I go to hug her. We take a few moments to just hold each other on a late sunny afternoon, letting the sounds of nature penetrate our ears.

I look down at her. "Are you okay?" I ask her, helping her get out of the car in the martial arts gear she's wearing. She nods. "Just a heck of a few days. I'm glad I'm not working this weekend!" she says. I smile.

"So am I," I say in a low tone into her ear as I nibble the side of her jaw. "I have a surprise for you," I add once I've thoroughly kissed her. Kissing isn't something I used to enjoy, but with Annie, I just want to kiss her all the time.

"Oh?" She makes that lovely sound when I've kissed her lightly too.

I nod. "Come on, let me show you," I tell her and take her by the hand and lead her into my house.

## 23 ~ Annie

Tony takes me by the hand and leads me up to his bedroom. On his huge bed are piles of clothes. Dresses, skirts, tops, jeans. A few versions of everything and they are all from a high-end fashion house. One of the dresses alone would buy me several more items from Primark. I almost protested that it's too much, then I remember I kind of did permit him, but it was for the chemises.

"I might have gone a wee bit over the top," he says as he sits on the bedroom chair and looks abashed. "But, what you don't want, I can send back on Monday." He stands and comes to me, cupping my face in his hands and kissing me gently. "You deserve someone to look after you, so take your pick of anything here."

"It's too much," I whisper. After the day I've had with the mood swings of the residents, the unprofessionalism of some of the other staff, I'm shot. I have no more spoons left to deal with this too.

"Think of it like this: The store came to you. You don't have to have it all. But I would like you to choose some things, Annie." He doesn't seem angry at me for being overwhelmed or looking a gift horse in the mouth, and I nod, then slowly start going through some of the things on the bed. The dresses are beautiful, wrap-around business-style attire that would look good in a pair of heels, or going out for a posh dinner. Not that we're going out anywhere in a national or global pandemic lockdown!

Morag appears at the bedroom door and quietly speaks with Tony.

"Ah, Miss Annie," she says, and I visually wince. My social filters, I realise, are gone, and mentally I kick myself. She smiles. "Sorry, Annie. You're here, I wasn't sure. Dinner will be served in forty-five minutes." She nods at me, then quietly says something to Tony and vanishes.

I raise my eyebrows at him. "What was that?" I ask.

He just smiles. "Dinner. Why don't you pick something to wear that you like and then grab a shower or a bath? I can run a bath if you prefer," he offers.

I shake my head. "A shower is just as good, thank you," I say, remembering how fabulous his shower was last weekend. I look at the dark blue wrap dress and pick it out, then Tony holds out a dark blue silk chemise with rose-gold lace on the breast and smiles.

"They'll go together," he says, and I nod with a smirk.

His shower is just as amazing today as it was last week, and I take a good quarter of an hour, allowing only thirty minutes for me to get dressed, apply some makeup, and join him downstairs. The clothes from the bed have vanished and I wonder where to. Kinky man has left out an option of a pair of dark blue Brazilian lace knickers with and without the g-string option. I'm forty-two for crying out loud, I'm not into g-strings, but then I wonder. Is he? I smirk and take the label off both pairs, tossing the non-g-string ones into my bag for tomorrow.

The man also ordered me shoes!? There's a pair of wedged sandals on the floor with the label still on them in my size. Sheesh, the shop did come to me! I slide them on to test them and they feel snug, new. I smile, bend over, and take the label off them. I look in his full-length mirror at the woman before it. It's me, but it doesn't look like me, not the everyday me I get to be at work or home. I kind of like this smarter, dressier version. I take my makeup bag to the bathroom and quickly apply some basic makeup. If the clothes are going to make an effort, so is the war paint.

I'm done in just over five minutes, keeping the makeup to a fresh-faced look rather than a nightclub look. Smiling at the reflection with my hair semi-dried already, I head downstairs to whatever awaits me.

Tony must have heard me at the stairs because he turns, and I see he's changed, dressed up. Gone is the polo shirt and jeans. On is a button dress shirt with no tie, dark blue chinos, and smart shoes. This is his house, but we're dressing up like we're on a date, and I suddenly realise, that's *exactly* what this is. We can't go out; we're in lockdown. So, he's brought the experience to us, enlisting Morag's help. I smirk now I've caught onto his game. For a date with him, I would have gone dress shopping and bought new shoes, lingerie included. He brought the department store to me, and I melted at his care.

I notice him watching me, and I can see his Adam's apple bobbing up and down as he tries to process through his thoughts and feelings at seeing me descend the stairs.

My anticipation is high, as it would be on a date, wondering how tonight is going to go, though I know where we'll end up.

As I reach the bottom of the stairs, he holds his hands out for me. All the lights in the house are on low. There's music playing somewhere, and I'm not sure what it is, but it sounds classical and it kills the silence. He takes my hand, turns it, kissing the knuckles gently, never taking his eyes off mine.

"You," he kisses the knuckles again, "look amazing," he says.

"Thank you," I reply, and he smiles. "You're looking rather handsome tonight too," I compliment. And he does. His ocean blue eyes dance, and he hooks my hand around his arm then gently leads me to a room I've not spent any time in. The formal dining room is littered with candles, the shutters are closed, and there are two places set. The wine is poured, and Tony pulls out a chair for me to sit before he takes the seat at ninety degrees from me. He takes a hand and smiles at me.

"I am so lucky you chose to help me that night," he says. I smile, there's nothing I can say in reply and anything I can think of doesn't do his words, effort, and planning tonight any justice.

"You started asking me about things on Wednesday," I say. Favourite Scottish bands were one topic we covered, movies were another. "What else would you like to know?" I ask.

He smiles. "I know a fair bit about you, but is there anything you'd like to ask me?" he questions. There are things about him I'd like to know, but not right now. Later, maybe, I'll ask how come he's divorced, what his kids are like, if they know about me.

"Books," I say. Let's start with one of my favourite subjects.

We talk through dinner about Arthur Conan-Doyle, Sherlock Holmes, Tolkien, Shakespeare, and the books that formed our views and those that influenced us. He goes back to a childhood book, *Spell for Chameleon*, which in hindsight, he says, almost documents the rise of Google. I talk about *I Am David*, and it's not one he's read. He talks about others I've not read, but there are a few things that we have in common, the love of a good story and the lives therein being one.

"*Silk Vendetta*. I didn't get that at sixteen; I did at twenty-six when I re-read it," I say.

"What's it about?" he asks, and we sit and discuss it whilst we eat the salmon-en-croute Morag has prepared and cooked to perfection. The sweet potato fries and kale are also expertly cooked, and I realise that he prefers clean food, not processed or out of a box. It's something I'll have to remember.

We talk as we eat, finding out more about each other, and once dessert has been consumed, he guides me to the library. There's a log burner that's going ten to the dozen, blasting out heat that can be felt from the hallway. Soon, we're curled up on the sofa, the bookcases behind us, the fire before us with the lights set low.

"How are things with your children?" I ask after we're comfortable.

"They're good. I won't see them until the summer holidays as travel is still not allowed. I spoke to them last week." I smile at his words. He doesn't seem to be a helicopter dad.

"And your ex?" I enquire. I'm not sure how or why his ex-wife let him go; he's been attentive to me since I pulled up at his home hours ago. He was when we met at Eastside too. He squirms, for the want of a better description.

"I neglected her," he says, laughing heavily. "I got caught up in making money, building a business. I didn't pay attention to her needs. By the time I worked it out, my neglect had killed our relationship, and she didn't want me to try to save it. So, we divorced." He looks hurt at his admission, and I feel for him.

"I'm sorry." I try to comfort him and reach out for his hand. Our fingers interlace, but it is what it is. Not everyone wants to fix things when they break these days. Relationships included.

He shrugs. "I don't intend on making that mistake again," he says, smiling at me. I raise my wine glass.

"Then let's make a promise," I offer. "We call each other out when we think that's happening. I get affected by work, and I don't always realise how badly until I'm fighting with said spouse, which was Jim for a while. You've been good at spotting that, and I've not once felt neglected, not by you." I somehow feel that any issues we have will be down to me, not him. He's got it all sorted out, unlike me.

He nods, and we clink glasses.

"I get what you do is emotionally challenging and sometimes, physically demanding. I think it's a wonder you remember where you live!" He grins. As he smiles this time, it's the first time I notice his dimples, and my sex clenches. Goodness, he's handsome!

"I do get my head down and just get on with it," I smirk in reply.

He pulls his phone out and the background music changes.

"Ah, Fleetwood Mac," I say as *Tango in the Night* begins to play. Tony sets his glass down and holds out a hand for me. I place my glass down next to his and allow him to pull me up, then he begins to dance and leads me with moves that befit the song title. It's not quite a full Tango as that requires me to lead part of it and I'm ignorant, but I'm twirling around, then pulled close as our hips gyrate sexually against each other. As the song ends, his lips lightly touch mine, and we kiss. I explore his mouth as much as he explores mine. His hands are behind my head, around my waist, and I'm pulled in close to him. My breasts pebble as they brush up against his hard chest, and I sigh into his mouth at the contact, allowing the lust and desire to build. I dig my fingers into his bicep, the other digs into his hair, keeping him close.

I don't care what the time is now, I want him to love me. I break the kiss and look into his eyes. They're dancing, exploding, full of passion. "Take me to bed," I whisper, and he smiles slightly.

"As ye wish," he says and turns the music and lights off. The fire will die down on its own, and he leads me quietly up to his room, this time closing the door firmly behind us.

# 24 - Anthony

Seeing Annie walk down the stairs, I struggled for a moment or two not to go and grab her, take her to bed, and make love to her until she and I were senseless.

The dress she chose is classy, highlighting her perfect waist, her breasts and her legs. A huge change from her bulky martial arts gear. I changed quickly as she showered, and I waited for her at the bottom of the staircase. I wonder if she realises that this is a date.

We eat, we dance, and then we kiss. Her command to take her to bed has me at almost full mast. Turning off the music and lights, I lead her to my bedroom, a room I'm rapidly thinking of as ours, and close the door behind me. Hera will have to find somewhere else to sleep tonight.

Annie turns to me as I gently close the door, and she's smiling. Her hands begin to undo the wrap of a dress and I stop her.

"Let me," I whisper. I've been wanting to undress her all evening. I take the tie and slowly undo the knot, releasing it with care. Her hands are on my biceps, bracing herself, and I push back the folds of the dress, revealing the chemise I knew she was wearing beneath it. She fills it perfectly, and I cup a breast, feeling the whole mound in my hand. I swear she was made for me; everything about her is perfect. She groans as I rub a thumb over her nipple, puckering it to attention.

I watch as she arches back, bites her lip, and calls out a "yes" at my ministrations. I stop to remove her dress, letting it pool at our feet. I pull her mouth to mine and kiss her again, deeply. Her fingers begin to undo my shirt, and I don't stop her until the last button has been reached. She finishes with the buttons, then I shrug the shirt off, tossing it behind me somewhere, and focus on Annie.

I slide a strap of the chemise off one shoulder, and she moves her arm so I can drop the other, then it falls to her feet, revealing her perfect breasts, the large areola and the now pert nipples. I take a breast into my mouth and play with the other as her fingers rake through my hair. I switch to the other breast, allowing my hands to trace down her torso to her knickers. I slide my finger under the elastic, following the path to the rear of them, finding that she's chosen the g-string style.

I moan a little and my trousers get even more uncomfortable as I react to her pert arse being in reach and bare for me. I crouch down and look into her eyes as I slowly draw her knickers down, to find that they're wet from her arousal. Already I can smell her, and she's glorious as she stands before me. I rise and kiss her as I walk her back to the bed, following her down as her knees hit, making her sit down.

She smirks and leans back on her elbows, and she smiles as I trail kisses down her neck, sucking on the soft skin to the valley of her breasts, between them to her stomach, and then to her sex. I push her legs open at the knees, holding them apart as my tongue begins to taste, lick, and tease her. Her fists grab the sheets, pulling at them, and her moans get louder. The muscles in her legs contract as I tease her with my fingers, thrusting them in and out. She arches up, she's close. I ease off slightly to strip, standing before her, feeling her lust-filled gaze scorch a path on my skin. Reaching into my back pocket, I pull out a condom, rolling it on before dipping down and tasting her arousal.

I lick from her arse up to her clit, slowly, delving my tongue in deeply, and I suck gently, then back down. The sounds she makes tells me she's close again. I kiss and suckle her, driving her to the edge, and I watch as she explodes in front of me, her walls clamping tightly against my fingers, her exclamations of pleasure filling the room. I rise and push into her before she can calm down. I'm in balls-deep, and I begin to move in her slowly, grabbing her wonderful hips to anchor me. Her legs wrap around me, and I watch as her breasts bounce with each thrust.

I love watching her move beneath me, and I lean forward to tease a breast with my mouth, anchoring myself to either side of her. I can feel her clamping around me, holding me within her as I thrust, and I know she's about to climax. I'm not far behind her, and I bite gently into her collarbone as her orgasm hits and she growls my name as her hands hold me to her. I follow right behind her as I empty myself into the condom, huskily calling her name.


I rise and find her lips, kissing her deeply as I slowly withdraw. She lets me up to take care of the rubber and follows me into the bathroom, cleaning herself up.

"Are you okay?" I ask. She's never followed me before, and she blushes as she starts the shower. She nods and I turn her to me, then I hold her.

"What's up, lass?" I ask. I close my eyes, hoping I didn't hurt her but pretty sure I haven't.

"I just...need to shower," she whispers, going pink in her face. I smile, lift her head, and kiss her lips, watching her chocolate eyes close as we touch.

"Yer amazing," I breathe as we break the kiss. I let her go into the shower before joining her. I wash her body from her neck down, slowly.

Morag added some ladies' shower gel so Annie didn't have to leave her own. A fact Annie has noticed and smiles about.

"Expect me to be here a fair bit, do ye?" she asks, rinsing the suds off her body. I moan slightly at the sight of her, and I can only grin as she takes some of my soap, lathers it in her hands, and begins to wash me.

We rinse off, still stealing kisses, and I wrap us both in some large towels before guiding us back to the bedroom. Annie picks up the blue chemise and slips it back on, making my dick get hard at the sight. I slip under the covers again and pull them back on her side so she can slide in next to me. We lie facing each other, holding hands with only a distant lamp casting any light on us.

"Thank you," she whispers, and I lean in to kiss her.

I'm not sure when it happened, but I've fallen for this remarkable woman. If she doesn't feel the same, I'm not sure when I'll ever recover. Or if I even can. I stroke and hold the side of her face, tempted to tell her how I feel.

"I have Elle's party to go to tomorrow," she says. "You could come with me, if you like?"

I hear what she's saying: She's ready and willing to present us both as a couple to her ex, his wife, her family. She's not where I am, but she's on that same path. My heart soars at this revelation.

"If you'd like me there, I'd love to come. I haven't gotten her a gift though," I say. Annie smiles.

"I've left the card and the gifts unsigned, but they're in the car." I smile at her. She's steps ahead on this.

"What time is the party?" I ask.

"Not until two," she says. We've time to pop to a supermarket and find something in the morning to add to the gifts.

"Did she like the flowers?" I ask. Annie nods.

"Loved them would be more accurate. She's never had anyone give her flowers before." I grin at Annie's words. "I loved mine too, thank you," she says, reaching across and kissing me gently. I can see she's starting to fall asleep and I continue holding her hand as she drifts off. I wait until she's asleep, then I creep out of bed and begin picking up our clothes, tidying away the towels onto the rack and turning off the light. It takes a few moments and I come back to bed to find Annie hasn't moved. I slip back into bed, pulling the covers tighter around us both before I take her hand again and let sleep claim me.

We awake leisurely the following morning, and I watch as Annie decides what to wear to Elle's party. I smile and beckon her to the walk-in, showing her the rest of the clothes, and she gasps.

"Tony..." She looks at the clothes then me and back again. "Honestly?!" she says, thumbing through some of them. I shrug.

"I wasn't sure what you liked in style or colour, so..." I let the statement hang.

She suddenly breaks into a laugh. "I gave you permission for the chemise," she says. I pull her close, she's still wearing it and the lace knickers that I'm tempted to pull off her. We have hours before we need to go to her daughter's party.

"It's not all for today, and what you don't like can go back," I say. She nods, and I'm glad she's not fighting me on this.

"That's just it; I love pretty much all of it!" she confesses, sighing. I grin.

"Then, it can all stay." I hold her face in my finger and thumb and focus her chocolate eyes on me. "I'll enjoy removing every piece off you, right before I take you," I tell her. She takes a half step towards me and kisses me.

"I'll hold ye to that!" she states and looks around the selection. She picks a casual hoodie that is similar to a sweatshirt but more like a dress. She picks out a new pair of jeans and smiles as she takes them to the bed. I'm half-dressed in fresh jeans and a blue button shirt that will just need a casual jacket to go with it later. For now, I'm ready.

I watch as Annie puts on one of the new bras, which is not like the ones I'm used to. I watch as she shrugs into it and fastens it across the front so that she's supported, and it makes her breasts look amazing.

Then she quickly slides into the fresh clothes and checks herself out in the full-length mirror. She turns to me in time to see me close my mouth, and she grins. "So I look good, aye?" she asks.

I growl, pull her towards me, and kiss her deeply. "Beyond good," I say when I've finished kissing her.

She nods confidently and her stomach growls. "I think I need feeding," she says, placing a hand behind my head, and she pulls me in for another kiss.

"Aye, I think ye do," I respond, looking around, and she sees me being slightly confused at the tidiness of the room.

"I do tidy up after myself," she scolds me. "The military makes a neat freak out of ye, even if yer not one," she explains as she opens the bedroom door.

The jeans she's picked look like they've been painted on her, and I can't help but smack her arse as she walks in front of me, both for her sassiness and her arse looking so good.

She turns to me and grins. "Later." She winks and heads off down the stairs. Damn it if I'm not grinning like a teenager.

Morag has prepared Belgian waffles with a variety of fruit for breakfast. The waffle maker beeps as another batch is cooked, and Morag carefully scoops out the four that have been made, then pours more batter in and closes it. I watch as she places the latest batch before Annie and me, and I smirk as Adrian pushes his plate away from him.

"Morag, that was fantastic! I'll have to work harder at the gym on Monday!"

Morag smiles. "If ye werenae such a wee piggy, ye wouldn't have tae!" she scolds. Annie looks at him and laughs. Adrian loves his gym; there's no way this brawny, bearded, tattooed, ex-military now security man will let his physique slip.

"Double payback in the gym, aye?" Annie says, and Adrian nods.

"I need to do some training this week," she states, and I smile. I hadn't realised she kept up her fitness level, but looking at her, it is obvious.

"I do have a gym out back," I tell her. Adrian nods, and Annie raises her eyebrows.

"Really?" she asks. "Can I use it later, please?" she requests. I nod, lean across and kiss her gently on the mouth.

"With pleasure," I reply.

"Fab!" she responds, helping herself to breakfast. I do the same as Adrian stands to leave.

"I want to check in with my crew on another job. May I use your office, Tony?" he inquires as he pours himself another mug of coffee.

I nod. "Sure," I answer, grabbing a waffle before Annie can take them all. Morag grins and warms the waffle maker back up, preparing two more with a wink and a smile.

We clear away breakfast and head out to the supermarket. They're the only shops that are open, and we have to wear a face mask whilst we go inside, as well as sanitise our hands as we enter. Morag asked that we get some items whilst we were here. Annie fetches those as I take a look at the non-food sections for something for Elle. I spy a decent-sized plush Leopard toy and grin. Grabbing it, I find a small bouquet and meet Annie by the tills. I pay for the shopping, and we head back to the car and home.

We've wrapped the extra presents, written the card, and the flowers are in a temporary vase until I can give them to Elle. I'm searching for Annie when I find her outside my office, listening to Adrian on his call. I go to ask her what she's doing when she holds up a finger to her lips to indicate that she wants me to be quiet, then she taps her ear and points to the office. She's listening to him. I find that rather disturbing, and I wonder what she's listening to. I join in, but I can't fathom why she's intent on listening and staying silent. I hear Adrian hang up and before I can challenge her, she's in the office with me hot on her heels.

"Adrian, who was the second voice in that call?"

Adrian looks up, not startled by her asking.

"One of my employees, why?" He leans back in the office chair, my chair, and I lean against the door.

"Annie, what's going on?" I demand.

She looks at me then back at Adrian.

"The night I encountered Tony, when he got knifed, I heard that second voice."

I'm stunned. How would she recognise that voice after all this time? Adrian has the same question it seems.

"You're sure?" he asks, leaning forward.

"Very sure," she replies in a cold, serious tone. "He was telling the guy who knifed him," she motions to me, "that he was still there, that your phone was telling him you were there in that building."

I look at Adrian and he nods. "I'll check it out. We didn't find any link or money flowing though," he replies.

"There's a connection; he was the second voice. I'd swear to it in court."

Adrian gives her a curt nod. "We struck out when we checked Alasdair and Duncan's background again."

Annie sighs. Then she looks at me. "You told me last week you were going to invest in two companies after I suggested you take the two on. How many others have you invested in, or done a Dragon's Den thing on their products?"

I shrug. "I get through about thirty applications a month."

I can see the cogs in her mind working. Then she looks me in the eye, and I can tell she's thinking of something we haven't thought of. "Do you keep their proposals, their applications?"

I nod and motion for Adrian to vacate my chair. Then I reach into the desk file my computer sits on and pull it out. "I have this year's applications here, but last year's applications are offsite."

I put the file on the desk, and she looks at Adrian.

"What if, for talking sake," she grins at Adrian, "that your employee is linked to any of these applications, somehow?"

Adrian looks at me and then back at Annie.

"You're serious?" he asks.

"Think about it. Nothing's happened since. You've had Tony on a tight leash and this lockdown is messing with everyone's ability to move about freely. The attack happened in Glasgow, and the attacker's helper had an Aberdeen lilt to his accent. It was one of your employees leading him to Tony. Start with companies over either way," she says, tapping the pile I placed on the desk.

Adrian looks at me, and I can only shrug in reply. We've had no leads so far; the money trail went dead. Adrian nods. "This is going to take a long time," he says. Annie just grins in an almost evil way.

"I best let you get started then!" she says, heading towards me. Then she turns to Adrian. "I'll keep him safe this afternoon and when you're still at it later, I'll give you a hand." She turns to smile at me, and I let her pass me. All I can do is shrug at Adrian who grabs the file and heads to the kitchen. I can hear him asking Morag for a pot of coffee and then I lose track of where he goes, as Annie is now by my side, gifts in hand, and her boots compliment her outfit. I gape at her; she's a few inches taller now, and her legs are showcased by those skin-tight jeans that I am just going to love peeling off her legs later.

She smiles at me. "Ready?" she asks, but I shake my head.

"Not quite, I need my shoes," I say. She nods and heads to the bench in the hall to wait for me, and I take all of five minutes to put on some socks, my shoes, and grab my jacket.

"Do you have all the presents?" I ask.

She smiles. "Everything, including the flowers," she says, pointing to the items beside her. I smile and we head off to the city centre.

## 25 ~ Annie

Hearing that voice again after so many weeks was like someone had dragged me by the scruff of my collar and hauled me straight back to the night I encountered Tony in that darkened, dilapidated room. There has to be a connection to Tony, though what it is isn't obvious. However, I was called Sherlock for more than one reason. This is supposed to be Adrian's investigation, his job, so all I can do is point him in the right direction and let him go at it.

I drive us in my car to Jim's, mostly because I know where we're going, but another idea strikes me about Tony's situation as I'm driving. When we get to The Mews in the Old Town, I find a parking spot and ask Tony to call Adrian.

"Not more work!" Adrian jokes at me.

"I just thought: Did you check the mobile calls into and out of your work numbers that night?"

I can hear the papers he's shuffling stop being shuffled. "Yes, but nothing showed up."

I ponder for a moment. "It's a pity that you don't have a mobile geek who can find out what calls were made from that location in that window of opportunity. I called Blythe when I was three streets away, but about ten, maybe fifteen minutes later? He was right above me when the call was ongoing and it wasn't a long conversation, so it had to originate from pretty much there."

I can hear folders being closed and a chair being moved on the hard floor.

"I have someone who can find that out," he replies.

"I'd get names, then check all that paperwork," I say. I've slipped back into MP mode, and I breathe deeply, letting it out of me.

"Yes, boss!" he quips, and I chuckle.

"Aye, sorry. Old habits," I apologise, and he snorts.

"Yer as bad as Bee!" he mutters.

"Aye, we did work together!" I remind him.

"I can tell," he replies, then the line goes dead.

Tony looks at me strangely. "He's not annoyed at you," he tells me.

I shrug. "I went into MP mode, so he might be a wee bit...unsettled," I say. "I forget that people don't want to be told what to do or where to look." Tony nods and smiles.

"I would never have thought to do what you've just suggested," he says. "I get lots of applications for business support." I nod, showing that I get it. He's able to put money in, but there's a contract needed on that investment and if people don't have the figures, then the investment isn't worth it.

"If that comes up bust, I would consider giving Adrian his notice," I say. Tony shakes his head.

"I've known Adrian for a lot of years. He's a friend as well as a businessman. He won't quit until he's done his job." Tony looks at me. "Which is why he might not say it now, but he'll appreciate the pointers."

I smile and nod ahead, grateful I might not have pissed off one of Blythe's lovers and Tony's friend. "Shall we?" I ask.

He nods, and we get out of the car. He's coming around to hold the door open for me and help me out. I smile and thank him, then we collect the presents together and head to Jim's house.

The hour or so that we're with Jim and Fiona passes quickly. Fiona shares with me the nursery plans she and Elle have come up with and where it's going to be. Tony seems to be okay being alone with Jim, who is supervising the birthday party on a Zoom call. I would never have thought of that, but it's a genius move!

Fee and Elle have made cakes, and our presents are by the pile of others downstairs. As the Zoom call ends, Elle descends upon them gleefully, giggling as she does so. However, she stops, sits down, and tears each open carefully, noting down what is from whom and places the wrappings in a bin liner to be taken out later. It's all very tidy. I comment to Fee that this won't always be how it is when she has two of them to care for!

Fee laughs. "Aye, I ken. But, she's a wee darling, and she's getting good at making a cup of tea." She winks at Jim, who seems to take the hint and half-fills the kettle before switching it on.

"I see you've got him trained with just a hint, nice one." I wink at her. I know Jim can hear me, and he just smirks. I half expect him to flip me the bird, but he doesn't.

Elle squeals when she gets to the leopard and jumps up to hug Tony. "I love it!" she proclaims in a high pitched voice. I give her that "too loud," look and she calms down a little, though not too much.

She gives off cries of "wow," "aah!" and "oohs," as she opens up all her presents, including the pink denim padded jacket I got her. She puts it on straight away and I have to prise it off her to take the labels off once I know it fits.

I grin as she puts it back on in double-quick time, before settling down again to open up the cards. She's taking a video call from my parents, and Tony comes to wrap his arms around me as we listen in. When the calls to my folks are done, I kiss her bye-for-now, and she hugs Tony one more time.

"Thank you for my presents and flowers!" she says, hugging him. He's bent down so she can throw her arms around his neck. My heart melts as she plants a kiss on his cheek before running off to play with her new toys and watch her new movies.

We say goodbye to Jim and Fee, then head back to his mansion. We've been out a couple of hours, and I wonder what Adrian has found whilst we've been gone.

# 26 ~ Anthony

The few hours with Elle and Annie's ex pass quickly, and before I realise it, the little girl is kissing me on my cheek and we're heading back to mine. Annie's a steady driver, confident. I can see similarities between Blythe's style of driving and Annie's. At least when the women in my life drive, I am not holding onto the car seat with white knuckles!

We're back at mine quite quickly, and we're inside with a hot drink in a few moments. Adrian hasn't been seen by Morag since shortly after we left, and it's not until dinner is over that we see him. He motions for us to head into my office and he turns on the anti-listening device. He looks at Annie with a smile.

"Yer were dead right, thanks!" he says, pulling out the files that I gave him earlier. There's one at the top that he opens up and shows us.

I nod. "I can have my PA check what paperwork we sent him, but I don't want to call him about it until Monday," I say. I refuse to put other people out for something that is important but not an emergency. Like Annie, my PA has a life, family, obligations. Adrian looks like he's about to argue, but Annie once again has an idea.

"Does your PA keep things that have been sent in a shared area, a cloud? Can *you* access that cloud?" she asks. I look at when his application came in and nod.

"Aye, shouldn't take me too long to see what we sent him. Should be the standard reject though," I say. She's right, the file is easy to find, and I print off the single page rejection we sent him at the start of December the previous year.

"So, what do we do now?" I ask. Annie and Adrian grin at me.

"Now, you let the police do their job," she says, nodding to Adrian. He takes the letter from me and grins.

"I've got some report writing to do, but I should have this ready to be handed to them on Monday."

I nod. "You can use the office if it helps," I offer. Adrian nods.

"I'll do that, thank you," he agrees and makes a call. I smile and motion for Annie and me to leave him to it.

I take us to the TV room and bring up Netflix. Annie shrugs. "Not fussed about what we watch," she says, and I pick a box set. Settling down with our drinks and snuggling each other, we get on with watching a drama series.


It's late when we head to bed, Adrian having retired at some point during our binge Netflix session. I enjoy burying myself in Annie before we sleep, and I'm smiling as we wake up cuddling each other. Even though it's early on a Sunday, we shower and rise.

Annie seems to be on edge, and I ask her why after breakfast. "I've not done anything really physical for a couple of weeks, well, beyond you." She grins, and I can only laugh in response.

"So what would you like to do?" I ask. "I have the gym out in the garden," I offer.

She nods. "Aye, that would be grand. Can we go and look at it?" she asks.

I nod and we head out. It's a large cabin unit that I had installed, but it's big enough to house a running machine, a multigym, and a matted area. Annie looks around and leans against the door as I stand in the middle.

"Decent floor space," she says and seems to be thinking; I stand and watch her work through whatever is going on in her head. "I can work with what's in here. Just means I change how I do what I need to," she says. I smile.

"So, you're okay with what's here?" I ask. She nods and smiles.

"Aye," she says, reaching up onto her toes and kissing me. "I just have to change my routine, but that's okay!"

An hour later, I watch as Annie heads down to the gym, and my curiosity gets the better of me. She's dressed in black gym leggings, a black sports vest, and a light coloured yoga top. When I approach, I can see her doing a routine on the small floor space with her phone on the ground, playing some fast music, and she seems to be copying moves from a video. There's a sheen of sweat on her brow, and she moves her legs, arms and torso as the video dictates; it looks like she's dancing but on the floor!

She stops, sees me and smiles, then takes off her baggy top, teasing me as she does so. I take a seat in my pergola and watch as she moves onto the weights but it's more the repetitions than any serious weight gain.

Lastly, she hits the treadmill, starting slowly, and in twenty minutes, she's calling it a day. She's been working out for an hour or so and she seems happier. She's certainly sweaty!

"I'm going to take a shower. Are you warm enough there?" she asks. She's left the door open slightly to let the room air and I don't blame her.

"I'm not as warm as you," I say, grinning. There's something about her that makes me want to pin her down and get all hot and sweaty with her.

"I'm sure the shower can sort that out for ye," she says, walking away. I pause for a moment, then watch as she winks at me over her shoulder and heads up to the house. By the time she's at the backdoor, I still haven't moved, but the look she gives me makes me hurry up to meet her in the shower.

# 27 ~ Annie

The weekend with Tony was just amazing. I might be forty-two, but I certainly didn't feel like it! The afternoon shower session at his lasted nearly half an hour with both of us getting off at least once by the other's hand.

I know I'm not far from his house where I am, but my four walls are not his. It's not where he is, and I feel unable to say anything, not yet. What we have is too new; it's only been a month, if that, not counting the first time I laid eyes on him. I don't want to be away from him; I feel more settled with him around.

Elle comes home on time, as scheduled, and Jim smiles as she darts off upstairs; I suspect to put some of her presents away in her room.

"Tony seems nice," he says as he stands a little further away than usual.

"Are you obeying the social distancing rules?" I ask. "In a support bubble house?" It's crazy, he's my ex and I was at his house yesterday, drinking tea as we have to be each other's support bubble. He blushes.

"Yeah, well—" he begins, but I cut him off.

"Going to be hard to maintain that if you need to come in for a better reason, don't you think?" I reply, exasperated; he didn't seem to be this careful yesterday. His eyes snap up, meeting mine.

"No need to be like that, Annie," he snips back. I sigh.

"Jim," I call softly to him. "I was standing in your house yesterday, drinking tea with yer pregnant wife. We have to be around each other because of Elle. That means you get to be in the house with me, in case you need to come in. Folks in support bubbles don't need to be so...aloof." He starts to argue with me then closes his mouth as he processes the point I've made. "Besides, if we get it, we get it. The other just needs to step up and help the other, aye?" I make that point then drop the subject when he nods.

"I'll be off then," he says, heading back to his car. I nod.

"Aye, she'll be at school on Friday, as usual," I reply.

He waves up to a window, Elle's window, then he climbs into his car and drives back to his home. I wish it were me driving back to Tony's.

Monday comes and things are back to normal. I check in with Holly, to find she's getting it on with the council removal man, and I smile, then send her back a "you deserve it" message. She so deserves someone who will love her for who she is. Elle does her school work, and I catch up on charity paperwork and invoices. Then I help Elle with her writing, and we pick out the first fountain pen for her to use.

I check my bank account and realise I haven't been paid. While Elle does more school work, I chase it with Julia.

"It should be there," she says when I tell her the reason I'm calling.

"I'm sorry, Julia, it's not." I can hear her sighing. "Is there something going on I need to know?" I ask.

"Not sure if it's something you can deal with, only, things have been a wee bit messed up with the salaries this month. I'll check and get back to you." She hangs up before I can enquire any further, and I shrug. I can't fix everything, and I try not to worry about how I'm going to pay for the groceries this week, or the fuel for the car; though my reserves are allocated to something else, I can divert them. Okay, we're not travelling anywhere, but we are eating; I do have my electric and other bills to pay. Goodwill isn't going to cut it and reserves don't last forever. Julia calls me at around four, asking me to check my account and I do. The money is there, thank the lord! Suddenly, I can breathe, but Julia still sounds worried.

"Talk with the bank manager? They might be working from home, but get the call in, see what the issue is and how it can be avoided," I advise. She agrees and we finish talking.

The sense of foreboding still doesn't leave me though, even when I'm at work on Thursday. On Friday, I'm at a safehouse and the feeling intensifies, then I understand why when we're called into a meeting room and given the dreaded news: We're now in isolation. One of the residents at the shelter I'm at has tested positive for this global virus, though they're not showing signs of it. Until they and everyone here gets the all-clear three times over the next ten days, we're not allowed to leave. I'm now on lockdown with twenty rescue women, three counsellors, and away from my daughter and Tony.

The phone call to Jim and Fee goes as well as can be expected, which is to say, it could have gone better. Jim's angry at me for getting caught up in it, even though I'm not the one infected. Despite me telling him I have no choice, that this is a directive by the local Primary Care Trust and Hollyrood, he hangs up on me angrily. Fee calls me back almost instantly and talks with me.

"Until they test negative, there's nothing I can do. We have to be isolated and tested for ten days minimum."

"I know," she says. "Jim gets it, he's been fighting with the workforce about it all week, and your situation..." She lets the statement hang.

"Straw that broke the camel's back?" I offer. Funny, it's always me with that damn straw.

"Aye," she breathes. "Here, Elle wants to talk with ye. She's got her bed here until you can get out of this, and we'll see where we're at with everything then, aye? We've got her covered." At least Fee gets that I have no choice in being locked away from my daughter and Tony. I'm grateful that she's got my back.

I talk with Elle and explain what's going on. She's sad that she won't see me, but I hear Fee say that we can video chat every night. I smile. Fee's a damn star. The call to Tony is much harder emotionally to do but turns out to be so much easier.

"Ach no! Ten whole days without ye?" he laments as I tell him. I've taken to the roof now; the other support staff are making their calls too. No one is having an easy time of it this evening.

"Aye. I was supposed to be out, helping folks get to the shelters this weekend, but I cannae. I'm as far as I can go."

"Do you have everything you need? Toiletries, clothes, food?" I smile. I'm locked away in the same city as him, and he's thinking about what I need, rather than what he needs or wants. Though, we both want the same thing: each other.

"I think we've got enough here. We've got folks around us doing the food shopping and getting essentials, so we should be okay. Clothes are an interesting one... I only pack enough for emergencies, and that's for two days."

"Do you want me to bring you some?" he asks.

I grin. "I can't be telling you where I am, otherwise it's no longer a refuge; they're on a-need-to-know. But, I can get a bag picked up from yours if you can pack me some casual stuff?" I can hear him shuffling around; I'm guessing he's in the walk-in.

"Aye, I can do that for ye. What do you want me to pack?"

I tell him the kind of clothes that work well for me here and what I need, which is jeans, t-shirts, tops, socks, underwear.

"I'll have that ready by tomorrow. Is that soon enough for it to be picked up?" he asks. I love how he just jumps in to help, rather than ranting at me and casting blame.

"Aye, should be. I don't know how quickly we can get someone out to pick it up, but I'll let you know?" I smile.

"Aye. How are you holding up?" he asks, and my heart just melts. We talk and then I head down into the building when we finish our conversation.

For two days, things are pretty routine. Everyone chips in and we get word that the runner we usually use can collect our personal belongings and drop them to us. Whilst we can wash things at the shelter, having spares is a good idea!

It's evening time, the bags have all been dropped off, and I smile as I check through mine. For some reason, there's one of Adrian's anti-listening devices. I tuck that back in the bag, wondering why it was packed, but I know it's something Blythe would have put in or asked to have put in.

I'm tidying the kitchen with some of the Polish women when they tense up. I look around and see one of the counsellors who has been caught up in this. I assume it's because he's male, but when he leaves, they begin to chat amongst themselves, not realising that I understand them.

"Say that again?" I ask in rusty Polish. I can't just listen in now, I have to join in. I need them to repeat what they just said in their native tongue, though I've not used it for over ten years. One of the women goes deathly white. I dry my hands and look at the small group.

"Listen, if he's involved in why you're here, I need to know. I can't get it fixed if we don't know."

The shorter of them all mumbles something but just loud enough for me to hear. "He was at the...hotel."

I go to the kitchen door and check he's not hovering around outside of it. I can't see anyone listening to us, but I motion for the girls to follow me and ask them to be quiet. I grab the device Blythe packed and take them up to the rooms just below the roof that we've not decorated yet. The sun is just setting and from the huge window, we can see a warm glow cast over Edinburgh. I take a few seconds to appreciate the view, knowing that it's going to be a long night. The shorter one looks at the device, and I smile.

"So we cannot be heard," I say. She nods and begins to tell me what happened.

"My name is Natasza. I work for rich man. One night, I am taken to a hotel. He was there," she nudges her head to the door and I get she means the counsellor, "They...shared me. I didn't want to." She starts crying and is hugged by some of the others.

We're still speaking in Polish so I try to get my words right.

"Who else was there? Can you tell me?" I ask. I've gone cold in sheer anger, and I know what I have to do before she's even finished telling me about that night. She nods and from the folds in her dress, she pulls out names. I blink. I recognise two of them. They're prominent figures, and I realise that this is bigger than even I can deal with.

Another of the women speaks up. "She is not the only one. I know of two others here who have been in that room."

"Other victims of his are here?" I ask incredulously. She nods.

"I need to speak with them," I say. She shakes her head.

"They Romanian, they do not speak much English."

I nod and tell her that I do need to speak with them, that I can use a translator app. Her eyes go wide and she nods. "I will ask," she says to me.

I look at the shortest one, Natasza, who has spoken up.

"I do not know how, but we *will* fix this. I promise." Suddenly, I feel like Atlas and I'm holding up the World. But this is a fight I'm not backing down from. I simply can't.

"Let's head down, but not in a group." We depart, and I tuck the piece of paper with the men's names on it into my bra, crick my neck. The vertebrae all snap back into place. In my room, I change out of my skirt into a pair of sports leggings. The anti-device looks like a blue-booth speaker, it's all very James Bond, and I place it on the table next to the bed I've claimed for the next ten nights. I call and speak with Elle, then

Tony. I keep the conversation light, but I send Blythe a keyword that will have her call me at midnight. Then I make the awkward call to Julia.

She's stunned at my revelations. "I can't just pull him out, damn it, not now," she says. "He checked out too!"

I grimace. "I know. But I'm going to be on patrol tonight. I might even lock him in his room, St Trinians style."

"This is a mess," she declares.

"Aye, but one we need to clear up. We can't ignore this," I say.

"I know. But, you're in isolation...how can we get him out?" I can hear her pacing.

"You call the police and let them know your findings. Once we're all clear, we need to move them to another unit. How secure are our computers and files with that data on it?" I ask.

"I'll change his password and lock him out," she says.

"Not yet..." I reply quickly.

"Why?" she asks.

"He doesn't know we know," I say, looking around the rooftop. "I'll keep an eye on him and get the other women counsellors to help out too. If he tries something, anything, we can stop it, get him removed by the police and charged." I hope I sound more confident than I feel, but it's just this simple: We have to.

I pace along the rooftop. "Julia, I know you didn't want to tell me as I'd have to do something about it, but I need to know who Sarah was working for."

She sighs and for a moment, I think she's hung up on me. "Henry Aikin," she says, and I stop dead. He's a local millionaire and his name was at the top of Natasza's list.

I go back down to the rooms we're using and the counsellor I need to watch isn't around. I played the question in Romanian about where he is on my phone, and seven heads turned to look at me, but there are no answers. I ask the same in Polish and get told that he's gone down to the laundry room.

I nod and head off to find him. I grab some laundry that doesn't really need doing as an excuse as to why I'm down there when he is. When I go down, I can hear him on the phone, and he's agitated.

He hangs up as I boldly go through the door, making a noise. I heard what he said, but he doesn't know I heard him. Now I want to know who he was talking with, and I know how I can find out.

"Oh, sorry, Chris, I didn't realise you were here," I say, putting my load into one of the three machines and setting it up. "Low on pants too?" I joke, and he nods with a weak smile. What I'd give for a listening bug! However, I'll have my answer soon enough as finding his number from the system takes me all of two minutes.

At midnight, Blythe calls me and I brief her quickly. She swears, and I give her the counsellor's name and his mobile number.

"Can you find out who he was talking to?" I ask.

"Aye, you can. I'm gonna give your number to Marcus."

"Listen, before ye do...dinnae say anything to Tony. I don't need him worrying."

She sighs and there's a few seconds of silence. "Aye, okay. Are you going to write this up?" she asks.

"Fuck yeah," I reply. I've already started on my mobile and saved the file to a secure cloud service so that it's not easily found.

"Be careful, pal," she says, hanging up. I don't think I am going to get a choice.

Marcus and a colleague call me at 1 am, and I go to take the call in the living room, leaving the door to the hall open. I can see and hear anyone on the stairs if they move about. It does also mean they can hear me, but my conversation is going to be very one-sided and very obscure.

"Hey, Annie," he greets me.

"Hello, you," I greet him.

"Are you alone?" he asks.

"For now. Though, walls have hidden ears, aye?" I reply. It lets him know I might not be as alone as I think I am.

"Okay, I have the number and I know who he was calling. Henry Aikin." I close my eyes and swear quietly.

"You know him do you?" I hear something being tapped against the microphone of the device he's using.

"Aye. Find everything out about them both, would ye? The whole nine yards. And then more. Dig dark if ye have tae." I hate the Dark Web and what it contains, but if there's stuff hidden electronically, that's where it's going to be buried.

Marcus whistles quietly in reply. "You know this fella?" I can hear him typing on the phone.

"Aye. That I do."

"I take it he's bad news?

"Something like that," I say. "Ye ken why I wanna know." I know Blythe will have told him; there's no secrets between the three of them.

"Do you need anything else?" he asks.

"Not for now," I reply. "Good night," I say, hanging up the phone and taking my seat back in front of the rooms that Aikin's victims are sleeping in. They came to us to get away from those creeps, to try and build a better life, or even to just rebuild. We're supposed to keep them safe, so how did Chris get access to the girls?

Until Marcus comes back with what he's found, I can only do what I can to protect them, and that means making them as safe as they can be. I hear nothing approaching their room for three nights. It's the night after our second medical test when Chris attempts to get access to the girls. The women and I, however, have other ideas.

I can hear the floorboards on the level above creak and footsteps quietly make their way across the landing. I've been snatching sleep during the day, the women counsellors are all on board with stopping him but keeping him on site until he gives us a legitimate reason to remove him. One of them thinks our plan is too risky, but I can't not do anything; we can't let him get away from here and run to ground. I hear the footsteps on the stairs and silently move to the darkest corner.

The girls asked why he was still around, and I said that we need a reason to get him out of isolation, arrested. They offered to give us one and make him start being accountable for the part he's played. So I wait in the shadows as he enters their room. I got a camera set up in the room thanks to Marcus and Blythe hiding it in another 'clothes' drop for me.

The cry goes up from one of Natasza's friends, and I enter their room to find one of Chris' hand over Maja's mouth, the other on her leg under the covers. The camera got it all.

"I didn't do anything, I was seeing if..." He stands up and holds his hands up and backs away from her quickly. Unfortunately for him, his actions are too late. The sheets are dislodged from the bottom and the friend is telling me that he had his hand on her leg beneath the covers.

"I think you were trying to see if they'd sleep with you," I state clearly.

"No," he claims, going white. One of the women counsellors would have already called the police, and I hear Natasza's friend, Maja, declare that he touched her without her consent in beautiful clear English, all for the benefit of the video.

The police arrive and they put on masks and disposable gloves before being escorted inside. I give my observations to the officer, stating that the girls were nervous around him and I was on night duty. One officer looks at me and snarls slightly.

"What are you dressed as?" he snorts, snarling his lips in disgust.

I grin. "Ask Wolf who I am," I say, pulling his name out of the ether. "Or perhaps, you'd like to go and ask Grey over there?" I call DCI Grey over and the officer goes white.

"I'd like this officer replaced please." I look at him and note his lapel number. "He seems to think that how I dress somehow impacts what I can do or see."

I see Chris being led away in handcuffs, and I know that any interaction he has with the shelters across the country is now in tatters. The officer is led away by DCI Grey, and he finds a competent policewoman to take down my statement. Hours later, when all the excitement is waning, the Polish girls come and hug me, thanking me for getting him out of there. I'm called to the side by one of the counsellors, Clare, when they finally stop thanking me.

"We've revoked his access, and I've removed anyone that isn't here tonight or needs to be here when the lockdown is finished with. You did well!" She praises me. I grin, but I have this sinking feeling that the proverbial shit hasn't even hit the fan.

I check in with Tony, chatting about various things, including a sexual position he wants to try with me. I also get an update on his situation. Adrian submitted his report and findings to the police who acted a few days after I had to be put into isolation.

The young entrepreneur from Glasgow was arrested and the gang member he paid to gas and slash Tony was found, confessing to all. Adrian's employee was harder to crack. Once he was presented with the fact that the gang member had revealed all, he too gave a more honest opinion of the matter, but his career in private security is over. I shake my head, wondering if it was worth the personal cost.

The police have them both in custody and bail was denied. Blythe and Adrian no longer have a reason to stay and guard Tony. His situation is over, but whatever I am involved in, it feels like it's only just beginning.

## 28 ~ Anthony

Adrian tells me the good news about my assailant being arrested in Glasgow. The gang thug told all, confirming the connection Annie had found. Adrian's employee, Duncan Hay, was arrested and bail for each has been denied. Duncan denied everything, until the gang member told all, tying up other loose ends that only someone involved knew, like why. It turns out Duncan is a cousin to the young businessman I rejected, Mark Hoggarth. Not that Mark's idea was bad, he just didn't have a clue about his business.

Adrian also explained that Mark had gambled money he'd already been given for the business, and lost it. When I didn't back him, he blamed me for his misfortune and debt, which was enforced, and he ended up in a hospital, severely beaten.

Annie and I speak every day, and I can tell that something has kicked off. She asked for a second bag of clothes, but whilst Blythe packed the bag, none of her clothes from here are missing. Adrian and Blythe have been talking in hushed tones around me, and I have no idea why.

Annie calls me, and the end of her now twelve-day incarceration is nearly here. There's one more medical test to do today and if everyone tests negative, they're all allowed to leave. I know Annie is supposed to be on retrieval duty this weekend, as she was when this all kicked off, but she greets me with the good news that she's not. Having just pulled a twelve-day stint, I'm as pleased as heck I get to have her to myself, no security guards or six o'clock shadows.

Blythe and Adrian have cleared out of the mansion, and I surprisingly find the whole place too quiet now. I'm sure it won't be once I've fed Annie; I have every intention of locking us both away in our bedroom and having my way with her as often as I can. Absence, they say, makes the heart grow fonder and I cannot disagree.

Annie calls me at around five o'clock. I'd been waiting for her call since around three when she said they were doing another round of tests.

"I'm free!" I can hear her laughter and smiles from here.

"Come here, I've missed you," I breathe.

"I've just been to see Elle; I'll be there in ten minutes!" I look at the phone and she's hung up. I've ten more minutes to wait until I can hold her and so much more.

The gate comm buzzes eleven minutes later, and I press the button to let Annie through. Morag has retired to her rooms with nothing more than a grin on her lips and a gleam in her eye. I stand at the front door, waiting for the engine to stop, and the driver door is open before the car engine has stopped. Annie strides up to me, full of purpose and passion, and I hug her tightly for a few moments before I drag her indoors, locking the front door behind us. I push her to the back of the front door and kiss her for a few minutes, exploring her mouth, reminding myself of how she feels against me.

I pull back and gaze into her eyes, amazed that she's here, finally. It's been too long!

"I need a shower first." She grins, pushing up to kiss me. I grab her hair, turn her head and angle her so I can plunder her mouth again. I wait until she's softened against my grip before I pull back from the kiss and let her hair go. If I had the inclination, I'd love her right here and now, all I've wanted for weeks is to be buried in her, have her in my arms. Then I move out of her way and swat her arse as she walks past. Her secret gift has arrived, and I'm keen to start using it if she's willing.

As I get to the bedroom, Annie's already in the shower; her work clothes are in the basket, and I grab the secret present, then strip off, taking it with me.

She smiles at me as I enter the shower with her, and I wash her down, then I hold out my hand, clenched in a fist. She gives me a puzzled look. I turn my hand and open it to reveal the smallest butt plug I ordered. Her eyes go wide and she looks up at me, mouth agape.

"You're serious?!" she asks. The water cascades over her, splashing me.

"Aye, if you're willing."

She looks at me and takes it out of my hand to examine it.

"Well," she says, handing it back to me. "I've been curious since we talked about it the other day."

I'm not quite sure what she means. "So, you'll wear it?" I ask. She looks at it for a moment and then nods.

"Once," she tells me. "I'll give it a try once. But if I don't like it..." She gives me a look that says I won't get another chance.

I nod, then kiss her deeply. "If you don't, then that's fine."

She turns from me and braces her hands against the shower wall. I grin and lean over her, then begin to play with her sex, rubbing my fingers up and down her. It doesn't take her too long to moan, and I use the shower to lubricate my finger before inserting it into her arse, slowly.

"Oh...my...God!" she growls as I get my finger up to my first knuckle whilst making her ride my fingers with the other hand.

"God, Annie...you're so tight!" I whisper. I turn her slightly so that the water from the shower runs down her arse, and I slide my finger out and back in again, loosening the muscles. She growls out again as her climax threatens to consume her, and I quickly grab the plug. As she orgasms around my fingers, I slowly and firmly slide the plug in until it's seated.

"Jesus H Christ!" she mutters, a few moments later. I kiss her back and let her turn herself to me before I kiss her deeply. I'm so turned on now that she's wearing it, I'm as hard as granite.

I gasp as her fingers grab me and her kisses demand the attention of my mouth. One of her hands goes behind my head, pulling me in.

"You," she says, nipping at my lips, "need to come too."

I grin. "Annie, I want to bury myself inside of you, right now. Either in here or on the bed. I've waited over two whole weeks to be with you," I tell her and kiss her neck by her collarbone.

"You decide," she says, smiling. She's kissing my pecs, then my torso, over my abs, and before I know it, her hot mouth is taking me in, swallowing, licking, sucking me. She makes me act like a horny adolescent and before I can fill her mouth, I pull her up.

"Here," I say, turning her around to face the wall again. She braces herself against it and the sparkly blue crystal of the butt plug twinkles back at me. I smile as I line myself up and plunge into her. She cries out another call for God as I thrust her again and again. Within moments, we're both coming hard, neither of us lasting long.

The shower washes us clean, and I kiss Annie deeply as we dry off. She asks me to take out the plug, at least for now. I kiss her shoulder as I do, then I rinse and dry it off.

"I'm glad I went onto the implant," she says. I had forgotten she was supposed to wait a month for it to kick in; she's another week and a period to go.

"Annie, fuck, I'm sorry. I didn't think..."

She smiles, places a hand on my pecs, and smiles. "I'm due on any day now, so we should be okay." She turns, holding up crossed fingers, then smirks at me over her shoulder as she slips on a chemise and a matching wrap. God, she looks as hot as hell in two little pieces of fabric.

I slide on a pair of silk pyjama bottoms, leaving my chest bare.

"I like this look," she says, kissing my chest again. I pull her head back and devour her mouth.

"As much as I like the one you're sporting at the moment?" I ask; the chemise and wrap hug her figure, her nipples visible through the thin fabric.

"Oh, for sure!" She grins. Then my stomach growls and hers follows. I chuckle.

"Let's get us fed," I say, letting her go. "Then I want round two," I command and pat a bum cheek.

We eat a light meal of cheesy chorizo omelette and salad, and Annie has trouble sitting comfortably.

She finds a way to sit that is more comfortable; clearly, her arse is still feeling it. We sit and we talk, but Annie doesn't go into details of what occurred at the shelter, and I feel I'm missing something. She has a hand on the table, and I grasp it.

"You don't have to hide things from me, Annie. You can tell me."

She shakes her head and quietly replies, "I want to...but I can't." Her eyes are sad, almost crying, but not quite. "You'll..." she doesn't finish her sentence and I have the tool that might persuade her.

I sigh then head to the office and grab one of those anti-listening devices that Adrian told me he'd leave behind. As I bring it back, I turn it on, then place it on the kitchen table.

She looks at me. "You really wanna know?" she asks in a voice I can just hear. Whatever it is, I know now that it's bad.

I nod. "I'm here for you. With you. Right beside you. Whatever you need."

She still looks like she's about to cry, but steals herself and sighs. "Okay. Don't say I didn't warn you."

She drinks half of the glass of water and begins to tell me what happened there with the counsellor, the ladies, and she mentions a name that makes me see red. Henry Aikin. When she's finished, I rub a hand over my face and look at her.

"He's a ruthless bastard in business, totally moral-less. I had no idea..." That he's involved in a sex ring like this doesn't shock me as much as I thought it would. I've seen how women react around him, how other men do. Now I know they must've been picking up on his true nature, or aware of his activities.

She nods. "I'm not sure what the counsellor has said to the police. I know he's still in custody and that bail has been denied. We've moved the girls around, but the IT systems aren't up to much, it won't take a brilliant hacker to hack into the database and find out where we've put them, even with the codes we use."

"Adrian could get one of his guys to look at that," I suggest.

"At what cost?" she asks, her voice rising. "Chances are, Aikin's already got access. Still has, most likely." She gets up and paces a little. "I've asked Marcus to take a look at it anyway, sod the car. He said he would do me a favour though, because of the girls; that he'd at least get the system secured." I nod and look at the device on the table.

"So now what?"

She sighs. "All the evidence is with the police, everything we've found, the videos... God, Tony, there are a *lot* of videos." She sighs and runs her hands through her hair. "Nearly thirty girls. The sound, the details..." She shivers, and I suddenly understand. She's seen some of the videos, though how, I do not want to know. I go and hug her, holding her to me. She squirms, full of agitation and anger. I don't let go.

"Shh..." I coo, stroking her head. "I'm here, it's okay."

She doesn't know how much of a dragon I am in business or life. She's not seen that side of me, the side that wants to protect her, love her. And I can. I am going to, it's time I showed her just who I am. She stops fighting me and lets me just hold her.

"I know, you're used to fighting the injustices." I pull back a little, still holding her as I look at her. "You don't have to do it alone."

"There's no one else," she whispers. I put a finger over her mouth, and she looks at me angrily for shushing her.

"There is. You just don't see all the other players on the board." I take my finger away. "The board is vast, Annie. Bigger than the fires you fight." I kiss the top of her head and keep her close to me. I've seen her when she's broken. She doesn't know I've recently contributed a healthy sum to the charity she works for. Finding out who it was wasn't hard, especially when there was a pickup of her clothes.

"Come, let's eat,"

We're nearly finished eating when we hear Annie's phone ring. She doesn't rush to get it, but finishes her meal and then heads off to grab it. She comes back to the kitchen with it glued to her ear. Then she swears like a pirate as the colour drains from her face.

"How the fuck in hell did he find out?" she spits. I perch against the countertop, listening in. I tap my ear, indicating I want to hear, and she shakes her head. I nod and tap my ear again. She sighs and transfers the call to the speakerphone. I recognise Wolf's voice the second he speaks again.

"From what we can tell, the counsellor got word to him via the lawyer he has, which Aikin's paying for. We can't control who his barrister is, but it's a top eagle in his corner."

"So the bastard went to ground with a warrant out for him?" asks Annie. I understand now. Aikin's done a runner, gone and hid like the coward he is because Annie's put the police onto his tail and empire.

"Yeah, we're checking what we can, but no sign of him yet.

"I might be able to help on that front, Officer." The sound of silence hits us from the other end of the phone.

"Sherlock, who is that?" asks Wolf after a few moments of nothing.

"Anthony McAully," I reply. I'm sure Wolf knows who I am. There's silence for a few moments.

"If you're offering locations, I'll take any anonymous tip I can get," he replies. I understand his statement.

"Leave it with me," I say.

Annie looks at me as if I've just grown another head. I wink at her, and she throws me back a gentle smile. She has no idea how close Adrian and I are. Wolf hangs up after a quick goodbye, and Annie stares at me.

"Who the hell are you?" she asks.

I step around to her and hold her close. "I'm who I said I am. Anthony Michael McAully." She pulls back and looks up at me. "And I part own Adrian's company." I smirk. "Well, forty-nine percent of it to be honest." Adrian and his brother own the other fifty-one percent.

"Really?" she asks. I nod in reply.

"I have my hands in quite a few companies," I share.

"The silent backer," she whispers and smiles.

I can see myself calling in a few favours to help Annie. Favours I don't mind cashing in. I pull my phone out and tell Adrian what I need. Then, I leave the rest to him as I take Annie back to our room, shut the door, and make love to her the rest of the night.

# 29 ~ Annie

Tony loves me throughout the night. From his fingers working their magic in my core, to him filling me, holding me down by my shoulders and taking me in various positions, I enter oblivion more times than I can remember. It makes me forget, at least for a while. He gets dominant at certain points, then he's loving, gentle, and giving in others. We play with the plug again, then he carefully removes it from me as I lay sprawled on my stomach, exhausted, sated hours later. He kisses me from my arse, up my spine to my neck, and pulls my hair back so he can see my face and draws me into a deep kiss. Then he pulls the covers over us and pulls me into his arms.

We smell. Of each other. Of sex. Of testosterone on Tony and goodness knows what on me. Whilst we didn't have anal sex, I've never come as hard from penetration as I have in the last twelve hours or so. I think we might keep this little toy.

Tony's revelation after Wolf's call that he part-owns Adrian's company surprises me; I hadn't realised he was always their silent backer. After the call that Aikin had evaded the police at his home and couldn't be found at his known addresses annoyed the hell out of me, I wanted to find him. I wanted to hurt him for all the hurt he's caused the girls I've vowed to protect. Aikin, though, is wealthy; he has the ability and funds to hide. Though I doubt he knows that Tony's in my corner, and I suspect Tony has far more at his disposal than Aikin has. The tension before, as I revealed to Tony the battle I was in, has gone.

"What are you thinking?" he asks as he holds me close.

"I just want him found and locked away. Do you think we can get him locked away in Alcatraz? Or give him concrete shoes and lose him over the North Sea?" I'm being semi-serious. Either of those options works for me.

Tony chuckles. "Alcatraz is a museum now, and concrete shoes are too good for him, as well as a waste of good concrete." He chuckles at me as he replies, and I smirk. Then I sigh.

"I'm going to have to be very careful until they find him." Tony looks at me and then kisses me.

"You carry on being you. I've got people hunting for him. The police are too. He won't get far."

I sigh. I somehow doubt that; I'm about to help tear down his little sex trafficking empire and hold him to account. Aikin's not a man who likes to be told no, or to be told he's done wrong: he's going to despise being told so by a woman. It's known that he plays dirty corporately and literally. Tony lifts my head and kisses me deeply.

"Annie, please, try not to worry," he utters quietly, looking deeply into my eyes.

I sigh. "Can't help it," I reply.

He grabs my hands and holds them whilst looking at me intently. He's not threatening, and I don't want to push him away. His mouth plunders mine, his tongue pushes into my mouth, dancing the tango with mine. He pulls back, though I wish I could stay right here for a good while longer.

"You can. It will be alright. We will find him. The law will serve him his papers and arrest him. Then we'll see to it that he rots in jail."

213

I nod. Aikin rotting in jail is my ultimate goal. Our stomachs growl in unison and I realise it's been hours since we ate, with a lot of calories burnt by our vigorous lovemaking.

"Come on, lass, let's go eat." He rolls away from me and heads for the shower, which makes me smile softly, and I follow him. Once we're both clean, we dress and head down to the kitchen. Morag is around today; she smiles and nods at me.

"I'll have breakfast for you in a jiffy," she says, bustling about the kitchen like a bee. Orange juice, coffee, and tea appear on the table, along with a rack of toast, butter in a dish, and jam.

Tony pours me a coffee then starts preparing his toast how he likes it. I sip my coffee and watch him, but I begin to follow suit as the hunger pains kick in and the smell of eggs and bacon hits my nose. It's late morning on a Saturday and other than going back to bed, I wonder what else we can do. I'm sore, and I want to get to know this rather secretive man before me. I thought I knew him, turns out I know jack shit about him. We're still on a national lockdown, I've been confined to one location for nearly two weeks straight, and I've not stretched my legs or exercised properly for weeks.

"Do you want to take a walk? We can walk into town, chill at the penthouse for a few hours, then walk back?"

I look up at Tony and smile. "Fabulous idea," I reply, appreciating that we're not just going to be bed bunnies all weekend, as wonderful as that is. "I was just thinking I didn't want to stay indoors all day. I've had enough of that."

Morag chuckles. "Aye, I've heard you've had a hard time with work recently. At least I have the garden here to potter about in. I'll have dinner ready for about six, is that okay?"

Tony nods and I just smile. I can't very well tell her not to bother—she's Tony's employee.

"I'll call if we're going to be later," Tony informs her, and she nods in acknowledgement.

My phone rings and it's Jim, asking how I am and what the plans for tomorrow are.

"Back to usual service. I'm just chilling out, unwinding at Tony's," I inform him.

"Okay, that's great. Just wanted to check. I'll see you tomorrow when I drop her off," he replies. The conversation ends after a quick goodbye from us both.

We finish breakfast, then I change footwear into something more suitable for walking. Tony has too, and I smile as he holds out a hand for me. He hands me a new raincoat, lined with a fleece that has multiple deep pockets. I look at the label and smile. He's gone downmarket, more expensive high street style fashion.

He comes over to me and pulls me up, then kisses me senseless. "I said I'm going to look after you, and I meant it. You and your bairn. So, come on." His tone is light but commanding. I put on the shoes and tie them by leaning on a step. He swats my arse and grins and leans in.

"You have a lovely arse, Annie, and one day, I will take it."

I clench at his words and shiver, still feeling some sensation from the plug, even though it's not there anymore, and my poor vagina that's had deep attention paid to in the last twenty hours.

He lifts my chin then kisses me sensually. "Come on, woman, let's go." I grab my phone and find a pocket I can put it into, then we're off.

Tony walks us towards Holyrood Park, past churches, over bridges, closed restaurants, empty play parks, then up past the Scottish Parliament Building and up to his penthouse. As we walk, we talk about his businesses, that he's got a stake in more than I care to list, backed even more. His interest in stocks and shares, as well as his attitude to things. If the company interests him and it can give its figures out with a plan, he's interested in hearing how he can help.

We talk about the McGowan brothers, Blythe, their connection and that I found Blythe the job, that Marcus created that credit transmitter because of what I was doing at the time Blythe started with them.

They set up the security firm, and Tony invested so that they'd have noted offices, paying the staff, a damn decent website, accountants, and the whole back office they'd need. Tony has a stakeholder investment in it, which is why when he started getting threats, Adrian was on hand.

"You're not just a handsome face," I say as he guides us through the penthouse doors.

He smirks. "No, I'm not. But I am very careful about who I reveal things to."

I hang my coat up and sit down to take my walking shoes off.

"So, question," I ask, looking at him. Now that I know of his involvement with Adrian, I have more questions.

He turns to look at me.

"Did you run a full check on me?" He comes to where I'm sitting, pulling me up.

"No," his eyes search mine, and they're the lightest blue I've ever seen. "If I want to know anything about you, financial or otherwise, I'll ask." He kisses me, and I melt into his arms.

Jim was already sniffing around my accounts at this early stage of our relationship when I wouldn't share my details freely, but I know now that Tony has access to more resources than Jim did.

"Thank you," I breathe out in reply.

"Why do you ask?" He takes a step back, and I explain Jim's mistrust of my pregnancy, finances, and that he asked for a DNA paternity test as Blythe saved my life with a transfusion. He winces and holds me.

"I wouldn't do that to you," he says. "But if you're struggling because of this pandemic, please, do let me know. I can have money in your account within hours."

I nod. I don't intend to tell him just how narrow my margins are. He sees the look on my face as I tidy my shoes away.

"Annie?" I look up and smile.

"Yes?" I reply. Damn! My face did the talking for me.

"Don't struggle. Be honest with me, please."

I realise he's giving me a chance, and I sigh. "It's tight, sometimes, but I manage."

He reaches out and cups my head, then brushes my hair away from my face. "Don't struggle." He stands up straight. "Give me your bank details, I'll sort it out."

I shake my head. "I'm doing okay for now," I protest. "Don't, please. Jim used to..." I shiver at how controlling Jim was with money. More so than I ever am and I have a resentment now every time I have to look at my account. He seems to relent, at least for now.

"Promise me," he says, his eyes searching deep into my own. "You'll tell me if you need some financial help."

I nod. The day I'm unable to afford to feed Elle and me, or pay the bills, I would. "Promise," I whisper as he looks at me expectantly.

The rest of the afternoon is lighter. He seems to have left that earlier discussion behind, and we check around the penthouse to ensure everything is in order. It is. Tony lounges on the sofa, the entire length of it, and beckons me towards him when I take the single chair.

"Come and cuddle, lass," he invites. The sofa is deep enough for two to snuggle up spoon style, and that's exactly what we do as he picks a Jason Statham movie I've surprisingly not yet seen. It's one of his earlier ones where he had slightly more hair, but still plenty of martial arts.

"You know, for a Cockney lad, he's done well," I say.

"He has. He's a nice guy too," replies Tony from behind me.

"You've met him?" I ask, incredulously.

Tony nods. "In London, as it happens, quite by chance. In the gents." He smirks.

"No way! I dinnae believe you!"

He pauses the movie, then reaches to the table behind him, grabbing his phone and after about five minutes, he pulls up an archived photo of him and Jason Statham in the lobby of a swanky hotel in Knightsbridge, London dated about six years prior.

"Well, I'll be..." Bloody hell, he has!

We settle back onto the sofa and carry on watching him beat people up, right the wrongs, hold a grudge. It's a little close to some of my work situations for my liking, even though I love Statham's movies.

Tony's arms are around me, his legs entwined with mine, and despite the fact Statham's on-screen, I'm dozing off as I feel warm, safe, loved. I don't get to see the end of the movie.

Tony's gently wakes me later on, chuckling at me that I am a lightweight. It's payback for *The Saint* movie, but I don't mind. I stick my tongue out at him, and he threatens to kiss it out of my mouth. I poke him again, and he grabs me, pushes me against the wall and devours my mouth for what seems like hours. By the time we're finished, it's a quarter to six and we won't be back for when we told Morag we would be. He calls ahead and smirks at me as we put our shoes and coats back on. Locking up, we walk back to the mansion, happily holding hands.

Sunday, we take an early walk over to Princess St Gardens, taking in Scott Monument and walking through Edinburgh University. The weather is colder today and even though it's nearly Easter, the weather is changeable. Today is a typical day in Scotland. We get all four seasons in two hours at one point. We huddle under a Yew tree to avoid the biggest deluge. We had sleet and hail before that. Twenty minutes later, we're back at the mansion soaking wet, cold but laughing and teasing each other as the sun shines.

Morag has prepared us a roast to enjoy together. Since our marathon sex session on Friday night, we've kissed and cuddled, but nothing more, and strangely, I don't feel neglected. We've spent time with each other, gotten to know the other better, eaten together. It's been intimate, sharing coffee, time, our lives. I had always thought that deep, primal sex was what I was missing, and I was so very wrong.

"Come over on Wednesday?" I offer. I for one have missed our midweek rendezvous; I'm missing him more every time we have to part.

He reaches across the small kitchen table and takes my hand. "Aye, I'd love to," he says.

I nod. "Excellent. I know Elle would love to see you," I say, sipping some water.

"How did she cope with you being away from her for so long?" he asks.

"Like a trooper. She knew that Mummy couldn't leave her work and why. We video called each other before bed, so it was as good as we could make it."

He smiles and holds my hand.

"I look forward to spending time with her on Wednesday," he says.

We finish eating then clear away our plates. All too soon, I have to go. We say our bye-for-now in the hallway as the weather is still rather unpredictable. I leave him with the taste of me on his lips, and I wipe the tears from my eyes as I drive home.

Sunday evening is the same as it was before I got caught at the shelter. Elle comes home, Jim is barely civil and leaves within five minutes, then Elle and I hug like mad and settle on the sofa. I order us a pizza; two weeks without significant time with my daughter deserves a treat.

We retire rather full of pizza, ice cream, and yes, singing songs from the sequel to *that* movie. I wish I could let that one go.

I spend Monday doing paperwork for the shelter, and Julia calls me whilst Elle is on a class call.

"I've decided to give everyone who was there for that fortnight a bonus. We had a generous donation recently, so we can more than cover it. And get our IT systems updated, which was one of the stipulations of the donation." She tells me how much of a donation. My eyes bug out at the figure she tells me: a quarter of a million pounds.

The bells go off in my head, but I say nothing to indicate I know, or suspect, who the donation is from.

"That's amazing! Have you picked an IT company or do you want me to go find you one?"

"Oh, would you?" She sighs. "I'd hate to go through that. You know more of what we need anyway," she says. I smirk. I know exactly who I am going to call and why.

"I'll see who I can find. There are a few ideas I have in my head already." And that's telling a small wee fib.

"I appreciate it, Annie, thank you!"

We talk about the weekend, that I chilled out, slept, walked, ate. I didn't reveal I was with someone whilst doing all those things or even that I spent my nights with a man and not just any man.

We end our conversation then I check on Elle, who has finished her class video call and is hungry. I make her some food and head into the living room after she's eaten. I make myself a cup of herbal tea and go sit on my favourite chair. Despite not being home for two weeks, I notice it needs dusting.

Tony answers me within a single ring.

"Hey, lovely lady!" he croons down the phone.

"Hey, you." Despite the fact I know he's just donated to the shelter I work for, I'm unable to stop the frustration from manifesting in my voice.

"What can I do for you? Miss me already?"

"Something like that," I say. He notices the silence and my tone.

"Annie, what's wrong?" he asks, concern sounding out in his voice.

"Did you happen to donate to the charity I work for?" I ask directly.

The silence on his end is deafening.

"It's very generous of you, but why? And I never told you who I worked for," I breathe as I ask him.

"Because they needed it," he answers without missing a beat. He hasn't said yes directly, but he's just told me why.

"Because I work there?" I ask him.

"Partly. I know first-hand the work you do, I know how it helps. With the charity shops being closed during this pandemic, it was the least I could do to keep something as vital as a women's refuge open. You're needed," he responds. He has no remorse and in his shoes, I doubt I would either. "And I simply asked the runner who fetched things for you, told him I was going to donate a decent six-figure sum, but I needed to know which one so I could surprise you."

"Those girls can't thank you. But I can." I close my eyes and sit back on the sofa. I can't speak, it's too much.

"Annie?" he calls gently. I remember to breathe.

"I'm here. I'm..." I pause. What can I say? We're not ungrateful. "Tony, I'll be honest, I'm stunned."

He chuckles. "In a good way, I hope?"

I rush to answer him. "Yes, goodness gracious yes. Just..." Quarter of a million. "It's a very generous amount. I just wished you asked me who."

I can hear him breathing so I know he's not hung up on me, not that he would.

"Perhaps. But the work you and that charity do is important. It deserves a generous amount."

"You stipulated that the IT systems need to be updated. That's a given."

He chuckles. "I have just the company to do it," he says. I smirk.

"I thought you might. Give me their details; I'll pass them to Julia later this week," I reply.

Wednesday arrives and I've had details from Tony about the specific IT company to use. I've passed the details to Julia, but it's her call. The house is clean and tidy, and Elle's already picked up that Tony will be coming for dinner.

"Will Blythe be coming too?" she asks.

I shrug in reply. "I don't know, sweetie, but I doubt it. She doesn't need to work that closely with Tony anymore." She just nods in acknowledgement and carries on helping me set the table and tidy things away. Soon enough, Tony is at the door with another small bouquet for Elle and another for me. He kisses me gently, which has Elle making gagging noises.

"What the hell, Mom!" I look at her.

"Sweetie, apologise now," I say. She glares at me and as I'm about to tell her off in a tone that brooks no argument, she sees the thunderous look on my face and sighs.

"Sorry, Mom," she says, walking off.

"Elle, come back here." She does, sulkily. "If I hear you using language like that towards me or an elder again, you'll find yourself punished, am I understood?"

She looks at me wide-eyed. I don't usually have to punish her. "Punished, how?" she asks.

"Lack of things. Movies, TV, books..." I growl out the last word and let it hang. She gulps.

She nods. "Sorry, Mom," she mutters, loud enough for me to hear her.

She heads off to the living room, and Tony is trying hard not to smirk. I just shake my head and chuckle.

"Mine were the same at that age, always have an answer to everything," he says, handing me a bag with a heavy dish in it.

It contains a crumble. I smile. "Thank you. I'll warm it up with dinner," I add, heading to the kitchen and putting it into the bottom of the oven. We head into the living room and sit with Elle, talking about the movie she's picked and what happened in the last Train Your Dragon one we watched with her.

She's in bed at the usual time, giving Tony and me time to talk, cuddle, and just be.

"You're working this weekend, aren't you?" he asks, and I nod.

"Aye, I'm going to be as busy as heck though," I say. "We've not had a quiet night for nearly a week now, and it's only getting worse."

He nods. "As I said, vital work needs vital resources." I smile.

It's late when Tony leaves, nearly midnight. He's not yet spent a night at mine.

"Soon," I say, looking up to where Elle is sleeping.

He nods. "I know," he says. He kisses me fully on the mouth, a promise of things to come next time we're together. It just won't be this weekend.

## 30 - Anthony

Blythe lets us into Annie's house. It's quiet. The place doesn't look touched, and I can't tell if Annie is even here, though her car is. We've not heard from her at all since Friday lunchtime, and it's Sunday afternoon now. She's never not back for her little girl, and I look anxiously at Blythe; until now, we've never missed a call between us. She wouldn't even answer calls from Blythe, who motions for me to stay and climbs the stairs quietly, knowing where all the stairs creak, avoiding them.

There are some dishes in the sink; though, the cup still has some liquid in it and it's cold. It smells like tea, and I hear Blythe descend the stairs, louder than when she climbed them.

"She's asleep. Spark out. Even me walking around hasn't woken her."

She holds up Annie's phone and puts it on the table, then she sits at the table, and I can see her thinking for a moment.

"I wonder when she got back," she muses. I point to the sink and lower my voice.

"Not too long ago, I think. The kettle is still semi-warm, there's some tea left in the mug, but that's cold. I think she came home, had a tea, and went to bed for a while before Elle came home."

Blythe checks the heat of the kettle and confirms what I've said. Then she checks her watch.

"I'll stay with you until she's here. Then I'll see if Elle is okay with you staying here as a responsible adult."

I nod. I promised Annie I'd be there for her, and whilst she's refused my financial help, there are plenty of other ways I can be there that don't involve money. My time and caring for her daughter are just as valuable. Annie's phone pings, and Blythe silences it quickly.

"Just sent her a text explaining why you're here; she'll look for her phone when she wakes up. She might go mad otherwise, even if Elle is here."

I nod. "Good idea." I look across to the kitchen sink and decide that I can be of use in many other ways too.

Blythe nods and tells me she's heading into the living room to tidy up. Between us both, the house is tidied up before Elle gets home, not that there's much that needs doing. The only chore left is hoovering, but neither of us wants to do that when Annie needs her sleep and she's not aware we're in the house.

Six o'clock comes around and Elle is dropped off. I am busy in the kitchen drying the last of the dishes by hand as Jim walks in. This is the second time we've met. I extend my hand out and greet him quietly.

"Why are we talking quietly?" he asks.

"Annie's been on the go since Friday, she's hardly slept, and she's taking a nap," explains Blythe. We don't suggest that it's going to be a really long nap, likely an all-night nap.

Jim nods. "You're going to be here with Annie?" he asks me. I take him in. He's taller than Annie, but a few inches shorter than I am.

I nod. "Aye, for as long as she needs and wants me."

He smiles. "What was it you said you did?" I can't fathom why he's asking, then Elle comes into the kitchen and I get it. I'm seeing his baby's momma. I smile at the child. "Investment banking," I say, not playing my hand totally just yet.

Jim nods.

I look at Elle. "Well, hello, Elle! It's good to see you again," I say. She smiles at me.

"Hello, Tony! Are you looking after Mummy?" she asks, throwing her backpack onto the dining table.

"Aye, I am. But, yer mom's had a horrid weekend working, so she's having a nap. We need to be secret squirrels and be as quiet as we can so she can sleep. Can you help me with that?" She nods her head and hugs Jim around his stomach as best an eight-year-old can. "Bye, Daddy! I'll see you next weekend!" She speaks quietly, but very enthusiastically, and my heart melts. She reminds me of my girl at that age, and I realise that it was almost two decades ago.

Jim nods at Blythe and me then he heads out, quietly shutting the door behind him.

"Do you have any laundry that needs doing, darling?" I ask Elle. She shakes her head.

"I keep clothes at Daddy's house, and Mummy Fee does all my washing."

I look at the backpack on the table. "So what's in yer bag?" I ask.

She smiles at me then rolls her eyes. "Uni and bunny, silly!" she says, pulling out two very well worn toys that clearly accompany her everywhere.

I grin at her, then kneel to her level. "Can you quietly go and put them away in your room? Then you can help me decide what we're having for dinner." Elle nods and then quietly goes to do as I've asked.

Blythe grins. "I forget you're a dad three times over," she tells me.

I nod. "Out of practice, but I'm sure it'll come back in a flash."

Blythe nods. "Right, I'll leave you to it. You've got my number?" she asks.

I nod.

"Bolt the door behind me. Annie will give you hell if you don't!" She smirks as she leaves. Elle comes back down, and they say their goodbyes very quietly on the stairs.

Elle joins me in the kitchen and we decide what she wants for dinner. I make double, but pick a chicken steak from the freezer rather than nuggets. It's not my usual style of food, but Annie is used to catering for her daughter, so her freezer is half full of kid-style food.

Elle tells me what she likes and what she doesn't, then we sit down quietly to watch some television whilst our dinner cooks. We get along quite well, and Elle is polite this time. She helps me set the table and asks why I've not made her mum anything when I serve our dinner up.

"I'll make something for Mummy if she wakes up for dinner. She might not wake up until breakfast though!" I say. Elle just nods.

"You know what Mummy does?" she asks me as she eats some peas. I've never had a child eat her vegetables without a fight. Elle, however, is a delight—a testament I'm sure to Annie's parenting.

I nod. "Yes. What do you think she does?" I ask.

Elle rolls her eyes. "She helps women who have been hurt get to safe places," she tells me. I guess that is what Annie does, though Elle isn't aware of how dangerous that can be sometimes.

We finish dinner, and I serve Elle some ice cream and let her chill out watching some more television. Any bath time can be saved until tomorrow, though Elle tells me that Mummy Fee made her shower last night and she "only washes three times a week as my skin doesn't like any more than that!" She's rather indignant with it and when I spot the eczema shower wash and cream in the bathroom later on, I get why. Elle is quite good at getting herself ready for bed when the time comes, and I sneak a peek in at Annie. She's still sound asleep, on her side as she so often is when we're together. I don't think she's moved an inch since Blythe checked on her earlier.

"Tony, are you going to be my second daddy?" asks Elle as I tuck her in.

I smile. "I'd like that a lot, button, but that's very much up to your mum. Would you like that?" I ask. I'm surprised partly by my answer; Annie and I have never discussed being more than exclusive lovers, though it's something that feels right. Elle is so easy to look after though.

Elle nods at me. "I have two mummies, but not two daddies. Mummy needs to have someone that will be my second daddy." I chuckle at her assessment and kiss her on the forehead.

"Good night, button!" and she giggles.

"Did you forget my name?" she asks, giving me a delightful but quite serious look.

I smile. "No, Elle, I didn't," I say and look the girl in her eyes. "But you've helped me hold things together tonight as a button does," and I watch as she slowly understands what I've said.

"I'm glad I could help you look after me," she says.

"We need to be a team," I explain. "Now, it's time to sleep and be really quiet to let your mum sleep as much as she needs. I'm going to sleep on the sofa so your mum gets the best sleep possible, okay?" I don't tell her it's because it's the first time I've been in the house overnight and Annie hasn't a clue I'm even here, or why.

Elle nods. "Do you need some blankets? I know where they are," she says and points to the cupboard in the hall.

"Thanks, button," I say and bop her nose gently. "Now, it's time for sleep. I'll see you in the morning." I give her another kiss on her forehead. I just hope Annie doesn't kick me out when she realises I'm here. I move a lamp from the living room to the kitchen to keep the light on.

It's nearly eleven when I make the sofa up for me, and though it's a tad short for my height, it's comfortable enough and I sleep soundly until the morning.

# 31 - Annie

I wake up, remembering I need to be up for Elle. I reach for my phone, but it's not there. I can hardly see; I'm still so tired! I check my fitness watch, but the screen is so small that I can't make out what it's telling me. My glasses aren't here either, and I sigh. I check what I'm wearing and notice I'm not wearing bedclothes, just a basic t-shirt and my knickers, stuff I can throw jeans over and look dressed in ten seconds. I clearly intended on having just a nap. I open the door and smell toast and head downstairs. Why can I smell toast?

The answer is in a six-foot-three hunk of a lover in my kitchen, feeding my daughter and drinking coffee.

"Hey," I say, spying my phone. Even though I've slept, I still can't see my phone screen clearly.

"Elle honey, do you know where any of my glasses are?" I ask her in an exasperated tone.

"I do!" She jumps up and runs into the living room and brings back a pair before I can do anything more than smile at Tony.

"Thanks, honey!" I say, and she sits back down.

"Tony has been looking after us, Mummy! I like him," she says. I smirk; she didn't like us kissing on Wednesday. She's a chip off the old block for her direct assessment of things.

I unlock my phone and notice it's at twenty-five percent. I didn't put it on charge, but there's enough power to see that I've got a message from Blythe.

*B: We got worried so I came & let us in. You were out of it, Sherlock, what the hell? What happened that you didn't even call* all *weekend? Tony is going to stay to look after Elle. He's got my number if he can't navigate his way around your house. Call me when you can.*

I look up at Tony. "Thank you," I say, then walk to him and hug him. It's so good to be held by him that I forget I'm wearing my glasses until they're knocked off by his hug.

"Since when dae ye need glasses?" he asks, kissing my head.

"Since I couldn't see words in the books when I read. Or dead tired. I have pairs scattered around all over. In the car, mainly." I grin. Honestly, I'm so long-sighted it's ridiculous. He smiles.

"You know you're cute when ye wear them," he says. I'm forty-two and I'm cute in my reading glasses?

"Oh, am I now?" I reply and I can't hold back the smile that I feel forming on my face.

"Mummy!" shouts Elle, and I jump. "You've not hugged me!" she wails. I chuckle and smirk at Tony. He's saved my bacon by looking after Elle for me.

I hug her, and she pulls back. "Eugh! Mummy, you stink!" she says, wafting her hand in front of her nose. I suppose I do, but I chuckle at her honesty.

"Go, grab a shower, and I'll sort ye breakfast, aye? Elle's doing her school work so she's sorted." I start to protest, but he cuts me off. "Go on, away ye go. We're good here, aye, button?" Elle nods, and I realise that button is an endearment he's using for Elle. It's also one she agrees with. That floors me.

"I'll call Blythe quickly and then I'll shower. Any chance of a coffee?" I plead. I am dead on my feet, still. The weekend was horrendous, seventy-five hours of retrieving women from their broken, violent homes, hospitals, bus stops, friends' houses, corner shops...a few confrontations, but every safehouse we have is in use and we're nearly at capacity.

"I'll bring it up tae ye, aye? Away and let Blythe know you're okay, then shower. I'll start ye breakfast when I hear you're finished." He kisses me on top of my head.

"Thank you," I whisper, reluctantly letting him go. I grab my phone and as I head upstairs, I dial Blythe.

Firstly, she's pleased I'm alive, though I find out she checked on me to ensure I was breathing! I apologise for worrying her and Tony.

"What happened, Annie? You never don't reply. We thought something had happened to you!"

I apologise again. "It went mad this weekend. Honestly, I dropped the car back here, and we got chauffeured around the city as I couldn't drive anymore, but those that could didn't have the retrieval skills we needed. We might have done some on the job training with most of them."

I recall one lady who was with me in particular. She was a designated driver in a Discovery 4, a huge seven-seater thing. One victim changed her mind, but my driver saw the bruise on the victim's arms, talked her into coming with us. It was whilst she was driving to a safehouse that the victim opened up, but not to me. I forget how long I've been awake by this point. Blythe's voice cuts through my fog, bringing me back to the present.

"Are you still there?" she asks.

"Aye, sorry. Just remembering something from the weekend is all."

Blythe sighs. "Look, I'm glad you're okay. We were really worried." She pauses. "Do you mind that Tony stayed over?" she asks gently.

"No. No, I'm not bothered. I couldn't function when I got back yesterday. I even missed my alarm to wake up for Elle coming home." I hear Blythe's sigh of relief. "Thank you," I say.

"I thought you'd be mad," she replies.

I go to the bathroom and start running the shower. It can warm up whilst I finish up talking with someone who has my back. "No, I'm not. Far from it. I'm glad you and Tony were around and helped. I..." I admit it, I should have asked for help. But I've been on my own for so long, I've forgotten how to. "I should have asked. You're right. Thank you for being there anyway." I smile, grateful, and I hope my voice conveys that.

Blythe chuckles. "You're welcome! I'll let you go and grab that shower. Oh, I've left Elle a small gift. It's in your shoe rack in the hall. Talk with ye later!" Blythe says as she hangs up. I think that's enough mushy emotions between friends for the day, and I wonder what Blythe has brought for Elle now.

I shower and take my time about it. I wash my hair twice and spruce up. Not that getting into bed with Tony is an option right now. Then I remember I need to change my bedsheets, given that I just collapsed into them in a sweaty, messy, exhausted state.

I exit the bathroom to find a mug of coffee on the side table, made just how I like it. I smile and feel loved; he's good to me. I dry off and dress, then I begin to remove the sheets and quilt cover, taking the whole lot downstairs. I throw half into the machine and set it going, and

I turn to see Tony placing a plate of food onto a tray. Elle is still at the table, doing school work, and he ushers me into the living room and makes me sit in the recliner seat with my feet up. He kisses me on the head after he's placed the tray of food in my lap with two coffees.

"Eat it all up, lass, you deserve it." He grabs the other coffee and sits at the end of the sofa nearest to me. I notice the folded up blankets on the other single chair, and I look at him.

"Where did you sleep last night?" I ask, but I guess he slept on the sofa.

"Here," he says, confirming my analysis. This isn't breakfast, it's the last three missed meals in one, and it's clear he's raided my freezer. I don't care though; it's food, it's there for eating, and he's stood and cooked me a huge Scottish fry-up. I might not get into my jeans again at this rate!

"Why down here? Why not with me?" I ask.

He moves closer to me so he can't easily be heard by Elle.

"Because you weren't expecting me and as far as Jim knew, you were having a nap, not that you were out for the count. I didn't want to push my luck or have you freak out at silly o'clock because I was in bed with you."

I smile. "You're too good to me, thank you."

He leans in and kisses me gently. "I told you I wanted to take care of you, not just..." He lets the statement hang and glances up. I can see my daughter being reflected in his cool blue eyes.

"Saved by the bell." He grins and stands up. "What's up, button?" he asks, heading over to Elle. I turn to watch them both, my food temporarily forgotten. He's good with her. The question is, what will his grown kids think of me?!

I need not have worried about what his kids would think of me. It turned out that they were the least of my issues.

~

That week went by like any other. Tony returns to his home, telling me he'll see me on Wednesday, which goes well. He tells me that Elle asked about him being her second dad. We're spooning on my sofa, which isn't as comfortable as his at the penthouse.

"I'm not averse to the idea," I reply, turning to smile coyly at him. "But we've not spoken about it, have we?"

He shakes his head at me, then grabs my hands while we're spooning. Then he kisses me on my head and pulls my arms back across me. I'm pinned to him from behind.

"What did you just do?" I ask.

"I looked at your hands," he says. We hold hands up against each other, and his fingers are longer and thinner whilst his whole hand is broader. Despite the size difference, our hands fit together well.

Elle goes off to school on Thursday and Friday, the days I work. This is the last time before the Easter school break and I'm looking forward to some time with her to read, catch up, and do things together. I see her off on Friday morning and kiss her fondly before she skips into school. It's a moment I'll never forget.

I get a call at the shelter on Friday just before I finish work, and my world collapses in a heap. Elle's been kidnapped, and Fiona's been hurt. Wolf is at Jim's, already dealing with the scene. I didn't think Aikin would be this stupid.

~

I drive home after calling Blythe and updating her. She's already got Marcus doing his thing. I know that whatever Wolf is doing, he's doing everything. I change into my tight-fitting dark clothing, then I pull my hair back and wait. I receive a call from Blythe that she's a street over and behind my house. I turn my phone off and leave via my backdoor quietly to meet her, kit in hand. She hands me an earpiece as we'd use in the military and then Marcus is in my ear, telling me what he's done to find her already as Blythe drives like a bat out of hell.

"You've got her?" I ask. I know he bloody well does, though I do not know how.

"Roger that, we're waiting to go in," says Adrian as his voice comes into mine at just above a whisper.

"How?" I ask, looking at Blythe.

"One of the team thought it would be a good idea to hide a small GPS tracker in something a child would use. Adrian, Marcus, and I didn't like the idea of our girl being hurt," she explains. "It's in the flashing shoes. They move, it pings." I gape at the information just issued to me, grateful to Blythe.

"Your job is to secure your girl." Adrian's voice cuts across our conversation. "See you in fifteen," he tells us.

238

"Acknowledged," I confirm and look at Blythe, understanding that this is his rodeo. I start binding my hands in my usul attire. Secure her? Oh yeah, we'll do just that.

~

I meet Adrian and his ex-special ops team outside a rundown hotel just north in the small town of Aviemore. He shows Blythe and I where to wait to go in to secure Elle. My hands are wrapped in pink boxing wrap, my knuckle dusters secure under them, my muscles tight and poised. I like the idea that guys get hit with something pink, or notice it right before I do what I have to.

One of Adrian's men takes out a watchman effortlessly, showing that the gang are lax in security. They're not expecting anyone to turn up, least of all a wee group of ex-military personnel, one of whom is a very pissed off momma. I keep my nerves about me, knowing that if I don't, I'll put Elle and the guys in danger. Blythe catches my eye and winks at me. I nod. We've got this. We have to.

The lights go out, the door at the back is blown open, and Adrian's men swarm in, Blythe and I hot on their heels. Elle's hidden GPS places her in this house and from the looks of it, I'm right where she is. I motion for Blythe to head up as I find stairs to a basement, so I head down.

There's one guard on the door, a young gang member, and he tries to box me. It doesn't take much to block his body blows and then hit him on the side of his jaw. I hear the bone crack, see the spit and blood fly out of his mouth as I break his jaw. He doesn't even try to get up; he's out cold.

"One tango down, basement," I say. Then I hear the best sound in the world.

"Mommy?" my daughter wails at me. She's on the other side of the door that is before me, and I search the guy for keys. My hands being bound in the wraps as they are make it hard to search, but I find them. There's a bunch and on the third key, I'm successful.

I push open the door and run in to find she's tied to the bed by her wrist by a thick rope a fish head would be proud of. I flick my wrist and a knife appears. Before I cut her free, I boot my phone up and take several photos for evidence. I hear footsteps behind me, and Adrian gives me the thumbs up. I nod.

"Do you want to go home, sweetie?" I ask. Elle nods.

"Yes please, Mommy!" she cries, and I cut the rope, hug her tightly, then take her by the hand and lead her back to Blythe's car. Adrian is already on the phone with Wolf, and I sit in the back with Elle cuddled to me in the middle seat. I've taken a window seat, and Blythe eases into the driver's seat.

I unwrap my hands and tuck away the ironwork that's been biting into my hands for the last hour and a half, then I hold my daughter as we drive back, kissing her all the time and letting her talk. For Elle, I'd endure a heck of a lot worse.

Wolf greets us at Jim's front door, and I'm looking slightly more work-related than a ninja. I throw on one of those hoodie tops Tony brought for me over my black shadow clothes so I don't look like I've just gone through hell. Though I have. So has Jim, more so than either of us.

"How's Fiona?" I ask as I guide Elle up the small flight of stairs. She's sitting on the sofa with a bag of peas wrapped in a clean towel that's being pressed to her face.

"I'm fine! You got her back!? How!"

Elle rushes to Fiona and hugs her tightly. "GPS," I say.

Fiona looks at Elle then to Jim, then to me. "How?" she asks. I point to Elle's shoes. She loves her light up shoes and every time she moves, they light up. They now also send out a GPS signal that Marcus can pick up. I don't tell that to Jim and Fiona though.

A police family liaison officer is waiting to speak with Elle, and with a cup of hot cocoa, she tells us what she went through.

"I tried to get away, Mummy. I did the tricks you told me; that's why they had me tied up. They didn't like that I kicked them in the nuts!" The officer holds back a smirk, and her eyes dance in glee.

I grin. "Good girl!" There's still a rope burn on her right wrist, but that will heal in time. Jim glares at me, and Fiona hugs Elle tight.

"What else happened, Elle?"

The officer is gentle in asking Elle a lot of questions, coaxing out of her what happened. The men didn't hurt her beyond tying her up. She heard them talking and she says that they were just to keep her until they were told to bring her back. Or leave her there.

I sit through it all, listening. Elle is cuddled up between Fiona and me as I'm holding one of her hands. Jim is standing against the corner wall of their open plan living room, looking like he wants to kill me. Or the gang that took Elle. I'm not sure which. An hour later, the officer is finished, and I watch as she puts away her notebooks and offers to make us another drink.

"I think you need to go to bed now, young lady. You've been *so* brave today!" she tells Elle.

She smiles at me and gives me a huge hug. "Love you, Mommy!" she says then goes to hug Jim, who picks her up and hugs her tightly.

Fiona stands up and together, my daughter and her stepmom, head up the stairs.

Jim turns on me as soon as Elle is out of earshot.

"What the fuck have you gotten involved in, woman?!" he growls at me.

I sigh. "Something...disgusting. And they don't want me to blow the whistle."

He marches over to me aggressively. "You put our daughter in danger," he accuses.

"What I *do* is dangerous. But if you think I'm going to cow down to someone running a sex ring and possibly trafficking women, you," I square up to him and wish I hadn't unbound my hands, "have another fucking thing coming."

The officer walks into the room and gets up close to us both.

"This is not going to help Elle," she points out.

"I'll file for full custody, Annie," Jim growls at me.

"No you bloody won't," Fiona announces from the bottom of the stairs. She's just starting to show her pregnancy. Jim turns to face her, and she marches up to him like a lioness.

"If you think that going up against anyone running a sex trafficking ring in this city isn't worth the risk, divorce me now. Pack your bags and get the hell out." I watch as Fiona stands up to Jim, and Jim refuses to back down.

"Our daughter—" he begins, but I cut him off.

"Yes, she got involved," I snap at him. "Because this arsehole thinks that women are a commodity, cattle. That solutions, like me, can be solved by breaking the law. Is that what you want our daughter to think?" I wait until he's facing me. "Do you *really* want her to think that the behaviour of the man that paid to have her kidnapped is okay? Acceptable? Because that's what you're telling her by telling *me* I brought this on her."

I walk up to him and get into his personal space. "Do not even think about telling me to back off from this fucking arsehole."

"Let's just all calm down," says the officer.

I back away and make my way to the door.

"What's it to be, Jim? Blame Annie? Or blame me? The person you should be blaming," says Fiona, pointing her finger at him, "is the bastard that thinks it's okay to hurt someone else, take what he wants, and not suffer the consequences of his actions."

Fiona turns to me. "Go, make this world a better place. Get him behind bars, whoever the bloody hell he is. The police are staying here tonight."

I nod and turn on my heel, eager now to catch up with Wolf and Adrian, and I march past the officer standing at the front door.

One call to Blythe and I'm heading to Adrian's offices in Edinburgh on foot, Jim's threat ringing in my ears, playing over in my head. When I get there, Adrian's crew are there, working on finding Aikin.

"Any luck yet?" I ask. My phone pings with the text notification. It's Tony, and my heart sinks.

Adrian shakes his head. I hold my phone up to ask if he's got a quiet space, and he points to the office behind me. I nod and duck in, then I call Tony.

## 32 - Anthony

The phone rings almost immediately with Annie's song and her number coming up on the screen.

"Hey, are you coming over?" I ask.

"Sorry, no..." She goes very quiet, quiet enough you can hear a pin drop. "You don't know, do you?" she asks. She sounds tired, exhausted, upset.

"What don't I know, Annie?" I sit forward on the sofa, disturbing Hera who is on my lap.

"Aikin got to Elle, took her from Fiona, and got Fiona hurt in the process."

I swear, and she chuckles at me for it.

"Elle's back home, we found her, thanks to Adrian and Marcus" she quickly adds, and I sigh in relief.

"Jim's not happy Elle got taken. He's..." I can hear the hesitation in her voice and then her voice drops off.

"He's what?" I gently remove Hera from my lap and slip on some shoes as we're talking. "Where are you?"

There's a long pause. "At Adrian's offices. It was his tech that helped us get her back so fast."

"I know where they are. I'll be there in ten minutes," I say, picking a coat up from the peg and putting it on as I grab my keys. "What did Jim do?" I ask.

Annie sighs. "He told me he'd file for full custody of Elle." I ache as I hear Annie begin to quietly cry.

"We can fight him on that," I say.

My heart breaks as I put her on speakerphone and start the car, heading towards the offices I know Adrian will be at.

"I can't afford to fight him, Tony. He knows that," she breathes between sobs. Her statement divides my attention. Do I go to her, or do I visit Jim? Annie wins.

"Annie, he won't just be fighting you; he'll be fighting us both."

"I can't ask you to pitch in," she says.

"Who said you were asking?" I scold in reply. I'm already close to his office and as luck would have it, there's a space out front that I can see from the junction I'm sitting at, waiting for the lights to change.

"Tony," she begins, but I've arrived.

"I'm here, I'm just outside." I slam the car door shut and lock it. "I'll be there in a minute, honey." I've never run up three flights of stairs before. I never had a reason to.

Adrian waves and points me to the office Annie called me from as soon as I walk through the doors; I guess he knows why I'd suddenly turn up, and I'm grateful for his perception. I walk in to find the room in darkness and a figure sitting alone on the sofa. As soon as she lifts her head, she's in my arms.

"What happened?" I ask her. There's some light coming in from the main area where Adrian and his team are working. Annie sighs and tells me what happened with Elle being kidnapped, then Jim's comments about going to file for full custody before Fiona told her to get Aikin behind bars.

"You're not the only parent in the world with a dangerous job, darling," I tell her, holding her hands. She nods, but I don't feel that she's on the same page I am. "If he tries it, we'll fight it."

She looks at me. "I can't ask you," she begins and for the first time, I snap at her.

"Damn it, Annie, you're not asking," I growl. "I told you, I will take care of you." She looks at me and even in the dim light, I can see her shocked look. "I want to. That means, being there when the going gets tough, supporting you however you need. Jim can throw his weight and money around. He's not the only one that can do that." I stare at her intently.

"You," I wait for her to look at me, not through me, "need to understand something, honey." I wait another moment, the need to say this burns through me. "I am in love with you." I wait for her to understand those six little words. She does, quicker than I thought she might. Her tears fall as she tries to smile, and she jumps into my arms, hugging me. I pull her onto my lap and cradle her to rock her gently.

"Thank you," she mumbles at me. I lift her head and look at her before I gently kiss her lips. They weren't the words I wanted to hear, but she's not in a good place to say them yet. I get it. Still, it hurts.

"Always. Let's go see what Adrian has found, aye?"

She nods and slides off my lap, but waits for me to stand up. She's holding my hand tightly, almost seemingly afraid to let me go.

Adrian does nothing more than nod at us when we emerge from that office. Blythe whisks Annie away to freshen up and, no doubt, find out what's upset her friend.

"Any clues?" I ask.

He nods. "Think he went to Aberdeen. Just double checking now." He turns to a member of staff as they bring him a tablet. A few clicks later and he's handing it back.

"Coffee?" he asks, guiding me towards the kitchen. I nod.

He pours me a black coffee from a fresh pot and leans against the counter.

"What gives?" he asks, nodding towards Annie and Blythe.

"Jim has threatened to file for full custody," I tell him. Adrian winces.

"Low blow," he says.

"I need to know everything about him," I growl in reply.

"Already on it; after tonight's shenanigans, we're running deep checks on everyone involved. Gang members, the bairn's dad. Even Annie." He looks at me as if he doesn't care if that bothers me. "You know she was an RAF MP?" he asks me. I nod and take a sip of the hot coffee.

"Yeah, why?"

He chuckles. "They call her Sherlock not just for her surname. She was good at working out the logic to situations, but she's a damn tigress apparently in a fight."

I grin. "I have not seen her fight," I say.

"Neither have I. Though one of the lads we found at the house Elle was being held at has a broken jaw because of her." He raises his eyebrows. So, she can fight. I know she does martial arts, I've seen her dressed in the suit, though what type is beyond me.

"And Aikin?"

We get interrupted by a team member, and he motions for me to follow. Grabbing my coffee, I do just that, but hang back. Blythe and Annie are back in the meeting area, both still dressed as I think modern-day Ninjas would be.

"Got money leaving Aikin's account as cash over the last two weeks. The maximum a day, that's fourteen-hundred total." He points to one of the photos they took before the police turned up. "Which is one hundred more than is in this bag," he says, tapping the photo.

"So they spent some?" asks Adrian. The team member, who is a short but stocky man, nods in reply.

"Local pizza place by the looks of it. They delivered there at around seven pm. We raided at around half eight. If Aikin gave them the money earlier in the day, he's had hours to be where he wants to be. With us being on lockdown, we know he's still in the country; even private jets aren't allowed to take off."

Another voice pipes up, and I look around for Annie. I beckon for her to come to me, and I hug her as the information on where Aikin is begins filtering through.

"He's at his place in Aberdeen. Remote place right up on the coast."

"So he'll see anyone coming," offers Annie.

The blonde woman nods. "Aye, but we're no the ones going knocking." She grins.

"Who is?" asks Annie, leaning forward.

Blythe cackles next to her and howls like a wolf. Annie snorts a laugh and then chuckles, before breaking out into a full laugh.

"Fuck! I'd hate to be Aikin!" she says, snuggling into me.

We get word an hour later that he's in custody, having tried to flee. They set the K9's on him as he ran over the moorland, and he was quickly subdued.

"I want to get you out of your house for a while, Annie. Away from here."

"I'm not hiding," she informs Adrian flatly.

He sighs. "He's already kidnapped your daughter. Do you want him to come after you? Or send some other goons to do it?" He also hands her a few sheets of paper. "We're linking all this into this guy too. That shit storm you thought was big, just got bigger."

Annie leans forward. "I can take care of myself. And I'll damn well make sure my daughter can too," she growls.

Adrian nods. "Okay, but Wolf would be happier if you were just not a target," he states. That stops Annie in her path. "Especially in light of this," he continues, tapping the papers in Annie's hand. She's not read them yet.

"What?" she asks.

I hug her. "It would make me happier too, to know you're not so easily found." She looks up at me, and I can see she's not happy, but tough. She's done a lot of work uncovering Aikin, she's had help from Adrian's tech guys to do it, but Aikin knows it started with her because of that damn counsellor.

"Annie?" Blythe is reading the same documents over Annie's shoulder. While Annie's not reading them, Blythe is. She touches Annie on her arm and that gets Annie's attention. "Hertford."

Annie looks at Blythe and the colour drains from her face, the light fades from her eyes. Then she closes them, breathes in, and when she opens them, there's a coldness about it. Annie nods.

"Not again?" she asks quietly, and Blythe nods, rubbing her arm. "Fuck." Annie draws in a huge breath, then turns to Adrian. "I need my family out of Edinburgh. Fiona and Elle especially." I notice she doesn't verbally include Jim, and I totally get why.

"I've got somewhere else they can go," I say. I do, but it's in England, down near Scarborough. Far enough away for Jim to maybe cool his heels.

Hours later, Wolf is meeting us and approves of the plan, though he's labelling it as Private Protective Custody for his records. I watch Annie, and I have this intense knot in my stomach; her attitude is different now, colder and Annie seems to be on a level I never knew people went to. I need her to be safe, and I'm not sure I want her to follow through on this plan.

Wolf tells us who Aikin's legal counsel is, and it's not quite the best in the country, but it's close enough. He also reveals that a local MSP is involved, and when the story breaks in the media tomorrow morning, the proverbial will hit the fan big time. Warrants are being signed ready for execution on very early morning raids.

A bail hearing is already set, and Aikin is being held at Her Majesty's pleasure until then, though Wolf hints that chances of bail being granted, given how he had to be arrested, would be almost zero. Wolf has his own tech guys to dig things up on Aikin, but he asks Marcus for the same.

Annie looks at me and smiles weakly then motions for me to follow her to a quiet corner of the open-plan office.

"I'm going to make them hunt me and find me. I need them to not go near you, or Fee and Elle." Again, I notice she's not mentioned Jim. I can only imagine her thoughts on him right now.

I nod. "I don't like it, but I understand why."

"It means I won't, cannot, contact you. At all." She waits for me to nod, to acknowledge this statement. "I've done this before. Hertford." And I understand. It was an op she was involved in somehow in her past, a solution for now. Her arms are crossed over her, her legs are shoulder-width apart, but I can see muscles tensing and relaxing as if she's ready to pounce. The fire in her eyes is something I love to see, but not for this reason.

"I guessed," I tell her. I hold my arms out for a hug and embrace her tightly. I try not to think of the next time I'll get to hold her, or see Elle. I just know that I will.

## 34 - Annie

Dawn breaks as we approach the far West Coast of Scotland on that
following Monday. Wolf and Tony relented when I said I wanted to see
the MSP arrested after I read the rest of the file. I watched as the police
smashed the door to MSP, Hamish McRae's house, arrested him, and
took him away just after four am. Dawn wasn't even on the radar that
early. I nod to the officer Wolf's assigned to drive me away once McRae
is in the police car and taken away. It's time to scatter the breadcrumbs.

We're near the town of Mallaig, which has the ferry terminal to
the Isle of Skye. My heart is heavy, leaving behind not only my daughter
(though she was in the care of her obnoxious father and fabulous second
mother) but Tony as well. I am not permitted to call them, talk with
them, interact with them, or reach out to them in any way. I am on radio
silence and it harks back to my RAF days on deployments. I didn't mind
the radio silence with my family then, no one knew where they were, and
there was no Elle. Now, my heart is heavier than a bar of platinum, and
the memories of what Tony and I shared are playing over in my mind.

My brief chat with Julia was a lie, personal time after Elle's
short-term kidnapping was a smoke-screen, though, if I wasn't about to
bring the end game on this, I might have used that as a valid reason.

The officer beside me has been silent the entire journey, and I've
not exactly been a huge conversationalist. We had a brief conversation at
a motorway service about coffee and what chocolate bar we each
required. The rest of my journey to Mallaig was in silence or with the
radio on. Goodness knows what I'll find on Skye itself. Skye was Tony's

idea, a friend of his who has a croft hidden away, hard but not impossible to find.

The boat is able to carry the car across, but that's not how I'll be travelling this leg. He walks to the boot and pulls my old RAF duffle bag out, leaving it on the floor. Then he hands me a folded piece of paper. Inside is a ticket for the ferry, foot passenger.

Written upon the piece of paper was an address and a name. I look up at the mountain of a man Wolf has assigned to bring me here. If Wolf was a wolf, this man would be a mountain bear.

"What's this?" I ask, looking at it, wanting confirmation. This is Tony's writing; it's the only thing of his I now have with me.

"Your contact. The boat leaves in twenty minutes and you're on it."

"Not going to keep me company?" I tease; I can see his jaw twitching. His amber eyes give nothing away. I knew exactly what Blythe meant when she mentioned Hertford. That was an op I'd rather permanently forget.

"Aye, just you."

"Damn, no babysitter," I counter, and he smirks.

"Like you need one, Sherlock," he growls, handing me my bag, indicating that our conversation is over. I grin and grab the bag from him. Why couldn't Tony have suggested somewhere in England? Somewhere near a library, civilization? Hell, even somewhere like London? There are plenty of places he could have hidden me as the trial against the politician built up, to encourage these gits to come after me. Why he picked the Inner Hebrides and Skye, I have no idea.

I walk to the ticket office, hand my ticket over, then I walk onto the Ferry, find a seat, and sit down. I resign myself to the fact that one way or another, this is going to end and soon.

The ferry journey is short, and I sit and drink something resembling coffee in the lounge area until we dock at Skye. I look at the paper and the details written in Tony's writing, focusing on his style of writing, trying to fathom what his style tells me about him. I walk down the gangway to find a busy port, small though it is.

There's someone there, holding up a sign with my middle name and my mother's maiden name of MacKinnon on it. Apt, since I'm on Skye, and I smirk slightly as I walk up to the slight but bearded man who is holding the sign.

I drop my bag at his feet and though I'm not short, he's a good head above me in height. "That's me," I say, pointing at the sign. He nods and begins rolling it up.

"This way, lass," he says. Picking my bag back up, I follow him and despite my many years out of the military, the discipline comes back into play.

I follow him to an old, battered but still working Defender 90. He opens the tailgate, and I sling my bag in the back, then get in the passenger seat. It's a two-seater in the front cab with only one bench in the back which is covered in a typical Land Rover canvas.

"Hope you dinnae mind the smell of sheep," he says.

I chuckle. "Tough if I did, isn't it?" I ask.

He nods. "You a city gal?"

I shrug. "Something like that,"

"There's a small croft on my farm where yer to stay. I hope ye brought some woollens with ye; if not, I'm sure we can find ye something."

I packed some when Tony told me I was staying in Scotland. "I've brought a few," I say.

"Aye, good." That was as much conversation we had until we reached the croft in question. Through back roads, dirt tracks, and cattle grids he drove, heading further across to the far side of Skye. This old car is rickety, but I guess if you're dealing with sheep, it's perfect. For a long drive, it would be disastrous for your body. I am sure our old defenders at Lossie were more comfortable than this boneshaker.

"Right, here we are," he says after I've been bounced around like a pea in a pod.

The croft is one of three old stone buildings angled together. Each is a single story dwelling, barely rising out of the ground against the hills of Skye, half-buried into the ground. Their metal roofs are fairly new I observe, certainly they've been replaced in the last five years. Two have a tall chimney with smoke coming out of them, but the third is silent and dark.

"Whilst yer here, I'd appreciate a hand with the sheep," he says.

"What kind of help do you need?" I ask. I know nothing about keeping farm animals, or farming. Guess I am a city lass after all.

"I need to move them in a few days down the hill. I've got the dogs, but another couple of bodies would help too, aye?"

"You know why I'm here?" I ask him. He nods.

"I've been told some story that I doubt is true, but I'm being paid well enough to house ye, so I dinnae need to know more," he says gruffly. Fair enough then.

I sigh. "I'll help out when I can," I say. There are no houses that I can see for miles, and we're nestled into the back end of a hill on Skye. No way is anyone going to be able to find me here unless they knew to look. Which was the intention.

The man opens the door and I realise I have no idea what his name is. "Sorry, I just realised I didn't ask you your name," I say.

He smirks, his white teeth just showing through his scraggly dark beard.

"Iain," he says, holding his hand out for me to shake.

"Amelia," I say. His grip is firm, his hands heavily calloused, but his dark work trousers and heavy woollen light-coloured jumper just add to the highland farmer look.

"Let's get you inside and I'll show you how the fire works," he says, opening the croft door.

"How the fire works?" I repeat, confused.

"Aye, it's fueled by peat and wood, so you'll need to know how to start her up. Once she's going, dinnae let it go out until yer leaving to go back, aye?"

I nod. He shows me how to start a fire, first with the basic wood, then the peat blocks on it which he says lasts for hours. There's a stack of peat blocks by the fire that would take up a bookcase, stacked as high as I am and wider than my arms will go. On the other side, it is the same in wood cuttings.

"You want about fifty-fifty of each in the fire. Put a peat block on and let it catch afore ye go to bed." He shows me the rest of the croft, which is rustic, simple but homely. The living room where you enter is an open plan with a kitchen and a heavy wooden front door. From the kitchen lies the only bedroom and bathroom the croft has. The bed is king size and the bedroom has its own fireplace. "Same rules on that fire as the main one," he says. The bathroom has a shower running into the bath, and it reminds me of home.

"You okay, lass?" he asks. I can only nod; my voice has left me. This is isolation, and my nerves temporarily take hold.

"Let's get the kettle on, aye?" he asks. I nod and go fetch my bag from the living room and take it to the bedroom, then I light the fire in the bedroom. I smile as Iain hands me a mug of tea as black as tar. "We've put some milk and stuff in the fridge," he says. "I do a bakery run every few days, but yer food is down to you after you've used up what's here. The nearest store is five miles, so you'll want to either come with me or use a bike." He leans across the counter where he's put my tea. "I suggest you come with." He winks. I smirk, but his humour doesn't change the fact I'm miles from home so that a sex scandal politician and his wealthy cronies get put behind bars. And a five-mile hike is only a stretch of the legs.

He's already tried to break me once, to get me to back off. I have no idea where Jim, Fee, and Elle have been taken, though Tony said he had somewhere for them to go that Elle would love. I wonder how Tony is, and I try not to let his absence affect me. I can recall his mobile number by heart, but his channels might be monitored too. The breadcrumbs need to lead to me.

Iain coughs to get my attention. "I'll come to get ye tomorrow to take you to the store, aye?" he says, and I nod.

"Perfect," I agree, determination kicking in. Iain finishes his tea and puts the mug into the sink.

"I'll see ye tomorrow, lass," he states and leaves me alone in the croft, and despite this being the plan, that's exactly how I feel. Alone. Isolated. Abandoned.

The following morning, Iain does exactly that. I stock up on provisions and use my card as normal. There are not many shops open at the time Iain has brought us here, and I know I'll have to hike it back so I'm here during the middle of the day. I check out the harbour master's office and see nothing out of the ordinary. I would love to know who the observer is out on this remote island, the one who is keeping an eye on the ferry and boats coming and going.

On the Hertford op, we had an observer, one who would discreetly alert the "mouse" that the "cat" was about. I was the mouse in this case; the cat was whomever the gang or Aikin sent after me. So far, our trap hadn't sprung.

For ten days, I eat, help Iain and his wife with the sheep herding, and hide on Skye. It is beautiful but so very quiet; I'm used to the buzz of a city. It also gives me too much time with my thoughts, and I don't like where they're taking me at night.

The heather-covered hills are great to take walks on and when the weather permits (which it does for a few days), I go and take a walk, exploring and stretching my legs.

259

I come across Castle Moal, a ruin of a castle once held by the MacKinnon clan, and I realise I've hiked the long way towards Kyleakin. The fresh air is amazing and the small town gives me some distraction to ease off the loneliness. It even has a bookstore, and I grin from ear to ear.

Books! My salvation, my escapism. It's hard to be alone when you've something to read. I spend the day in Kyleakin, enjoying being with people, being alive, drinking coffee from the small cafe, even with a face mask on, then I hike back via the harbour, arriving back at the croft just as the cold darkness wraps the island in its soft velvety blanket. The trap still hasn't been sprung.

The other days, I hardly see another soul, unless I go to the general store, which I manage to find on foot one day while out walking. I return by nightfall on my second hike day, and I am glad I got back when I did as the weather breaks with typical Atlantic force howling wind and hammering rain. Maybe it's because of the metal roof, it sounds heavier than it is, but the fire more than makes things cosy and warm to read my books by. The anticipation begins to build, the crumbs must be leading here, to me, by now. The nerves and adrenaline begin to kick in. They're taking their time.

What turns out to be the last evening on Skye starts out like the others. I eat something light, hike down to the harbour, and there's a small pirate flag flying near the bins. My trap may have been sprung, but I can't stand and dance about it. As I head up to Castle Moal again, I stand on the rocky outcrop and look down at the town. Whoever was sent, I can't see them, but then, I don't need to. I just need to know they're there.

I hike back and settle down for the evening, eat some fruit, and I pick up a book, the fire burning away, throwing out a regular heat. I hear scratching at the front door, as if someone can't find the keyhole, long after the sun has set, and I grin. It's not a sound you'd expect to hear, unless you were expecting it.

I carefully put the book down and make my way behind the kitchen counter so I can see who dares to enter. I hear two voices, hushing each other; the door opens and then closes quietly. I quickly ball my fists but hold my position, keeping my breathing quiet and slow. They motion to each other, and one heads to the bedroom, the other around to the fireplace.

As the one guy comes back from the bedroom, I launch at him, knocking his knee out from under him, hearing and feeling it break. He screams in agony, curling up into a ball. I know he's going nowhere for a while.

His accomplice, though, is on me in moments, yanking me back by my hair. I can feel his hot breath on my neck and he leans in.

"Going to do to you what I should have done to your daughter," he growls. He yanks me to the sofa and throws me onto it, and I turn. My eyes are already adjusted to the low light cast by the fire, I know that his won't have quite yet; it's much brighter in here than it is outside. I grin and adjust how I'm laying, and I move just enough that he doesn't pay attention, but enough so I can lash out. He starts to undo his jeans, and I tense up; I've got one chance to take him out, and I have no intention of missing.

His friend moans. "She broke my fucking knee!" he screams, which causes Mr Hopeful before me to glance at his friend. That glance alone is enough. Pushing myself up, I aim a kick to his groin, connect with his balls, pull back and swing a hook with one hand, guarding with the other, aiming for his temple, his jaw, his throat. One punch after another land on him, and he recoils, unable to stop my assault. He collapses onto the floor, whimpering like the child I know he is.

I stand up to full height and head to the bedroom, taking out the two pairs of cuffs Wolf made me pack. Why two, I have no idea, but it's enough. I cuff one to a radiator and Mr Hopeful to the iron grill of the fire. Then I make a call to Wolf. It's finally over.

The officers that Wolf called to my scene aren't used to dealing with this; though, neither is Wolf. Just before dawn, I hear the blades of another helo fly overhead, then fade to a distance, but not completely. There's a knock at the door about twenty minutes later, and one of the local officers opens it up to reveal one of the faces I've wanted to see for nearly ten days, but not the one I want to see the most.

I nod. "Hey, Wolf," I greet him. He takes a look at the medics that Mountain Rescue has had to bring in to tend to these two attackers. I even left the guy near the fireplace in his half undone jeans. Wolf just raises his eyebrows at me, and I shrug. A medic quietly briefs Wolf, and I see him chuckle, then whisper something to the medic, who just casts me a glance, and swallows; his eyes are wider and I'm sure he's just turned pale. I think I scare him.

Wolf motions me to the kitchen counter, hands me a newspaper, dated yesterday. The headline makes me collapse onto the floor, missing the chair I was aiming for. No one is sure what to do, until Wolf makes me stand up.

The headline is simple, cutting. "Local MSP found dead in his cell," it reads. Then I'm placed on a chair and I realise I need to breathe. I look at yesterday's news, not sure what the hell it all means quite yet.

"Does that mean there's no trial? Was all this for fuck all?"

He sighs heavily. "Against the politician, there's no trial. The counsellor and his police friend though, that's still going ahead. We've tied Aikin to Elle's kidnapping, as well as all those rape and sex offender charges you uncovered. Seems one of the Polish girls had a cousin on the inside who got wind of what happened. A big brute of a man, ex-forces too. Aikin's battered and in intensive care. That's now being investigated, thankfully, *not* by me."

So that was what the paper couldn't allude to. It was either Natazsa or Maja's cousin who served justice out the old fashioned way. I feel sick that the MSP is dead. There would still be answers to be found, but the fear for the witnesses, for those of us who fought for justice, was now far less. The threat was gone.

"That's... Hell, I wanted him to rot slowly, painfully!" I spit. Whilst I waited for the 'head officer to come from the mainland,' I had packed my bag, stripped the bed, and got the laundry on while the local police officer watched me from a distance.

It's given me time to reflect. This time away from the charity has me thinking, and I'm not getting any younger. I don't want to keep on doing what I am, but I need a change, although I love why I do what I do.

"So I get to fly in the helo home?" I ask, trying to hold my nerves and anticipation together.

"We have got a flight to Stirling, as I need to update you." I nod in reply, but I really don't like that look of foreboding he has engraved on his face.

"Oh aye?" I reply, rallying myself. Wolf simply nods at me.

The helo is a police one, borrowed from Strathclyde. Wolf switches us to the non-pilot frequency when we're in the air.

"Yer not gonna like what I've got to tell you," he begins. We're a good thousand feet off the ground; travelling by helo is something I don't miss about my military days.

"What's happened?" I ask into the headsets, fearing the worst. "Is Elle okay?" I lean forward, eager and keen to hear whatever the hell it is.

"We think it's those two," he thumbs back to the croft I had been staying at, "tried to burn down your house when they couldn't find you there." I sit there, stunned, aware that my home and my life as I know it are over. Jim will fight for full custody now, and he has resources I don't. To his five million reasons, I have fifteen thousand, and I no longer have a permanent address. The odds aren't looking good, then I remember Tony, what he told me when Jim threatened me with the custody battle two weeks ago; even if Fiona would divorce Jim, he'll make good his threat. I decide in a heartbeat that this isn't something I can drag him into; I can't use him like that. Why would he want me now?

I breathe deeply, hold it in, and then let it go.

"When and how much damage?" I ask.

"Front door, mainly. Your friends had someone watching the house, so it was caught and dealt with quickly." I can only nod in reply, the sick feeling in my stomach threatens to empty out onto the helo floor, but I manage to hold it back, desperate now to see just how much more fucked up my life has become.

## 35 - Anthony

The news of Councillor McRae's death at the hands of one of his victim's cousins in jail leaves a heavyweight in my heart. The news that Aikin is in intensive care for the same reason somehow doesn't bother me as much. Annie laid a trap after the arrests, Blythe telling her that there were other gang members wanting to "finish the job." Hence the "*Hertford*," statement the last time I saw her. The fact I paid for the location on Skye for three months and was willing to pay for more is incidental.

Adrian and his crew came back to ensure I wasn't harmed whilst the police took me up on my offer to also hide Jim and his family. At least now they could get back together. I look up as Blythe enters the office with a bounce in her step.

"Thank goodness that's over with!" she says as she, too, watches the TV screen with the breaking news of the MSP's demise.

"It's not quite over yet," I say. There's still a trial to be had, but it is no longer the big circus that it was promising to be. "Annie's not home yet."

Blythe nods. "Wolf is going to let me know when she's back," she says, standing up as if to leave. Then, Blythe does the most curious thing. She sits back down, grabs the remote and mutes the television.

"I need to warn you about Annie," she says. She's looking at me like a corporate barrister would.

"What do you mean?" I ask. I just want Annie home.

Blythe sighs. "Annie's not going to be in a good place. She might have set the trap for the last of these swines and it paid off. Her head,"

266

Blythe taps her temple, "isn't going to be focusing on what you two had before. The creeps found her as intended, and she has dealt with them. Broke one guy's knee and incapacitated the other, Wolf tells me. He's going to tell her about the fire."

I sit back and listen, encouraging her to go on.

"Sherlock's great, don't get me wrong. But this to her is going to feel like she did when we came back from deployment. She's going to be out of it, not thinking straight. That fire will not help her in the fight against Jim, and she'll not want to fight a battle she can't win." Blythe stands up and looks me squarely in the eye. "You're going to have to remind her that you love her, that you're in her corner."

"She already knows that," I say, but Blythe holds her hands up.

"She knows what you *had,* two weeks ago. I know how she thinks, how she was after a tour. She'll have gone deep and dark into herself; that is how she copes with the shit she does. Do you think her freaking out on the bench that night was a one-off? We all do it. You've not seen one until you've seen someone come back from what she has, or a war zone. She's been through hell, and it'll feel like she's been on a deployment."

I suddenly get what Blythe is saying.

"So how do I help her?" I ask.

Blythe sighs. "Counselling. I know a good one that understands vets and this type of situation. Book her sessions, don't let her get out of it. And, be there for her. She's going to push you away because her thinking will be that she's protecting you; she won't ask you to fight for her." Blythe opens the office door. "And, Tony, you're gonna need to push back, fight back. Hard. Her barriers *will* be as high as the Castle walls and just as bloody stubborn." She emphasises the word will, then nods at me as she exits, leaving a card on my desk for the counsellor she mentioned and a fiery need for me to get to Annie before anyone else.

I sat outside her fire-damaged house at the end of the first day of the news breaking. I've parked within sight but not directly in the drive she had tended to for seven years. I don't know what the insurance has to say about the fire, about rebuilding the part of the house that was damaged, replacing her items, and I don't care. I do know from Blythe that the fire was caused by arson and it was tied to that damn MSP. I don't know how Annie has taken the news that someone tried to torch her home yet. By the time darkness falls, I know Annie's not coming home tonight. I turn my engine on and head home, needing to rest to start my vigil again tomorrow.

I get a text through at five am to say that Annie will be at her house in just over an hour, that Wolf has briefed her about the fire. I wash, dress, and grab a coffee to go for us both, and within thirty minutes of rising, I'm once again sitting outside her fire-damaged house.

I see a large BMW pull into Annie's driveway a little while later and Annie gets out, looking ashen with her fists clenched. Wolf is in the driver's seat, watching her. I turn the engine off and walk over, being careful not to startle her. Wolf just nods and quietly closes the car door, then walks to the other side of her gate, giving us some privacy.

"Annie?" I called out. She turns to me, and she's fighting back the tears, her hands by her sides, still clenched in fists. She's taking in the house, the damage to it. It's mostly the front door and hallway that was burnt, but still, it's not liveable at the moment.

"Tony, you shouldn't be here," she mutters. I take a step towards her.

"Why not?" It's chilly this morning; our breaths cloud before us, then dissipate. Annie doesn't answer me; she turns and hangs her head a moment, before looking up at her house. The front door and hallway were the parts the fire reached before the fire brigade turned up, and are boarded up with horrible looking security grids.

I take another step towards her, trying not to crowd her, but recalling every word that Blythe said to me yesterday.

"Annie, why shouldn't I be here?" I ask again.

"I'm not right for you; I bring way too much trouble to your door." She chokes, and I can tell she's trying not to cry. God, this is a brave, stubborn woman!

"Why not?" I insist. I know she can't give me an answer because she hasn't got one that I haven't spent the time thinking of a reply to when I was keeping my vigil yesterday.

"Because," she counters emptily. She turns her head to speak that one word, then goes back to staring at her damaged home.

"Because of what, Annie?" I plead. If it weren't for Blythe's warning yesterday, I'd likely be walking away by now, very frustrated and confused. I know now she's trying to push me away. I may have told her I loved her, but I know she hasn't said those words back to me, despite how I know she feels.

She says something that I can't make out, and it feels important. I take another step towards her. "Tell me, Annie. Tell me why."

Her head slumps and her shoulders roll forward. The dam has burst and in two steps, I'm there, wrapping my arms around her, holding her tightly.

"I've got ye," I say into her hair, quietly. There's an old comic book I recall from my youth about *The Watchmen*. I often wondered who watches the Watchmen. I hear the boot of the BMW open and then close behind me and a gentle thump as a heavy bag is placed nearby. I see Wolf out of the corner of my eye, and he nods to me, then his car starts and he gently pulls away, leaving Annie and me alone in the cold.

"Come back with me, Annie," I plead, kissing her head again. The tears have stopped flowing, and thanks to Blythe, I know the job of putting Annie back together is going to be tough. However, it's a task I want and I'm willing to do.

"Why?" she asks, but she's turning away, trying to hide.

"Because ye can't stay here," I say. Then I recall what else Blythe said. "And because I want you with me."

She shivers as the cold hits her and the sobs slow. "No, ye don't. You don't want a fighter, a brawler in yer bed. I'm a whole load of trouble."

I hold her to me tightly, and the words of her song that we shared so many months ago come to mind. "Aye, I do. You fill up my senses, like a walk through Princess Street Park." I cast my mind back to the walk we took through the old town that one sunny afternoon. "Like a walk down George Street in the rain, or through Holyrood park when the rainbows come out." I feel her lean in against me and feel I'm getting through to her, breaking down those walls that Blythe thankfully said would be there. Walls I would have otherwise left up.

"I want you with me, Annie, always." I kiss her head again. "I love you."

The tears start to fall again, and I hold her to me tighter, turning her around. I had wanted her to turn to me on her own, but I realise now she's not able to; even if her heart wants it, her head is ruling her here.

"It's been hard, darling, I know. But, you don't have to fight on your own anymore. I told you at the start I wanted to look after you. Even after all this crazy, legal situation, I still want to." I kiss the top of her head. "I know you left to protect me, made them hunt you out. I know you insisted that Jim, Fee, and Elle go for the same reason." She looks up at me, her eyes still full of tears, her face all red and blotchy from the crying. My heart breaks at the sight of her still hurting, still fighting. "I get it. But. You. Are. Not. Alone."

I am in love with her. I know when she's in a better place, she'll tell me that she feels the same about me; she's shown me that before, and I suspect these walls are a part of it.

"Not anymore. Not for a long time."

"I don't understand," she whispers. "Why?"

I curl my index finger under her chin and lift her face to mine. Then I kiss her gently.

"Because you deserve everything, Annie," I reply when I break away. "You fight for everyone else, but not yourself." I watch as she closes her eyes in defeat, admitting finally that I know her, that I see her. All of her. As stubborn as she is, she's a fighter. Beautiful like the Highlands, wilder than the winds and as destructive as any Atlantic storm. Right now, that storm has wrung itself out.

"What does the devil say to the warrior?" She looks at me blankly as I ask. Then I continue. "The Devil tells the warrior they can't withstand the storm. The warrior replies that they are the damn storm." I search her eyes, and she blinks away another loch of tears. "You are that warrior, Annie. Those women are safe, because of you. You challenged their attackers, and they tried to break you, not once but twice." I nod towards the house. "They failed. Both times. You've withstood it all, Annie. Let someone else fight the next battle, let me help you prepare for the one after. Be brave for me." I pause. "For us?"

The reply is almost silent, significant and powerful like a leaf falling from a tree, or a butterfly flying past. "Aye," I hear her breathe. I gently guide her to my car and take her home.

# Epilogue

It took months of therapy and Aikin's trial to start putting Annie back together. There are still dark moments, but they are short-lived, thankfully, and getting rarer. Annie is still as stubborn as ever, but she lets me fight for her when we both need it.

The first big step I saw her take was with Elle. She wanted to hug her daughter, but at the same time, she didn't, scared she had hurt her little girl beyond repair. Elle, though, was perfect and didn't care; she just hugged her mother and treated her like, well, her mum! Getting her to see her mum was a challenge, and as I watch the pair of them play Connect Four, I recall the confrontation with Jim.

~

The day I decided enough was enough and went to see Jim, Annie had fallen asleep on the sofa in the library. I had taken to using the security cameras to keep an eye on where she was, more of a suggestion from Blythe than my own idea.

Her phone had lit up, but she hadn't responded to it. I went to go and see what it was on the screen, and I baulked when I saw it was Jim. Elle was supposed to have been back at ours on the Sunday after Annie and everyone had returned. She hadn't been dropped off. Annie wouldn't tell me why, but I had an idea it was because of Jim. Behind Annie's back, whilst she was on Skye, I had retained four of the best family and court solicitors Edinburgh had to offer, given the threat Jim had made, even at the risk of losing his current wife. Jim would fight, sure, but he wouldn't have the best of the best on his side. The fact I had done that, would send warnings out to the other solicitors too. Take his side, face the best four in the business and my incredibly deep pockets.

I sat and waited until she woke up, which with my fidgeting around her, wasn't long. Usually, I left her to nap, knowing that what had happened had drained her physically and mentally. She threw everything she had at everyone. Everyone, but Jim.

I smiled at her when she woke up. Dressed in jeans and a silk V-neck blouse that highlighted her figure, she looked amazing, though underweight. It had taken me two days just to be able to hold her in our bed, and she was slowly becoming her old self. Until these messages came in.

"You had a message," I pointed to her phone and saw her grimace. A few moments later she looked as if she was chewing on a wasp. I held my hand out for her phone and she resisted for a moment. "Come on woman, no secrets, aye?" I told her. I watched as she closed her eyes and tears silently poured down her cheeks. It broke my heart to know that she was this upset but won't, or feel she can't, confide in me. I have the information file Adrian pulled together on everyone, including Annie. I'm sure her bank has told her how much money she has in her account now, though a hundred thousand so she could do what she wanted was nothing to me.

"Please?" I pleaded with her and held my breath. I saw her sigh deeply, sob, and then unlock the phone, then she handed it to me and I read the messages from Jim. I clenched my jaw and narrowed my eyes as I scrolled down all the messages from him over the last three days.

I leaned across and kissed her on the forehead. "Leave this with me," I commanded her. I don't usually boss her about, but whilst she's involved in this fight, Jim's not bargained on me taking him on head first. It's time I showed my hand.

"I can't ask," she sobbed at me. I sigh, frustrated. She still doesn't get that I'm here for her. I leaned into her and lifted her chin with my fingers. Taking a handkerchief from my pocket, I dried her eyes, then kissed her mouth gently.

"Yer not. He's not the only one that can throw their weight around," I growled. "He needs to understand that you need to be appreciated for being Elle's mum and all the other work you've done and still do." I watched her gape at my words, then as she closed her mouth, she mumbled a word or two I couldn't understand. "I'll be back, away ye go, dry yer tears." I kissed her nose, stroked her arm, smiled at her the best way I could, whilst I imagined just how much damage I could inflict on Jim.

"Do you remember what you told me, the first time we were together?" she asked me as I stood. I paused, trying to remember what I had told her, but clearly, Annie remembered.

"You told me you had money, influence." She was getting her words out through sobs and it broke my heart. "That people use you. I cannae do that to you." She wiped her eyes, but the tears didn't stop.

"Ach, Annie," I groaned, taking a seat on the sofa next to her. "That was afore; I've learned you'll not ask me for help unless yer back is against the wall. And it is. Only, yer *not* asking. I can see what needs to be done, but this isn't your move to make, sweetheart." I pulled her into a hug and just gave her the handkerchief. "Now go, sort yourself out while

I go and do this." I kissed the side of her temple and waited a moment until she took a breath, composing herself. I could feel her still holding back.

I sighed, I wanted - needed - to make her understand I was there for her. I unbuttoned my shirt and grabbed her hand, putting it where she stitched me up months before.

"You," I told her. "You did this. You made me better and you didn't have to. You were there for me when I needed you, and I didn't ask. I'm here for you, in exactly the same way." Her eyes began leaking, which I wiped away with the handkerchief, then our foreheads joined. "I need you in my life," I whispered to her.

"You are," she breathed back as her eyes closed and the tears fell even harder. I pulled her to me and held her, vowing to stitch her back together again — starting with Jim.

Morag appeared and guided her to the bathroom, nodding at me as I tucked my shirt back in.

"Four for meals going forward, Morag, aye?" I asked her. I gave Morag a firm, decisive nod, received one in reply, then I headed to the key locker, grabbing my already prepared case.

I grinned to myself as I pulled the keys for the Maserati off the hanger and fired her up a few moments later. I got a deep, internal satisfaction at the growl the car put out as I stomped on the accelerator and cleared the exhaust. It matched my determination and mood. Knowing that Jim was still on the waiting list for this car, this model, I intended to use the car to show him just exactly who he was dealing with.

Fifteen minutes later, I managed to pull into a space a few doors down from his Mews house. Fiona opened the door on my knock, and she seemed surprised to see me.

I leaned in and gave the lady a kiss on the cheek. "Pack the lass up for me, aye? We're going back to the agreement as of today," I told her. She gaped at me, then closed her mouth and looked around me. "Annie's not here. I'm the one here to see Jim."

"He's in his office if ye dare to enter," she quietly told me.

I nodded. "Aye, I dare. I ken he's going to be a wee bit frustrated," I replied to her, not hiding the smile breaking free on my lips.

Her mouth dropped, then she pulled it back up and pointed to the door in question, the only closed door on this level.

"Pack the bairn, please," I repeated my command. She's gotten bigger now as her own pregnancy kicked in. "And if you need out," I offered. She pulled her shoulders back and nodded.

"I ken where to find ye," she told me, her response clipped, short, but there was a fire in her eyes that wasn't there a moment ago. I only nodded, my message to her conveyed. She headed off in one way, and I marched into Jim's office without knocking.

"I told you," he bellowed but stopped when he saw it was me. "What the hell are you doing here? Is she here with you?" he demanded, looking around me, expecting to see Annie. I closed the door quietly behind me, then I took a seat on one of the sofas in his office. It's not quite like mine, but the idea was similar. I unbuttoned my suit jacket, then I sat on the sofa as if I owned it. If he's not careful, I would and in short order.

"Having a bad day?" I asked without preamble or malice. For now, I needed to keep my cool.

He leaned back in his chair, his eyes watching me like a hawk. Pity for him I've already made several moves on a chessboard he's only just worked out he's playing on.

"Not too badly," he retorted.

"Really? Had trouble getting a decent family lawyer?" I began. The first salvo was let loose and I watched him as the colour drained from his face.

"What do you know?" he asked.

"Oh, I know plenty. The four top family solicitors and their practices are on my retainer." I watched as he swallowed, his Adam's apple bobbing. "I know your company is in difficulty, mainly because of this pandemic. I know several of the avenues you've tried to raise funds to pay your staff haven't worked out and, before you ask, I had nothing to do with that. I didn't need to." I watched as he understood what I was telling him, that I'd done a full financial background check on him.

"You can't afford the best four, you can't afford even one of them. You might have had five million excuses to fight Annie for custody of Elle, but I've got about thirty-five million more of my own. Every one of them," I leaned forward to ensure he understood, "Annie now has at her disposal." I punctuated every last word. His eyes went wide as he realised that I had given Annie seven times more firepower than he was waving around and that was just disposable cash.

"Keeping the bairn from her mother, after all her mother has done to bring this trafficking sex ring to an end, is spiteful. You didn't appreciate her or see her when she was with you, but I do. Now, yer not going to carry on being a spiteful man, are ye, Jim?" I asked the question calmly, leaning back on the sofa that pretended to be a Chesterfield, but wasn't.

"It was because of her Elle was taken to begin with!" he growled at me.

"A judge might see that. But the counter to that is, she was taken on your shift. Your pregnant wife was hurt as a result, you weren't able to protect her. You do know it was Annie that pulled her out of that basement? Broke the jaw of the one guarding her? Broke the knee of one of the other gang members when they went hunting Annie on Skye and threatened to rape her, after telling her that he should have raped your daughter?" I watched as Jim absorbed what I'd told him. He gulped and hid his expression, but not before I'd seen it.

"Now, the fact that Annie has physically gone after those who dared hurt her daughter and you did..." I let the statement hang. I gave him a few moments to think. "The fact that Annie and I are together and that she's temporarily living with me whilst the insurance sorts out the fire damage on her house, which, by the way, you'll *encourage* them to resolve this week, then you will step back from talking with them." I looked at him, letting him know that I knew he'd been playing arses with her insurance and persuading them to not fix her house. How he'd persuaded them he was involved with her, I'd never know.

"I have no idea," he began, but as he started talking, I pulled out the file Adrian had put together on him. I waved it at him and put it on the desk. I watched him pick it up and read everything about himself, his finances, loans, the car order, the conversations with the insurance, though Adrian's team had to do some questionable hacks for that angle.

"You can't afford that Maserati, not if your company fails," I reminded him. "You don't need to be fighting fires that you don't need to fight. Annie is one of those." I leaned forward. "She always *will* be one of those. Even if she and I don't get married as I want, I will always have her back from now on." I didn't let him know that the words I'd originally planned to say weren't those; they'd come from the heart and they were honest.

Jim sighed, chewed on the inside of his mouth, and after a few moments, he picked up his phone. I listened as he cancelled the legal counsel, telling them that he'd reconsidered about changing the agreement that's already in place.

"You're a wise man, Jim." I knew I was patronising him, but he was making the only decision I'd let him make. I pulled out another file and took back the file I had on him. "There's a proposal for a friend of mine who can step in to advise you on your business. How you've operated before won't work right now. He's got experience in running your type of business in sanctioned countries, skills you could do with borrowing. Read that, contact him."

I stood, and Jim did too.

"I'm glad you came around to my way of thinking," I told him. "And you need to talk to someone about how you deal with your temper." I dropped a different counsellor's details on his desk. "That's not a request." I nodded to the file he was holding. His jaw twitched, but I saw recognition in his eyes. He was so angry and I wasn't sure why. Whatever it was, he needed to deal with it and not hit out at Annie, Fiona, or use Elle as a weapon.

"I'll see myself out, and I'll be taking Elle to see her mum. I'm glad you agreed to go back to the agreement and *not* charge Annie for the extended privilege I granted you whilst she fought for justice." I'd put the investigation file back in my case and left him in his office, closing the door quietly behind me. That he might even charge Annie for not being able to take care of their daughter or take her as agreed due to extenuating circumstances had crossed my mind. I was just stunned he'd tried.

Elle was packed and waiting for me in the living room. She was sitting on the sofa quietly next to Fiona. I'd never known her to be so mouse-like.

"Hey, button, shall we go make your momma smile?" I asked. Elle jumped up and ran to me, throwing her little arms around me.

"I get to see Mummy?" she asked me, her voice rising and her eyes wide.

"You sure as heck do. Shall we go?" I took her hand and grabbed her case, and I heard the office door open. Jim stood in the frame but nodded.

"See you on Friday," he told her.

"I suggest you read your emails," I replied. "Elle will have an extended catch-up break with Annie and won't be back here until a week from Friday." Jim threw me a look, but I knew the email had landed, I felt the ping from my solicitor copying me whilst we were talking. Hands-free kits were rather helpful.

His jaw twitched and then stopped. I hoped he finally worked out that I do not play games.

Annie was in tears again when Elle barrelled in through the kitchen door and into her arms, making it clear she had missed her. Annie mouthed the words "thank you" to me as she hugged her daughter tight. That night, after Elle was in bed, she finally revealed why she hadn't confided in me about Jim's threats from the start. His nine-year control over her about money, finances, and the house, as well as what she'd told me before about the birthing part, made me almost as angry as I've heard Annie can be.

"It's not where I wanted to live," she told me as I paced around the library, the room she'd taken to be her sanctuary. "Not originally."

"So sell up," I instructed her. "The insurance will move on the repairs this week; that I know. When they're done, sell up."

"And where do we go?" She looked at me with the saddest of eyes.

"Stay with me, pocket the money," I told her. I moved to sit next to her, and she let out the biggest sigh, the tension ebbing away. I pulled out my phone and let her watch as I logged into my banking app and showed her just how much I had at my disposal. She swore, then covered her mouth quickly. I chuckled softly as she swore like the scuffer she'd told me she was.

"It's not mine to pocket," she told me, sadly.

"Oh, but it is, the house is in your name, not Jim's," I told her, then I showed her the entry to her account. I knew her financial situation better than she did. She gaped and looked at me as if I were mad.

"Seriously?!" she asked me, incredulously. I nodded.

"I told you, I want to be there. Please, start understanding that."
I saw the emotions in her eyes, the fear, but I also saw the need for her to
believe. At least, that's what I was hoping I was seeing.

"Jim will," she began, but I silenced her with my finger over her
lips. Her eyes widened and she let out the breath she'd been holding for a
moment.

"Play nicely. Trust me," I finished off her sentence. My voice
was low, edgy, and I wouldn't tell her the details of what had transpired
between us when I went to fetch Elle.

"What did you do?" she breathed at me as she pulled back. Her
eyes were wide, her nostrils flared, her hands folded up into themselves. I
forgot she could read people like a book.

"Made him see sense." I sat back on the sofa and adopted the
same position I had with Jim, though this time I was not battling an
adversary, I was trying to make the woman I was in love with see sense
and see what she had around her. Nine years to not have anyone
significant in your corner, nine years of being torn down from the inside,
not being in any financial control, was going to take a lot of undoing.

"How?" she demanded of me, her voice husky and fearful.

"By reminding him I'm in your corner, Annie." She looked at
me and then at the phone.

"You showed him your accounts?" she asked, taking an
incorrect guess at what I'd done. I shook my head.

"I had other ways to persuade him." I almost told her what I'd
had Adrian dig up, but I didn't. What I did, our talk, was between me
and him

"Tony," she began, but I silenced her with a kiss.

"No. How I do my business, take care of those I love, that's for me to do. You and Elle are a part of it."

She leaned forward and her forehead met mine. Her eyes were closed, her breathing slow and deep. "My trodaiche," she whispered. Yep, I guess I am.

~

The first time I ever meet her parents is as a part of her healing journey. They travel up from Dumfries as soon as the first travel restrictions are lifted, though I had talked with them before thanks to Annie. They leave their home early one evening and are in the penthouse by one am the following morning, waiting for Annie and I to visit for lunch the following day.

Morag takes care of them for me so that their visit will remain a surprise. Annie doesn't know that they travelled up to see her so soon, and her siblings are due in a few weeks. It is heart-warming and again, the tears from Annie are cathartic. Her parents are as proud of her as I am.

A conversation whilst clearing the dishes away with them that first evening tells me Annie is perfectly aware of what my talk with Jim entailed. As she answers questions from her parents about the house, its repairs, the new car she's looking at, she looks at me whilst giving some of her answers. I'm not sure how she found out, but she did. What I'm more surprised about, is that she's not angry at me for how I did it.

"You fought for me, for *us*, when I hadn't any more fight left in me regarding him. I'll *never* forget you did that," was all she had to say about it later that night in bed. I'll never underestimate her, it chills me that she found out specifics, including my business support proposal to Jim.

Her old boss calls too, though that conversation I am much less happy about. It was never clear in my head if Julia had a hand in the girls all being located together at that particular safehouse, if it was just sheer bad management or if the counsellor was manipulating their location. However, she has pulled in new regional managers to manage the main Scottish Cities the charity operates in, with plans to expand. They talk for hours, or it seems like it is setting the world to rights, and Annie challenges Julia back, fighting again for what is right.

I am as proud as all hell when Annie tenders her resignation for the role that she did with that charity which meant we crossed paths, and takes up the offer for one of the senior regional managers. Whilst she doesn't need to work anymore, she wants to continue to fight for the social unbalance that there is against women, but lose her dark thief get up. There are so many battles on that field, she can do it however she wants. I just like to remind her of that fact each day. I did find that outfit rather appealing when she eventually showed it to me, knowing now that she was wearing it on the evening she stitched me back together and sewed herself into my heart.

She does, when needed, go out and do that work, but it's a rare occurrence.

It takes a few weeks before Annie is able to physically enjoy me again, and I give her the time to give the signals. Treating regular moments with her as a date, expecting nothing from her but her company helps. Creating a routine for us both also helps, as does Annie getting stuck into changing the structure of the charity. The routine we create appeals to her military background and training.

Her therapist gives me the ideas to begin with when I ask how I can help what she is doing. It's hard, I'll admit, not to have her from the first moment we returned after her protective custody ended. However, I'm not such a cad as to take a warrior when she's down.

Now, we're six months ahead of that returning moment and I'm nervously getting ready for a going out date evening. My birthday was a few days ago, and Annie is taking me out now that some restaurants have opened back up. Mentioning my name apparently opened a few doors, and I smile at myself as I follow her instructions on how to dress.

"Are you ready?" she asks from the doorway. The insurance finally settled on repairing her house when the trial was in full swing, and once Jim got his head out of his arse and backed away. I'm pretty sure Annie had a word with him too, their dynamic has changed for the better. Now, the repairs are nearing completion, and Annie has been there daily picking out fixtures for it. Jim even relented on her pocketing the money from any future sale, not that he could do anything but acquiesce. However, I have something very important to ask her that makes where she and Elle live a moot point. Elle thinks it's nice to have three homes. If only the child knew.

"You look gorgeous, darling!" I say. Annie's picked a fifties style dress in a royal blue that just exudes both sensuality and classic sexuality. It shows her figure off perfectly, something she's been maintaining these last months, using exercise as additional therapy. Thankfully, she's less bony and looking much better for it. She is still as fit as a fiddle, having picked her training back up.

She twirls around for me, and I love the clothes show. The soles of her shoes are the same main colour as her dress, and the heels give her a few extra inches.

"Come on, let's go, the taxi is waiting," she bosses me.

I smile. "Taxi?" I ask. I could drive us.

She nods. "Aye," she says, holding out her hand for me whilst grabbing a shawl. I smile and let her lead me on the date she's carefully planned. "So we can both have a drink!" She winks at me.

We're at a table at our favourite Italian restaurant. Well, it's my favourite, but due to the lockdown, we haven't had a chance until now to indulge in eating out, and this is our first as a couple out in public. I'm glad she picked here above the other places I like. We're led to our table wearing our masks, and the waiter holds the chair out for Annie and asks us to choose the wine. It's still unsettling that we have to wear masks when walking around or in the taxi, but the world is a very different place these days. Annie opts for an Italian white, and knowing the main course I'm having, I choose the same. As soon as he leaves with our order, we remove the masks.

"So," we both say, together. Annie's cheeks go red, and I sit back, sighing contentedly.

"You first," I offer. Ladies always come first.

"Okay," she says, taking a large gulp of wine. "It's been hard," she pauses, trying not to break down as she tells me what she needs to, "so bloody hard, learning to trust. Not just you, but in general. I have never been good at it because of...well, a hell of a lot of things! Jim being one." I watch as she takes another drink of wine and takes a huge breath. I can feel the nervous energy pouring off her, and I wonder why. I take the hand that's not holding the wine and rub my thumb along her knuckles, gently sending reassurances to her as best I can. I notice that her hands are softer, her nails are in better condition, and I'm pleased she's looking after herself again.

"It's been me, myself, and I for most of it, save a chosen one or two." She looks me squarely in the eye, and I love the depth her eyes show. "But I have come to trust you. More than I ever thought I would, or needed to." She stops herself from saying anything more and fights back tears. I squeeze her hand, letting her know I'm here. "But I want to admit it now. To you."

She looks me straight in the eye, and I see the love that she feels for me shine through. I need to let her say this in her own way, though I've felt this way for months. "I love you," she finally whispers, just loud enough for me to hear her.

I pretend, cruelly perhaps, that I didn't hear her.

"I'm sorry?" I say. She glares at me; she knows I heard. "What did you say? I didn't quite hear you."

"You heard. I said I love you," she repeats, clearer this time. The tears are drying on their own as she verbally spars with me. I grin; there's my fighter once again.

"That's what I thought you said," I say and slide out of my seat to go to her and kneel before her right before I kiss her senseless.

"Tony, people are watching us!" she hisses, embarrassed. Her neck and décolleté are going red, and I can't help but smirk in satisfaction at that.

"Let them, I don't care," I retort. I reach into my pocket and pull out the small blue velvet box that's been on my person for a few days, the one I managed to sneak into my pocket before she dragged me out of the house tonight. Her eyes go wide, and I grin. It's not quite what she's thinking it is, and I cannot wait to see her face. I open the box and show her the ring that I have picked out, along with a spare front door key.

"Annie, I told you months ago I wanted you by my side. I knew it when we spent that first night together. I said I wanted to protect you, to care for you, to be the one to hold you up when you needed it and, honey, I want to make it all official. Will you do me the double honour of not only officially moving in with me but marrying me, as soon as we can?"

She's silent for a moment, and I think she's forgotten how to breathe. The only way I know she's still alive is that her eyes are glued to the ring and the spare master key I ordered for the mansion and penthouse. I'll add her biometrics when we get back, though that is likely to happen tomorrow. I have all-night plans for us when we get home, and they do not involve updating our security.

"Annie?" I see her chest heave, and she's finally remembered to breathe. I smile. My knees are getting sore, but I don't care.

"Yes," she breathes huskily. Then a louder "abso-fucking-lutley yes!" erupts from her. She reaches forward and kisses me, and I know that things can only get better for us both from here on out.

*THE END*

## Glossary

There are a lot of RAF military terms in here, especially in chats with Blythe and Annie. If you've ever heard military people speaking to one another, you'll understand how these two talk. You can find most of what I've used on this site:
https://en.wikipedia.org/wiki/RAF_slang

Trodaiche (tro-ditch) is a Scots Gaelic word and the title of the book. It means Fighter and the title was inspired by Lockdown 2020, Christina Aguilera's song by the same title, combined with The Boxer by Simon and Garfunkel. Both these songs ear-wormed me at the time. Then, I saw an image of *@hernandrago* on Instagram, and I had my hero. My heroine? I still don't "see" what she looks like; so, she's over to you all.

I have put together a Spotify Music List for this duet, I listened to it a ***lot*** when I was writing these; you can find it here: bit.ly/TDDMusic

This work and any/all others are listed on my website (louisemurchie.com) where you can sign up for my FREE Newsletter. I'm Scottish, I like things that are free - I hope you appreciate them as much as I do too!

*Louise*

MURCHIE

Thanks for reading this story/duet and for any reviews you leave. I deeply appreciate it!

## *Statistics:*

- According to the Office of National Statistics (ONS) Domestic Violence was up 6% to 910,985 incidents in England, Wales and Scotland due to the Pandemic.

- One in four women and one in six men will be affected by domestic abuse during their lives.

- On average two women are murdered every week and thirty men are murdered every year.

- 18% of violent crime reported during 2020/21 was related to domestic abuse, although it is least likely to be reported to the police.

- With that domestic abuse, other crimes such as vandalism and criminal damage occured at the same time.

Sources: ONS & Gov.Scot

---

24-hour National Domestic Violence
Freephone Helpline
## 0808 2000 247

www.nationaldomesticviolencehelpline.org.uk

Mens Advice Line
0808 8010 327

Printed in Great Britain
by Amazon

79076479R00169